More Than a
Wise Woman

To Lil ......
Enjoy & Blessed Be !!
EMaddox

More Than a Wise Woman

Elaine Gugin Maddex

Artistic Warrior Publishing

www.artisticwarrior.com

ISBN 978-1-987982-00-8

Library and Archives Canada Cataloguing in Publication
Maddex, Elaine Gugin, 1955-, author
More than a wise woman / Elaine Gugin Maddex.
Issued in print and electronic formats.
ISBN 978-1-987982-00-8 (paperback).--ISBN 978-1-987982-01-5 (epub)
I. Title.
PS8626.A3144M67 2015   C813'.6   C2015-903556-2
                                               C2015-903557-0

DISCLAIMER
This is a work of fiction. The information in this book is for entertainment
purposes only and should not take the place of your physician or health-care
professional.
The publisher and author are not responsible for any adverse effects or
consequences resulting from the use of any of the suggestions, preparations,
or procedures in this book

To my husband, Wayne: Thank you for your love and support,
and for preparing all those awesome meals and pouring my wine.

And to my sister,
Diane: Thank you for all the helpful suggestions,
unwavering encouragement, and love.
It's not easy living so far from my best friend.

Contents

The Aura of Tessy McGuigan   *1*

Moving In   *7*

Tessy Meets the Tuckers   *12*

Kindred Spirits Prevail   *21*

Woe-be-me Correspondence   *28*

Recipe for Friendship   *37*

Blooming Yule   *49*

Humbug   *57*

Joy to the World   *63*

Plain Out of Sorts   *73*

Grandpa Comes A-Courtin'   *79*

A Fresh New Day with

Not One Mishap . . . Yet   *93*

Bittersweet Feelings and New Beginnings   *104*

Fond Farewells and Heavy Hearts   *115*

Not Goodbye . . . Just . . .

See You in My Dreams   *123*

And Life Does Go On   *130*

Tessy Presents Her Crusade   *136*

Victory for a Wise Woman   *143*

Come East, My Ladies . . . Come East   *148*

Winnipeg-on-a-Whirlwind   *157*

Ghosts, Goblins, and . . . Gorillas?   *168*

Six Weeks and Counting   *180*

Christmas Riddles

and Sound Advice   *189*

Final Riddle . . . Yet No Clue   *198*

A Frosty Start   *204*

A Magical Moonlit Affair   *209*

"Attitute" and Patience   *216*

All Things Revealed   *223*

The Recipes

Refreshing Foot Bath	6
Solace Foot Salve	6
Summer Afternoon Iced Tea	11
Herb Jelly	11
Sore Muscle Sachet	20
Lovely Lavender Lemonade	20
Vibrant Herb Vinaigrette	27
Microdermabrasion	27
Lemon Thyme Tea Loaf	36
Revitalizing Citrus Mint Tea Blend	36
Hand and Nail Repair	48
Screaming Headache Salve	48
Lemon Lavender Shortbread Cookies	56
PMS/Menopausal Spray	56
Magick Mist Moisturizing Spray	62
Berry Blessed Lemonade	62
Iced Spiced Apple Cider	72
Foot and Body Scrub	72
Foot Refresher Spray	78
White Musk and Ginger Scent	78
Chewy Peanut Butter–Chocolate Macaroons	78
Bruschetta	92
Soothing Herbal Bath Salts	92
Gentle Insect Repellent	103
Heavenly Dream Pillow	103
Berry Banana Boost Smoothie	114
Herbed Soda Bread	114
Lamb Shank with Fresh Mint Chutney	122
Fresh Mint Chutney	122
Mango Salsa	129
Serenity Bath Oil Blend	129

Light Lemon-Lime Mousse 135

Spicy Herbed Cheese Ball 142

Pesto 142

Tender Mend Antiseptic Salve 147

Campfire Fun Banana Boats 147

Stay Alert Scent 156

Spiced Rhubarb Muffins 156

Travel Protection Pouch 167

French Canadian Popcorn Balls 167

Autumn Herb Tea 179

Lice Eliminator Treatment 179

Eczema Salve 188

Yuletide Potpourri 188

Simple Shepherd's Pie 197

Yuletime Tea 197

Peppermint Hot Chocolate 203

Olde English Wassail 203

Christmas Eve Casserole 208

Yule Nog 215

Christmas Breakfast-in-a-Pan 222

1

The Aura of Tessy McGuigan

Most everyone in Ladyslipper, Saskatchewan, is accustomed to seeing the widowed Tessy McGuigan adorned in a long peasant dress, flowing wrap, and wide-brimmed hat, with gemstone amulets and crystals draped about her neck and limbs. The good folks find her invariably a bit peculiar . . . sweet, but harmless. It's not just her Irish brogue and eccentric ways of freely handing out herbal remedies and helpful hints, or even her unorthodox attire; it's her spirited aura that most notably stands out in their minds. However, there are a few of the prominent society ladies that whisper, "witch" when they think she can't hear. Tessy is always amazed at what fear and ignorance can conjure up but carries on with a prayer of tolerance and acceptance for them — to a point.

Today, Tess's attire consists of her favourite cotton shirt tucked into her denim bibbed overalls, indicating that she was focused on some intense yardwork. Raptured by her gardens of herbs, perennials, birds, and butterflies, she delights in the "Magick of the Faeries and Mother Earth."

Enveloped in the branches of her majestic maple tree, standing on the top rung of a stepladder to hang a bird feeder, she heard her front gate open and someone whistling up the walk. Her two loyal canines, Duke and Darby, paid little attention to the intruder, so she figured that it had to be the postman on his daily delivery.

"Good mornin' to you, Roger," she called down from her perch without turning to see.

"Oh, good morning, Tess! I didn't see you up there," answered the startled postman as he leaned down to tussle with the dogs. "What are you up to today?"

"Oh, it is a busy day I've been planning. 'Twould keep even the quickest leprechaun on his toes," she gaily replied.

Roger chuckled as he continued to play with the dogs. "Did you hear that the Tuckers are moving in today?"

"Aye, I did hear that today is the big day. A fine wee family, I understand." Tessy stepped down a couple of rungs in time to observe Roger hobbling back down the walk. "Roger, what have ye done to yourself?" she asked.

"Oh, new boots," he said, shaking his head. "And of course I didn't think to bring along my old faithfuls to switch into."

"Oh, a painful experience, to be sure" she sympathized. "Well, now, when ye get home, fill an old wash basin with warm water and add some Epsom and sea salts, then add a few drops of peppermint, eucalyptus, and lavender essential oils [Refreshing Foot Bath]. While you're at it, throw in a handful of marbles to roll your feet over; soak them for a time, pat them dry, and apply some of my Solace Foot Slave that I delivered to your Connie, and you'll be fixed right up!"

Roger laughed. "Well, I'm not sure we have all those ingredients but I could check with — "

"Never mind, Roger, I'll ring up your Connie — she'll know," Tessy chuckled.

"Well, sore feet or not, I best be on my way. The sooner I finish my run the sooner I can get home and try that remedy of yours. See you Monday." And with that, Roger reached into his pocket, pulled out a biscuit for each dog, and limped off, leaving Tessy to her task at hand.

"Good day to ye, Roger!" Tessy called after him.

Just as Tessy finished hanging the bird feeder and was on her way down the ladder, she noticed something strange in one of the branches. She reached over and plucked it out. Of all things, it was a large, fresh, sprig of holly. "Now, what in St. Paddy's name would a fresh sprig of holly be doin' in my maple tree? Our Garden Groupies Club has toured just about every garden in the county, and there's not a single person in these parts that I know of growing holly." She carried the sprig with great care and puzzlement into the house and placed it in a jar of water and set it on the kitchen windowsill. It held some kind of meaning . . . but what? She knew that in Celtic lore holly is a plant of protection and luck; also it is a plant for a man to increase his ability to attract a woman; and, of course, a plant for Yule. After giving it another perplexed look, she shook her head and returned to her gardening tasks.

Tessy was busy dunking buckets into the rain barrel to fill the bird baths when she heard a truck rumbling down the road. She turned in time to see a very large moving van rolling past her house. "Aye, heading to the Tuckers', I'd bet," she said out loud to Duke, who was standing nearby.

Tessy's rhythmic Celtic brogue seemed to poetically roll off her lips, making even the soberest of people smile. As a schoolteacher, she did try to slow down and enunciate properly but more often than not her accent popped through. Whenever it was brought to her attention, she would say, "It's up to your English teacher to be teaching ye English. I'm here to teach ye history." Her accent was especially fervent when she was in a hurry, when her Irish temper was up, or when she was tired. Today, she was tired. She hadn't slept very soundly, and the heat of the day was upon her.

Tessy decided to take a well-deserved break from her yardwork. The day was proving to be a bit warmer than she had anticipated and this was slowing her progress; *however*, she thought to herself, *one can expect this kind of heat at the beginning of July*. As she was about to head into the house, the dogs started barking. She turned to see a small group of people entering her front gate so she called the dogs to come close and sit. She suspected who they were but waited for them to speak first.

"Good morning. How are you today?" they greeted.

"Good morning. Fine, thank you," Tessy politely answered.

"We have come by to drop off some reading material on our beliefs for you," said one of the ladies, offering a handful of booklets and pamphlets.

"How kind of you. Let me go and fetch some reading material on my beliefs, and we can share ideas."

"Oh, no! We've heard about you and we've come here today to save you," she gasped.

"Well, now, come to save me, have you? How nice of you. Thank ye kindly, but the Lord and Lady do a fine job of looking out for me. May I ask who it was that told you I might need saving?"

"Well, I guess there's no harm — it was Mrs. Chamberlain who told us to come and get you to repent."

Tessy smirked, knowing the true intentions behind the town's infamous busybody, Mrs. Chamberlain, and said, "That doesn't really surprise me. I truly respect all religions and beliefs but I expect that same courtesy to be shown in return. And I do thank you for your good intentions. Good day." Tessy turned, walked up the front steps, entered her house, and closed the door.

It was a kind gesture, just the same, Tessy thought as she headed for the kitchen. Tessy loves living in Ladyslipper, Saskatchewan. Not only are most people kind here, but Ladyslipper is so beautiful; Tessy calls it "the hidden gem of the prairies." It looks like a scene that was dropped out of a Norman Rockwell painting, and that is why a young, mystical, eccentric Tessy stepped off the train many years ago and remained. When she hopped on the CN Rail from Winnipeg back then and headed west, she had fully intended on getting a bit farther; but when the train descended into a grand valley and stopped in Ladyslipper, she was overwhelmed at how much the little community somehow reminded her of her beloved village in Ireland. Maybe it was the old stone houses they passed on the way in, or the quaint little shops that surrounded the church with the tall steeple in the centre of town. Whatever it was, it loudly called to her.

She met and married a wonderful local boy by the name of Dermot McGuigan, a second-generation Irish descendant. Dermot, also a teacher, was "the only spark in me lighter," as Tessy put it. When asked about her husband, to this day she will tell you: "My husband was a wise man — talked little, listened a great deal; never missed a conversation worth hearing." That was over thirty-four years ago, and now Dermot's gone, having succumbed to cancer. He passed over to the other side three years this September. At times, Tessy feels like it was just yesterday, and other times it feels like centuries ago. She often senses his presence, sometimes in the greenhouse where he loved to putter, but always in the room they called the library. That's where he would sit for hours marking papers, looking up references or just pondering. When she needs to talk to him or just be with him, that's where you'll find her.

Tessy wandered into the kitchen to retrieve a pitcher of homemade iced tea from the refrigerator and glanced over at the holly sprig. As she sat on her veranda enjoying a welcome breeze and sipping the tumbler of refreshing iced brew, she pondered the mystery. What was this misplaced, odd little plant trying to tell her? She watched her two cats, Merlin and Cordelia, curled up on their favourite cushion lazily soaking up the warmth of the afternoon. No respectable person of the Craft would be without a feline or two. She reached over and stroked their silky coats, and, as she did, they lifted their sleepy heads, yawned, then stretched. They got up, circled around one another, curled up in their new positions, and continued on with their nap. Tessy chuckled and rebuked them, saying that after such a relaxed afternoon, she was expecting at least one mouse to be delivered on the doorstep the next morning. And with that, she set her empty glass on the wicker side table, gave each of them another affectionate pat, and promptly headed back out to her garden.

As Tessy lovingly puttered about her lush gardens, down the block, quite a different scene was taking place.

Refreshing Foot Bath

1 1/2 cups (375 ml) Epsom salts
1/2 cup (125 ml) sea salts
1/2 tsp (2 ml) vegetable glycerin
12 drops eucalyptus radiata essential oil
10 drops lavender essential oil
8 drops peppermint essential oil

Mix ingredients well in large bowl; spoon into airtight container. Scoop 2 to 3 tablespoons (30 to 45 ml) into basin of hot or cold water; swish with feet to blend. Add a handful of marbles and gently roll feet over them while soaking for approximately 20 minutes.

Solace Foot Salve

1 cup (250 ml) organic all-vegetable shortening
20 drops calendula essential oil
20 drops lavender essential oil
10 drops peppermint essential oil
6 drops tea tree essential oil

Mix (at room temperature) vegetable shortening with essential oils. Whip for 2 minutes and spoon into container and cap. Use within 6 months.

2

Moving In

The Tuckers had finally arrived. Ladyslipper had been without a local pharmacist for the past few months, since the passing of old Mr. Graham. Jim Tucker had been an assistant pharmacist in a neighbouring town. He heard the pharmacy was up for sale, so after careful deliberation and a number of trips to Ladyslipper, he became the town's newest proprietor.

This was a bittersweet move for Jim and Penny Tucker. Their three children — Sarah, fifteen; Matthew (Matt to family and friends), twelve; and little Emma, who had just turned seven — found it very difficult to leave their school and friends. But they knew this was an incredible opportunity for their father to own and manage his very own store; so after many family discussions and numerous sleepless nights, they made a unanimous decision.

Moving day was just what one would expect. Both the SUV and the car were packed to the roof and beyond. The SUV pulled a small trailer, and out on the street, a large moving van was parked. A steady stream of furnishings and belongings paraded up the front walk and into the lovely, two-storey home. The children each ran upstairs to scout out and claim their new bedrooms. Matt, taking possession of the room overlooking the backyard, already had the window open and was proceeding to climb out onto the roof when Sarah came in, grabbed him by the seat of his pants, and hauled him back. Loudly protesting, Matt was handed over to his mother, who, after a stern scolding, instructed him to get back downstairs and help. An hour later, Penny called for everyone, including the movers, to come to the backyard for a break and a bite to eat. The picnic table displayed an array of sandwiches, a tray of fresh vegetables, and plenty of ice water and pop. Appetites were hearty, and everyone stood milling around, eating and discussing the move.

Matt had already made fast friends with Brendon, the boy across the street, and, with a sandwich in each hand, they were inspecting the ruins of a long-since decayed tree house in the back bushes. As they ate, plans were being made to resurrect the structure as soon as possible. A pact, with NO GIRLS ALLOWED, was being drawn up and rules were being discussed for the new clubhouse. To Matt, it was plain to see that Ladyslipper was a very cool place, and this was going to be a fantastic summer.

As soon as they had had their fill of food and drink, everyone returned to work, and before long, all the large pieces of furniture were moved into place, and the moving van was gone. Boxes were stacked up along the walls, leaving only a small path leading from one room to the other.

It was late afternoon, and Jim was getting tired. He found Penny in the kitchen up on a chair putting some dishes in the cupboard. He stood watching for a moment admiring her and how she had handled the move with such ease. He walked over and gently placed his hand on the small of her back. Startled, she jumped and turned. "Oh, I didn't hear you come in. How are you doing?"

"I'm bushed," he sighed as he helped her down from the chair.

"I'm getting a little weary myself. How 'bout we stop, enjoy a nice glass of wine on our beautiful new deck, then start the barbeque. I picked up some chicken thighs when I went to the store this afternoon. How does that sound?" Penny asked.

"You are a brilliant woman. I knew there was a reason I married you," Jim chirped as he gave her an affectionate peck. Penny smiled and shook her head as she gave him a smack on the butt.

Sarah and Emma were both in their rooms unpacking. Necessities were unpacked first and now they were on to their treasures. The bedrooms were all equipped with built-in shelves, so while Emma was busy displaying all her stuffed animals and Barbies, Sarah was dusting off cherished mementos: pictures of her old cheerleading squad and classmates, and one in particular named Eric. Sarah was sitting on the floor with her back leaning up against her freshly made bed. As she dusted off Eric's picture a tear rolled down her cheek and fell onto the glass. How was she ever going to make it here without her friends, and especially the captain of the volleyball team? She was trying so hard not to make a big scene, mostly for Dad's sake. She knew that he and Mom were already feeling bad enough. But starting a new school, not knowing a soul, how would she ever manage? She looked up and noticed Emma standing at the door staring at her. Emma ran over to Sarah and put her little arms around her neck and said, "It's okay. You don't have to be sad. I'll be your friend even if I am your sister!"

Sarah wiped the tear away and, smiling, she hugged her little sister back. "Thanks, Emma, that makes me feel lots better. Let's go downstairs and see what's going on."

"Okay," answered Emma. "But I came in to find you 'cause I can't seem to find Buster Bear anywhere."

"I'm sure he just got put in a box that ended up in one of the other rooms. We'll look for him tomorrow until we find him, okay?" promised Sarah.

"You're the best. I'm so glad you're my big sister!" Emma grinned, grabbing Sarah's hand on the way down the stairs.

The girls found their parents relaxing on a couple of lounge chairs out on the back deck. "Hey," said Sarah.

"Hey back," Penny replied. "Thanks for all your help today, girls. You were wonderful."

"No problem," answered Sarah. "It went much smoother than I thought it was going to."

"I agree. I was expecting at least a glitch or two, but there just didn't seem to be any. Not that I'm complaining," Penny retorted.

Emma, who was sitting quietly on her daddy's lap, piped up: "But we did have a one really big glitch."

"Oh? What was that?" her parents chimed in unison.

"Buster is missing, and I'm not sure how I am going to go to bed tonight without him."

"Ooh, my, now that *is* a big glitch," her mom agreed.

Just then, Matt came flying around the corner of the house, skidding his bike to a stop on the sidewalk. "Hey, what's for supper?" he called, dropping his bike, wheels spinning.

"Matt, go put your bike in the stand by the garage, please — that's what it's there for," his dad said as he got up to flip the chicken. Matt, dropping the top half of his body and shaking his head, turned and complied with his father's wishes.

"Did you get some of your room done today, son?" Dad asked.

"Yep," Matt answered, grabbing a carrot stick as he passed the table.

"Good — then you can help me with the garage tomorrow."

"Ahh, Dad! Brendon, Jason, and I were going to work on the clubhouse tomorrow."

"Well, not until we get a good chunk of the garage done first. So you best be getting up early so we can get a good start on it."

Matt dropped his head into his hands and exhaled a huff of frustration, to which his father responded, "And there'll be no attitude, or you will be spending the entire day unpacking."

"Yes, sir, sorry," Matt sheepishly replied.

"Thank you!" Dad smiled and tousled Matt's hair. "Now, who's ready for our first cooked meal in our new home?"

Summer Afternoon Iced Tea

Steep 1 large fresh bee balm flower with approximately 3 fresh lavender flower sprigs in 2 cups (500 ml) of hot water for 10 minutes. After it has cooled, pour into tumbler over ice cubes and enjoy!

Herb Jelly

- 1 cup (250 ml) fresh sage
- 2 cups (500 ml) hard apple cider
- 1 cup (250 ml) water
- Juice of 1 lemon
- 1 pouch (85ml) liquid pectin
- 3 cups (750 ml) sugar
- 4 one-pint (500 ml) sterilized jars and lids

Place clean, chopped herbs in an 8–10-quart (8–10 L) Dutch oven and add apple cider and water. Bring to a boil over high heat. Boil uncovered for 5–6 minutes, remove from heat, cover, and let stand for ten minutes. Strain herbs through cheesecloth, add the lemon juice, and add more apple cider if necessary to equal 3 cups (750 ml) liquid. Discard herbs. In the same Dutch oven, combine the juice mixture and fruit pectin. Heat on high, stirring constantly, until mixture comes to a rolling boil. Add sugar all at once and boil for 1 minute, stirring constantly. Remove from heat and skim off foam with a metal spoon. Carefully ladle hot jelly into hot, sterilized jars, leaving 1/4 inch (0.5 cm) room at top. Wipe rim and threads of jar with a clean, damp cloth. Place lids on jars and screw down evenly. Process 5–10 minutes in a boiling-water canner. Remove jars and cool on racks. Label and enjoy!

3

Tessy Meets the Tuckers

Tessy takes it upon herself to hand deliver a welcome basket of goodies to all newcomers to Ladyslipper. The Tuckers were not going to be an exception. She got up a little earlier than usual to complete her morning grounding and meditation ritual, followed by twenty minutes of yoga. Feeling refreshed and filled with gratitude, she began to wander about her gardens, deciding which labours of love she would surrender today. With Duke, Darby, Merlin, and Cordelia all underfoot, Tessy methodically meandered through her flower beds, lovingly inspecting every plant. She stopped to gently touch a massive castor bean leaf then bent to brush her hand over a carpet of chocolate mint, releasing its intoxicating scent. "Aren't you just beautiful, now. Thank ye for your gifts, Lord, and thank ye, wee faeries, for watching over them." She couldn't imagine life without her gardens or her pets. They give so much and ask so little in return.

Tessy always had a few things prepared and on hand for last-minute gifts or emergencies but she wanted to assemble a unique basket to welcome the Tuckers. Putting a great deal of thought into what she was including in the basket, she decided to prepare a few of her speciality herbal formulas. She had chosen: a dozen Sore Muscle Sachets for the tub; herbal Summer Afternoon Iced Tea in a small, decorative tin; a quart sealer of Lovely Lavender Lemonade for the children; Herb Jelly from last fall, which always tastes better after setting a spell; a corked bottle of Vibrant Herb Vinaigrette mix; fresh Lemon Thyme Tea Loaf; homemade Hand And Nail Repair; and a small jar of Screaming Headache salve. Aye, that would be perfect.

She had put the tea bread in the oven early that morning while the house was still cool. The oil and vinegar mix was already set, but she needed to go out to the garden and cut some fresh herbs to place in the decorative bottle. The jar of jelly was wiped fresh, and she placed a floral fabric topper on it, tied with some jute. She was quite pleased with the way things were coming together. For the herbal vinaigrette, she decided to try a blend of rosemary, sage, thyme, and lemon verbena, with a few garlic cloves and peppercorns added for that extra little nip. As she clipped her herbs, she enjoyed inhaling their individual fragrances and relished the moment. *What a blessing it is to have such a moment,* she thought to herself. She smiled, shut her eyes, and took in a long, deep breath to appreciate the scent one last time before she got up and headed for the house.

She chose a beautiful large basket with a double woven handle and she lay in a small yellow gingham tablecloth she had made and began placing the items on it. During her morning meditation, she called upon her spirit guide to assist her in choosing some specific crystals and gems to add: amber, bloodstone, and carnelian for cleansing, grounding, and protection; emerald for friendship; and amethyst and rose quartz just for all-around good measure. She then wrote a brief note of characteristics on each, placed the stones and note in the bottom, and continued to arrange her gift of welcome. With the basket soon filled with jars, tins, and formulas, she gathered the gingham cloth around the attractive package and tied it with a wide cloth ribbon. Tessy stepped back and looked at the delightfully wrapped bundle with great satisfaction. She carried it into the main kitchen, walked over to her writing desk, picked out an appropriate card, and composed a note of welcome to the Tuckers. She looked at the clock. It was 11:30 a.m. She decided she would fix herself some lunch and deliver the basket in the early afternoon.

Before proceeding on her kindly errand, Tessy thought a nice bouquet of flowers to accompany the basket would be in order; so, just before she left, she ran out to her cutting garden. She snipped off some gorgeous fuchsia-pink peonies, snow-white Shasta daisies, and a couple of colourful lupines to add a little contrast. With a few sprigs of baby's breath, it was quite a spectacular arrangement. As she hurried back to the house, she shook off the peonies a number of times in hopes of removing the ants from the magnificent blooms. She took the flowers over to the kitchen sink and stripped off some of the bottom leaves, tossing them into her compost bucket. She then artfully arranged the flowers in her hand and secured them with a rubber band. She pulled out a clean plastic bread bag, placed in it a paper towel, dribbled in some water, inserted the flowers, and tied it securely. "There, that ought to get ye there just fine," she concluded out loud. And with that, she gathered up the bouquet in one hand, the basket in the other, and she was off.

However, not before grabbing one more very important item that she always left hanging by the door and never went anywhere without: her suede pouch of special herbs, oils, and precious gemstones. This was Tessy's emergency kit and the answer to any obstacle she might encounter on her daily travels.

It was such a beautiful day, Tessy never even considered driving her vehicle. As a matter of fact, she very rarely drove anywhere about town. She most often rode her large trike and, if she was running errands, she would attach her wagon on behind. But today she decided to walk and pull the wagon, as she planned on just picking up a few things after her stop at the Tuckers'. She had devised a little compartment at the front of the wagon to hold her handbag, cloth grocery bags, and some plastic bags for any garbage she might come across along the way. Setting the gift basket in the wagon, she gently propped up the flowers next to it, grabbed the handle, and headed down the lane. When she reached the end of the lane, she securely latched the gate and reassured Duke and Darby she would be returning home soon with a treat for them and to be good and watch the house.

So, with her long cotton dress flowing in the breeze, wide-brim reed hat carefully placed on her swept-up curls, Tessy hummed a cheerful tune and headed for town.

The first part of her journey was on more of a footpath than a sidewalk, as the blocks had all but disintegrated over time and had not yet been replaced this far out of town. It was, however, a well-travelled path, as it was the way to Ladyslipper Beach, with a steady stream of kids headed there both summer and winter. As Tessy made her way to town, children dressed in their beach apparel passed her by, some riding bikes and some walking hand in hand. Having taught for so many years, she knew and chatted to some; with others, she just exchanged a smile and a friendly greeting. She heard the odd snicker behind her and knew, without a doubt, that she and her wagon must look a peculiar sight; however, Tessy joyfully accepted and embraced her differences, beliefs, and eccentricities.

Before Tessy knew it, she was strolling down the familiar, cracked sidewalks of Ladyslipper, enjoying the heavily treed avenues and manicured boulevards. As she sauntered, she was captivated by her surroundings, which never ceased to delight her. When she stopped to get her bearings, she realized she was two houses past her destination.

Chuckling, she turned and retraced her steps to the Tuckers' front walk. She made her way up the walk past telltale remnants of a move and parked her wagon at the bottom of the front steps, slightly off to the side. Collecting her offerings, she proceeded up the steps. She shuffled a few empty boxes out of her way to reach the door and firmly grasped the door knocker. Just as she was about to give it a hefty crack, the door suddenly flew open virtually yanking Tessy right into the house. Startled, Tessy jumped back to see an equally startled, wide-eyed, lanky young boy. Tessy gathered her wits, straightened her hat as best she could, smiled, and said, "Well, hello, young fellow. Ye must be Matthew."

"Y-y-es," was all the boy could muster.

"I'm Tessy McGuigan. And I'm here to welcome you to Ladyslipper."

"Thanks!" Matt replied.

"Would your mum be about?" inquired Tessy.

"Yep . . . MOM!" hollered Matt

A very pleasant, yet drained, looking woman came smiling to the door, saying, "Matt, honey, please don't yell. That's very rude."

"Sorry, Mom. I've finished helping Dad, and my room's almost done. Going to meet Brendon and Jason. See ya later. 'Bye!" Matt yelled as he ran past Tessy, leaping down the last three steps, then over Tessy's wagon. While at a full sprint, he scooped up his bike with ease, hopped on it, and was headed down the street before another word could be spoken.

Both women stood in a moment of awe until Tessy broke the silence: "My, quick as a rabbit, that one!"

"Oh, I'm so sorry about that. Hi, my name is Penny Tucker. Please come in. Excuse the mess." Penny stretched out her hand to welcome Tessy when she realized Tessy's hands were full.

"Oh, that's fine, dear, I won't stay but a minute. I'm Tessy McGuigan. Here to welcome ye to Ladyslipper. I've brought you a few wee things that I thought might come in handy this week and some flowers out of my garden to brighten up your new kitchen." As they entered the foyer she handed the flowers to Penny and set the basket down on a cube box marked "DEN."

"Thank you so much! How thoughtful! And the flowers are beautiful. They're out of your own garden? They're so vibrant and healthy."

"Aye, thank ye but I can't be taking all the credit. God makes them, I just plant them and the wee faeries watch over them." Tessy chuckled "But ye might want to hand them back to me for a minute while I take them outside and give them one more wee shake. I can see another ant or two, which I'm sure won't be welcomed guests in your new home." With that, she took the bouquet from Penny, walked back out to the veranda, and shook the flowers over the edge. "There, hopefully that's all of them now." She returned to the foyer and handed the flowers back to Penny with a smile.

"Would you like to come in for a cup of tea, Ms. McGuigan?"

"Oh, no, you're busy, to be sure, but thank you—and please call me Tessy. Everyone does."

"All right, Tessy," Penny repeated.

Just then, Emma came bounding down from upstairs clutching a stuffed bear and chattering with much delight. "Mommy, look! I found Buster—oh, hello . . ." she stopped on the bottom step staring at Tessy.

"Well, hello, there. And what would your name be?" Tessy knew darn well this was little Emma but she wanted to nudge the child into conversation.

"My name is Emma, and this Buster. He's been lost, but I found him. He has been my very best friend since I was one . . . well, 'cept for maybe Julie. She's my friend back where my old house is, but I didn't know her when I was one, only when I was five. I miss her, but Mommy says I'll find a new friend here." Emma finally had to stop and take a breath. Tessy walked over and shook hands with Emma then Buster.

"A pleasure to meet you both. My name is Tessy. And I'm sure you'll have no trouble finding lots of new friends. There are plenty of wee girls your age in Ladyslipper."

"Really! Oh, Mommy, did you hear that?"

"Yes, honey. See, I told you."

"Yah, but Matt already has friends and stuff," pouted Emma.

"I know, honey, but sometimes it just takes little girls a bit longer to make new friends," Mother sympathized.

"I'll tell you what—do you like dogs?" asked Tess.

"Oh, yes. Someday I'm going to have a puppy. Right, Mommy?"

"Well, if it's okay with your mummy, ye can come out to my house and play with my dogs, Duke and Darby, someday soon. They would love to be your friend. Would ye like that?"

"Oh, yes! Could I, Mommy, please?"

"Well, I'm sure that would be fine, but we'd have to see when it's a good time for Tessy"

"I also know a lovely wee girl, about Emma's age, by the name of Becky who comes to visit me quite often. Maybe I could invite her to join us as well," Tessy offered.

"Oh, Mommy, this is the best day ever. First I found Buster and I'm gonna have dogs to play with and now my very own friend named Becky," Emma burst out.

All of a sudden, Penny was beckoned from the back part of the house.

"Excuse me," Penny apologetically glanced at Tessy. "I'm out at the front, Jim," Penny called. From around the corner, conversation in midstream, Jim Tucker appeared.

"Oh . . . pardon me . . . Hello, I'm Jim Tucker." He stretched out his hand as Penny jumped in to introduce Tessy to her husband and directed his attention to the gifts. "Well, that was extremely kind. Thank you so much." Jim smiled.

Then little Emma started up, "And I'm going over to play with her dogs and she has a lovely little girl for me to meet and her name is Becky and she is going to be my friend, and oh, Daddy, I found Buster. This is the best day ever . . . I'm so happy!"

"I see that. Boy, lucky you," he replied as he threw his wife a look of bewilderment. He then excused himself and said, "Honey, Sarah's in the kitchen filling the dishwasher and can't seem to find the rinse stuff, so we were wondering if you might know where it is."

Penny sighed and said, "Oh, we're right out, and I forgot to pick some up yesterday."

"Oh, no worries, my dear," Tessy piped up. "Some vinegar will fix ye right up."

"Vinegar? Really, how's that?" questioned Penny.

"Well, now, ye just pour a little vinegar in the compartment where the rinse solution goes. It'll get your dishes sparkling clean . . . no spots . . . cleans your dishwasher, AND it's much better for Mother Earth."

"Really, just vinegar? That is amazing. We'll give that a try for sure. Thank you, Tessy," Penny said gratefully.

"Good, good, good, glad to be of help. Well, I best be off, then," announced Tessy.

"You're sure you won't come in for tea?"

"Oh, no, thank ye, dear, I've more errands to run and I'm sure you have many tasks yet to tend to," Tessy replied, turning toward the front entry. "I'll be in touch, Penny, so we can plan our visit."

"Goodbye, Ms. Tessy. Please, please don't forget to invite that little Becky girl," begged Emma.

"Oh, never, my dear," assured Tessy, patting the child. Tessy proceeded down the front walk with little Emma skipping merrily beside her until they reached the hedge by the main sidewalk.

"Goodbye, Ms. Tessy," she repeated as she threw herself around Tessy's middle and hugged her most earnestly. Tessy leaned over the child's head and hugged her back. At that moment, a genuine, mutual bond immediately developed between the two. They waved goodbye to each other until Tessy turned the corner and was out of sight.

Feeling lighthearted, Tessy continued on her way, smiling and exchanging salutations with anyone who crossed her path—until she looked up and saw three women heading toward her.

"Oh, great, here comes the devil herself, Mrs. Chamberlain, and her two sidekicks, Curly and Moe," she said quietly; then scolded herself for the unkind thought.

Tessy knew that Mrs. Chamberlain was not an advocate of hers in any way, shape, or form and was never afraid to voice her opinion—and whatever that opinion was, her two sidekicks wholeheartedly adhered to. As they approached, Tessy centred herself, put a protective shield of white light around her, took a deep breath, looked them straight in the eye, and said "Ladies, have ye ever seen such a fine, bewitching afternoon?"

They all gasped at such a comment and scurried past her. Tessy knew she shouldn't taunt them like that, but after so many years of their badgering, sometimes it was just too hard to resist. After they had passed, she heard one of them say, "She must have traded in her broom for a wagon," then heard them all laugh. Tessy's Irish blood started to bubble, but then she considered their fear and ignorance, placed herself deeper into her white light until she was calm then carried on with her errands.

With her shopping completed and her wagon full, she headed for home. It was just as pleasant, but seemed a little longer with the heavier load. It was hot, and she was feeling a little weary so she stopped to rest on a park bench under a large poplar tree. She dug into one of her cloth grocery bags and retrieved a bottle of water, cracked it open, and took a couple of generous gulps. "Ahhh . . . there's a reason the good Lord put water on this earth," she said aloud. Just as she said it, she noticed Matt had ridden past on his bike.

"Hello again!" she called after him. Matt waved a hand in return and kept on riding alongside his new friends.

Tessy sat enjoying the park's activities. She revelled in watching the children at play, sliding down the slide, bouncing on the springy toys, and playing soccer. At the far end, some were on those skateboarding loopity-loop things. She really didn't know what else to call them, but they certainly did look like fun. "I wonder if the Tucker children have one of those boards?" she mused out loud. "I might just ask if I can give it a try — on a much flatter surface, mind ye," she chuckled.

Feeling well refreshed, she continued on her way. As she trekked along, she thought about how excited the Tuckers must be about their big move. She reflected on the first and only house that she and Dermot had bought. They had lived most of their lives in the last house on the edge of town. The charming, turn-of-the-century, Victorian home, painted a cheery yellow with white trim, displayed detailed gingerbread gables and a huge, inviting front veranda. The elegant structure sat on five acres of rolling lawn with massive trees and gardens. When they were first married, they would walk past this property and fantasize about one day owning it. Tessy would dreamily gaze at it, laugh, and say, "I shall name it Ashling Manor when we live there." The Irish meaning for Ashling is "a vision" or "a dream," and Tessy held to that vision. A few years later, the owners of their dream home retired and decided to move to the West Coast. The property was never even listed. Tessy called it positive affirmation and Divine intervention; Dermot just called it plain luck.

She was now on the path close to her home when she noticed some pop cans and candy wrappers caught in the hedges. She took out one of her plastic bags and began to clean up the garbage and as she did so, she was wondering how she could get people to realize that littering was such an insult to Mother Earth. She had already placed a garbage container down at the end of her lane for folks to use as they passed by but obviously more had to be done. Someone needed to make a stand against litter, promote community awareness and defend Mother Earth. She decided, right then and there, that she would be the candidate to take on the challenge. She would devise a strategy and present it to the Town Council. "Aye, that's what needs to be done," she said out loud as she finished picking up the last of the trash. She sorted out all the cans and placed them in her wagon for recycling then dumped the plastic bag of garbage into the bin at the end of her lane. Elated with her decision, she continued on up to Ashling Manor.

Sore Muscle Sachet

A one-foot square (about 30 cm by 30 cm) of cheesecloth with
  yarn
1 cup (250 ml) Epsom salts
1/2 cup (125 ml) sea salts
1/2 cup (125 ml) baking soda
2 Tbsp (30 ml) vegetable glycerin
1 Tbsp (15 ml) chamomile flowers
1 Tbsp (15 ml) lemon balm leaves
1 Tbsp (15 ml) lavender buds
1 Tbsp (15 ml) pine needles
1 Tbsp (15 ml) sage leaves
2 tsp (10 ml) peppermint leaves
20 drops eucalyptus radiata essential oil
3 drops ginger essential oil

Place all dry ingredients into centre of cheesecloth. Add essential oils.
Gather into a pouch and tie with yarn. Drop into tub while filling with
warm water, ease yourself in, and soak for 20 minutes. Relax!

Lovely Lavender Lemonade

A 6-inch square (about 15 cm by 15 cm) of cheesecloth or 1
  organic coffee filter with string
1 Tbsp (15 ml) dried lavender buds
1 cup (250 ml) boiling water
6 cups (1.5 L) mixed pink lemonade
Lemon slices
Sprigs of fresh mint

Place lavender buds in centre of cheesecloth/coffee filter, gather and tie
with string. Place in a large measuring cup and add boiling water. Cover
and let steep for 5 minutes. Pour liquid into a 2-quart (2-L) pitcher and
squeeze excess out of the mesh pouch and discard. Stir lemonade into
mixture in pitcher, cover, and chill for at least 2 hours. To serve, pour
lavender lemonade over ice cubes and garnish with a lemon slice and a
sprig of mint.

4

Kindred Spirits Prevail

Tessy had to put her little crusade on hold for the time being, as during the summer months, Town Council took a two-month break. However, that would not stop her from brainstorming and researching solutions to her environmental campaign. It actually felt invigorating to feel this passionate about a cause again. She already had a plan to contact the school and get the kids involved and she knew with that kind of backing, the Town Council would be even more likely to take a positive approach. For now, however, she had a more personal assignment to attend to.

It had been close to a week since her visit with the Tuckers, and she was having difficulty contacting little Becky. Apparently, Becky had gone with her father to visit her cousins in Alberta for ten days. However, she was due home tomorrow, and Tessy was on it. She had made arrangements with Susan, Becky's mom, for Becky to spend Saturday over at Tessy's. Tessy had become Becky's surrogate grandmother when Becky was about four. She and Susan would take walks to the beach past Tessy's house and they would stop for a chat and that was when Becky adopted Tessy as her "special" grandma.

Tessy had called Penny and explained the situation and even though Penny did her best to reassure Emma that arrangements were being made, Emma was getting a little discouraged and thought that Saturday would never come. But Saturday did arrive, and a beautiful day it was. It had rained the night before, which turned everything lush, and the scent was incredible. Tessy was up early to perform her yoga routine out in the backyard. After a refreshing rain, she loved to spend time in her gardens listening to the birds and enjoying the aroma of a damp floral morning. Penny and Susan were dropping the girls off around one p.m., as Tessy planned for them to spend the afternoon playing and getting to know one another.

"I haven't hosted such a gathering in a very long time," Tessy told her pets. She was relaxing out by her pond enjoying the soft tones of her wind chimes and her breakfast tea. "Does a body good to know you're helping folks along with their journey, but I best be getting back to the house and preparing for my guests." She raised herself slowly from her spot so not to startle the nearby butterflies and the goldfish in the pond and headed back to the house with Duke and Darby at her heels.

The morning passed quickly as Tessy made her preparations. She had decided on serving lemonade with Lemon Lavender Shortbread Cookies. She wondered if it might be a little too much "lemon" but concluded they would complement each other very nicely. She went out to the garden and picked a huge bouquet of fresh shasta daisies and arranged them in a beautiful antique pitcher. She then placed them on the round wooden picnic table out on the backyard stone patio. When she stepped back to take a look, she was pleased with the setting she'd created. The gingham tablecloth with coordinating napkins and the pitcher of flowers looked even better than she had anticipated. Tessy thought having the rendezvous outside in a more casual setting would allow her young guests to relax and really enjoy their visit.

Tessy glanced at her watch. "Oh, my stars, it's 11:45 a.m.! I haven't stopped for lunch yet, and they'll be here in a jig." She bustled about the kitchen fixing herself a wee bite and then hurried up the stairs to get dressed. It was another warm day so she picked out one of her lightest sundresses, which was loose and very comfortable. She never liked to be bothered with anything ill-fitting or that needed to be tugged and pulled at. She reached her arms into the airy frock, slid it over her head and straightened it out with a few strokes of her hand. She then stood back to view herself in her long, oval, mahogany framed mirror, swooshed her skirt back and forth feeling very much like one of the little girls she would soon be entertaining. She let out a contented sigh and a soft giggle, fixed a few loose strands of hair from her neck, pinched her cheeks then turned and danced off down the stairs to play tea party hostess.

Everyone arrived as promised and pretty much simultaneously. They were all ushered through the gate into the backyard where introductions were performed, and small talk commenced. Emma and Becky were both shy and giggly at first, but before long were off playing with the dogs and getting royally acquainted. The two younger women were comparing the girls' likenesses and discovered they had many of the same hobbies and interests. Susan announced she had just been hired to work in the office at Becky's school come September. This was a wonderful turn of events for her as a single mother and she was extremely excited. She mentioned that they will be looking for volunteers in the coming year and asked if Penny might be interested. "You know, that might be just what I need," Penny mused out loud. Although Tessy didn't say anything at the time, she, too, was interested and found her wheels in motion, thus leaving her visitors to their conversation.

Meanwhile, Emma and Becky were enjoying their own little tête-à-tête.

"I'm going into Grade 2 next year!" Becky boasted.

"I'm going into Grade 2, too," Emma replied. Then both girls doubled over with laughter at the two-too comment; in their giddy state, it didn't take much to set them off.

"Wouldn't it be wonderful if we could be best friends, next year, and maybe forever?" sparkled Emma.

"Well, that would be great—but I better check with Megan first," replied Becky.

"Who's Megan?" asked Emma.

"Oh, she's my best friend . . . well . . . sometimes. But I always to have to check with her first, 'cause sometimes I am and sometimes I'm not 'cause she might be best friends with someone else that week."

"I thought that if someone is your best friend they are always your best friend," Emma piped.

"Well, I kinda thought that, too, but that's not what Megan says. Megan says it's whoever she decides, and you just have to wait. Sometimes I feel really sad when it's not my turn; but when it is my turn, we have lots of fun," Becky reminisced.

"I'm not sure I'm going to like Megan," Emma thought out loud.

"Oh, but you *have* to!" Becky gasped. "Everyone has to or she gets really mad!"

"Why?"

"I'm not sure, but those are the rules when it comes to Megan."

"Well, those won't be the rules for me," Emma announced. "Let's go get some lemonade and cookies."

"Okay!" Becky said, running after Emma; and with that, no more was spoken of Megan.

The ladies wandered about the cottage garden admiring the lush beauty and the incredible scents of the huge clusters of double peonies against a backdrop of six-foot-tall delphiniums. As they chatted and finished their refreshments, Susan looked at her watch then placed her glass down on the picnic table. "I have a hair appointment in about ten minutes, so better run. Tessy, are you sure you don't mind watching Becky for a little while this afternoon?"

"Not at all, my dear. The girls seem to be getting on just grand, and I have a project for us to attend to. We'll be as fine as frog's fur." She waved her hand about, sending Susan off with a chuckle.

Susan called out as she walked backwards toward the gate to the front yard, "Penny, it was wonderful meeting you and Emma. If you don't mind, I will get your number from Tessy and give you a call. We can get together soon and the girls can play while I explain more about the volunteer program."

"That would be great. It was really nice to meet you, too. 'Bye!" Penny called out with a wave.

Penny turned to Tessy. "She seems like a lovely person."

"Aye, she is. Poor thing, she and wee Becky, they've had quite a time of it." Tessy leaned over close to Penny and whispered, "I'm certainly not one to judge but I understand that her ex-husband is a bit of a bad egg — at least when it comes to being a husband. Had a few 'scons,' if you know what I mean! But people like that always get their comeuppance. He seems very good with Becky, though . . . bless his heart."

Penny, trying desperately to hide a puzzled smile, tilted her head close to Tessy and questioned, "Scons?"

"Oh, yes, dear . . . oh, amorous encounters," shaking her head. "But enough of that talk. How are ye getting on? Is there anything I can help you with getting settled in?"

"Oh, that basket you sent over was a great hit, thank you again. Jim used the Sore Muscle Sachet the first night, along with the headache balm, and he said he was absolutely amazed at how good he felt the next morning. He laughed and said he was going to have to get you to supply a truckload of them for our store. Sarah and I have been using the hand and nail butter, and our nails have never looked better. And there isn't a crumb left of the tea bread. It was so delicious. Would you consider giving up the recipe? Actually, everything in the basket was so helpful, thoughtful and delicious."

"Well now, that's bang on," chortled Tessy. "I have the tea bread recipe just inside the kitchen door. Let's go in, and I'll get it for you."

"Will the girls be okay out here?" asked Penny.

"They'll be just fine. Won't miss us a bit. Duke and Darby will take grand care of them."

"We'll be right back, girls. Tessy and I are going into the house for a moment. Behave yourselves," called out Penny.

"Mothers have to say that, you know." Emma felt the need to explain her mother's instructions.

"Oh, I know," Becky gravely replied. "I'm really surprised Mom didn't say that when she left. Probably just forgot 'cause she was in a hurry, but I bet she'll ask when she gets back."

Penny wrote down the recipe and then left on a few errands of her own, leaving the girls contentedly entertained by Tessy. Tessy had cleared a little area in the backyard for a new rock garden and she and the girls were making a plan. The girls had come up with some wonderful whimsical ideas, which prompted Tessy to tell them all about God's nature angels that watch over and protect the gardens. Which she prefers to call the Wee Folk or Faeries.

"There's really fairies?" Emma whispered.

"Aye, of course! They're as real as you and me," Tessy assured her. "Ye know how God sends angels to watch over us . . . well, He also sends nature angels to watch over His plant and animal kingdom, and they are what we call Faeries or Wee Folk. Ye can't always see them, because they are very shy, but they help us with all of nature. They guard the plants, the animals, anything to do with keeping Mother Earth's environment safe and clean, as well as many other things." The girls listened wide-eyed and intently as Tessy went on. "They love it when ye believe in them and spend time talking to them. They want us to play and have fun, but above all, they want us to respect and be kind to all of nature and for us to pick up rubbish people have left behind. They also want us to use Earth-friendly products."

Tessy believed it was never too early to teach young ones about Mother Earth and environmental respect. Tessy had talked faerie lore many times with Becky, and now Becky was thrilled to have someone her own age to share these tales with. The girls were entranced with Tessy's stories and enthusiasm for the "elemental realm." The afternoon flew by as the three of them delighted in digging, planting, and playing. While the girls conversed with each other as well as with their new invisible friends, the rock garden seemed to magically transform before their very eyes.

Susan returned first, with Penny not far behind, to pick up two very elated, exhausted little girls. Susan walked over to see their work-in-progress. "Hi, girls! How was your afternoon? I trust you behaved yourselves?"

Becky looked up at Emma and said, "Told ya she'd say that!" She raised her hand and the girls did a "high five" then continued on with their planting. Susan laughed and said, "Come on, honey, we have to get going."

Tessy stood up when she saw Susan approaching and was now brushing off her knees. "They were as good as gold all afternoon. We've had a grand time together. I hope you'll let them drop by again real soon." By this time, Penny had made her way over to the little garden as well.

"Sounds to me like the afternoon was a hit," she smiled.

"Oh, Mommy, I had such a great time! I've learned all about faeries, and we planted flowers for them to live in!" Emma exclaimed as ran over to her mother for a hug.

"Really! Well, you can tell me all about them on our way home," she replied, giving her daughter a big hug in return. "Tessy, where would you like the girls to put their tools?"

"Yes," Susan said, "Becky, please help clean up. Then we must be going."

"Okay, Mommy, coming," Becky said as she and Emma placed their gardening tools in Tessy's wagon.

"Come back to see me often. We've plenty to do in our garden yet," Tessy said as both girls ran over and hugged her waist.

"Can we come back tomorrow?" Emma asked.

"Yah, can we?" repeated Becky.

Both Susan and Penny looked at Tessy with questioning eyes, but before they could say anything, Tessy spoke up. "That would be wonderful; I would love to see you tomorrow."

Susan, still looking at Tess, asked, "Are you sure they aren't going to play you out?"

"No, no, not at all. They are a delight to have around. They keep my inner child close at hand," Tessy chuckled.

"How about I'll call you in the morning; we'll see how you are feeling then," Penny said as she and Emma were headed toward the front gate.

"Well, now, if ye ring me in the morning, and I don't answer straight off, I'm probably in the garden—but I will return your call."

The girls each took turns petting and hugging Duke and Darby and stroking Merlin and Cordelia, promising to return soon. And with that, they all had final goodbye hugs and waves with vows of more tales and new adventures to be discovered. As Tessy watched them off, she turned to her animals and sighed with great satisfaction for she knew she had had a hand in creating two long-lasting friendships.

Vibrant Herb Vinaigrette

3/4 cup (175 ml) extra-virgin olive oil
1/4 cup (50 ml) red wine vinegar
1/4 tsp (1 ml) Himalayan salt
1/2 tsp (2 ml) peppercorns
1–2 garlic cloves, minced
1/2 tsp (2 ml) lemon verbena
1/2 tsp (2 ml) thyme
1/4 tsp (1 ml) rosemary
1/4 tsp (1 ml) sage

Whisk together olive oil and vinegar in a small mixing bowl. With mortar and pestle, grind salt and peppercorns and add to oil and vinegar mixture. Add minced garlic to mixing bowl. Add herbs and whisk thoroughly. Pour vinaigrette into a decorative bottle and store in refrigerator overnight to blend. Shake well before use. Add sprigs of fresh herbs to make it even more attractive!

Microdermabrasion

1 Tbsp (15 ml) baking soda
1 Tbsp (15 ml) sugar
1 tsp (5 ml) distilled water
2 drops lavender essential oil

Make a paste of the four ingredients. Dip fingers into paste mixture and very gently begin to massage on face and throat using small, circular motions. Do not rub with any pressure. After approximately 5 minutes, rinse thoroughly and apply moisturizing spray.

5

Woe-be-me Correspondence

Penny was upstairs sorting sheets and blankets into the linen closet when she heard the front door slam and someone thundering up the stairs. She looked up in time to see Sarah stampeding toward her.

"Sarah, what on earth — "

"Sorry, Mom," Sarah said as she practically knocked her mother over on the way past. "Roger just dropped off the mail, and there's a letter from Jen, and since we don't have our new computer yet, this is as good as it gets. I've just got to go read it right now. I'll be in my room." And the door slammed behind her.

Penny left what she was doing and went downstairs for a cup of coffee. On her way past the front door, she stopped to pick up the array of mail left strewn across the hall table. She flipped through it as she made her way to the kitchen. *Not much,* she thought . . . just the usual junk mail along with a couple of the hookup confirmations. She poured herself a cup of coffee, sat down at the kitchen table, and gazed out the bay window. She smiled as she watched Matt and his new friends busily repairing the old tree fort out in the back. "Oh, for the days of simple pleasures," she said out loud and opened up the latest flyer for Kessel's Grocery Store and slowly thumbed through it.

Upstairs, Sarah anxiously but carefully opened her letter from her best friend, Jennifer Bettray. Jennifer lived in Sarah's old neighbourhood and was now the only person, as far as Sarah was concerned, who carried any and all knowledge of importance. This was her first letter since the big move, and she just knew it would contain all the latest news of whatever was happening in the world she wished she were still a part of. Sarah jumped on her bed, propped up every pillow and stuffed animal she could find, lowered herself into them, and began to read.

Dear Sarah,

My life is a shambles without you!! (By the way, I really miss you.) I'm forced to hang out with Marci and of course, wherever she goes Sharon has to go, especially now that she and Peter have broken up. I know you didn't mind hanging out with them but they never bothered you because you knew how to handle them, I just don't fit in as well. It was soooo much easier when you were here. Since you've been gone they're just so bossy and intolerable. They treat me like a peon. And if that's not bad enough, my bratty little brother Mic (surprisingly not Morley this time) has decided he has this enormous crush on Marci and wants to hang out with us too. How embarrassing!! This, of course, ticks Marci off having someone his age tagging along and she blames me. She does, however, seem to like the attention and flirts with him shamelessly even though she has nothing but contempt for him. It really is quite sickening. "HELP!" Please, Please Come Back.

The other Jennifer (Jen #2) which I wouldn't mind hanging with is spending most of the summer at this special music camp and won't be back until sometime in August. Judy got caught smoking so she is like sooo grounded — like forever!! So I have no one else. Life is just so unfair!! Come Back, Please, Please, Please!!!

In your letter you asked about Eric. I don't have much news other than he's on holidays with his family and I don't think he's home yet as far as I know or care. You are so much better off without him anyway. Sorry, you know how I feel about him!! I'll try and keep you posted but only because I luv you!

I'm thinking, since my summer is a disaster anyway, I might as well work and make some money so I'm going down to Heavenly Scoops tomorrow to see if they could use another ice cream scooper. Not very exciting but Ray got a job there and you know how "smoke'n hot" I think he is! Working alongside him is the only thing that could possibly make this summer bearable, that and the fact that I could then afford to buy those adorable capris we saw down at Barbie's Boutique.

Oh, better go. Mom's yelling at me to come down and set the table. Come Back, Pls, Pls, Pls. Maybe you could just come for a visit if nothing else. You also mentioned maybe me coming to see you too. Hopefully something will work out soon. Miss ya bunches.

Love & Bestfriends Always,

Jen #1

P.S.

When are you getting your new computer hooked up??

P.P.S.

Have you met any cute guys yet??

After reading the letter through three more times just to make sure she hadn't missed anything, Sarah dropped it into her lap "Poor Jennifer" she sighed out loud. "But no news of Eric. I sure wish she liked him." She folded the letter back up, placed it in the envelope, and tucked it into her nightstand drawer next to her diary. She walked out into the hallway and was about to step over a pile of blankets and pillows when she called down to her mother: "Mom, would you like me to put this stuff away for you?"

"Oh, thanks, sweetheart, that would be great! I got busy down here with some other things and forgot all about them. Too many things on my brain lately." Penny wasn't sure if the last part of that sentence was meant for Sarah or more for herself.

The doorbell rang, and Penny opened it to find three rather solemn, well-dressed ladies roosting on her front doorstep.

"Good day, ladies. Can I help you?"

"Well, quite frankly, Mrs. Tucker, *we* are here to help *you*. My name is Mrs. Chamberlain and this is Mrs. Wright and Mrs. Mason. We understand that you are allowing your children to spend time with that voodoo, spell-casting witch, Mrs. McGuigan! We want to warn you to keep them as far away from her as possible. Heaven only knows what she is teaching them."

"Well, Mrs. Chamberlain, thank you, but my husband and I feel our children are perfectly safe with Tessy, and, quite frankly, she has become a dear, treasured friend of our entire family. Also, how we raise our children is none of your concern, and I will be extremely upset if I hear you have spoken to any of them regarding this matter. So now, if you will excuse me, I am very busy right at the moment. Good day, ladies!" And with that, she shut the door.

When Sarah had finished putting things away, she came down to the kitchen to see what her mom was up to. Penny was still huffing and puffing, not quite believing what had just happened.

"Who was at the door?" Sarah questioned.

"Just a couple of town busybodies trying to make trouble," Penny huffed.

"About what?"

"Oh, it's really nothing, honey—never mind. Thanks again for putting the rest of the linens away. So, any news from Jen?" her mom casually asked, wanting to quickly change the subject yet not wanting to seemingly pry.

"Oh, you know Jen, always a bit of a drama queen. It really does sound like she's having a rough summer, though. Marci and Sharon are being a bit hard on her."

"That's too bad. Marci can be rather . . . demanding, shall I say. You never seemed to allow her to get away with that, which I was very glad to see. You really have come into your own, sweetheart. I'm so proud of you."

"Thanks, Mom." Sarah reached over and hugged her mother. "Awful quiet around here. Where is everyone?"

"Matt's out in the back renovating, and Emma and Becky are over at Tess's, as usual. I'm so glad Tessy introduced Emma to Becky but I do hope they are not wearing out their welcome over there. Becky's mother, Susan, seems like a wonderful person. I'm thinking she and I could become good friends. By the way, I hope you don't mind, but she asked if you do any babysitting, and I told her you do from time to time—so I'm thinking she might ask you."

"No, that's okay. I don't mind and I could always use a little extra cash."

"That's good," continued Penny. "She's a single mom and I think it would be good for her to get out and socialize a bit; and Becky is a sweet girl. Susan has done a great job with her from what I've seen."

"I'm sure glad you're not a single mom. Not that you wouldn't be terrific at it, but I'm just glad we won't ever have to find out, right? You and Dad are good, right?" Sarah had never really thought about it before now even though quite a few of her friends had divorced parents.

"Oh, honey, your dad and I are more than good. We are still as crazy about one another as when we first met—I promise."

"That's good, but just keep it under control, okay? Don't go getting too lovey-dovey and stuff!" Sarah scrunched up her face.

Her mother laughed and hugged her. "Okay, I'll inform your father that we have to try and keep the 'lovey-dovey stuff' under control."

"Good, thanks!" answered Sarah, quite relieved.

"Would you please go and collect the girls? When you drop Becky off, maybe you could mention to Susan that you don't mind babysitting once in a while but not on a school night before any big tests."

"Okay, be back in a bit," Sarah said as she let the screen door slam.

Just as Sarah walked out the door, the phone rang. Penny, still fuming over her unwelcome guests, answered it with a little less relish than usual.

"Hi, Penny, it's Susan. How are you?"

"Oh, fine," Penny offered.

"Are you sure? You don't sound fine."

"I am so mad. Three busybodies just had the nerve to come to our door and suggest that Jim and I forbid the kids to see Tessy!" Penny huffed.

Susan started to laugh. "Oh, that had to be Mrs. Chamberlain and her two cronies. They have been trying to run Tessy out of town for twenty-five years. Don't pay any attention to them—they love to get into everyone's business. They came by my door shortly after Joe and I separated, giving me all sorts of advice, and then told me I should just close my eyes to what Joe was doing, be a good wife and mother, and go back to him. I couldn't slam the door in their faces fast enough!"

"Are you kidding?" Penny was astonished.

"Nope! Welcome to Ladyslipper—you have just been officially initiated!" Susan laughed again.

"Thanks a heap, neighbour!" Penny sighed.

All the way to Tessy's house, Sarah couldn't stop thinking about Jen's letter. Something just wasn't sitting right. She was positive that when she talked to Eric before she left that he said he would be home from his holiday this past weekend and that he would phone when he got home. Now, Jennifer says she doesn't think he's even home yet and just kind of brushed it off. She also seemed more ticked at Eric than usual. No, something is not right. Well, one thing was for sure: Sarah would be sending off another letter as quickly as she could get it written. "Sure wish our new computer would hurry up and get here," she grumbled out loud.

Sarah had been over to pick up the girls on more than one occasion so she had no qualms about opening the gate to Ashling Manor and letting herself into the yard to play with the dogs. After she had thrown the ball for Darby a number of times, she ran up the steps, and knocked on the screen door, yelling hello on her way in. Tessy was in the prep kitchen and didn't hear her on the first call. "Hello?" Sarah called louder.

"Oh, hello, Sarah dear, come in, come in," beckoned Tessy, wiping her wet hands on her apron. She gave Sarah a heartfelt hug. "Can I get ye something, love? Lemonade . . . iced tea, maybe?" she asked.

"No, I'm not feeling that great. Well, maybe an iced tea would be nice, if it's no trouble."

"Trouble? Of course not, no trouble at all — sit, sit. Why aren't ye feeling well, dear? What seems to be troubling ye?"

"Oh, cramps right at the moment, among other things," Sarah moaned.

"Poor dear . . . well, a warm drink would sit better for you than cold. How about a nice cup of orange ginger and yarrow tea?"

"Okay, thanks, that sounds good, too."

"Have you tried black cohosh or evening primrose for your cramps?"

"No — what are those and what do I do with them?"

"Black cohosh is a root from a plant native to right here in North America and it's a wonder for the plights of us women. I usually have some caplets but I'm all out at the moment. I do have some root in the back kitchen but it has an unpleasant odour and tastes just as ugly. One has to add a fair bit of honey and lemon to it to make it taste like something you might want to put in your mouth. It does come in caplets, and I'm sure your dad will have some at the pharmacy. I do have some of my PMS/Menopausal Spray that should help for now, though. Wait right here, and I'll get it." Tessy disappeared into the back kitchen and returned with a small spritzer bottle. "Here, close your eyes and spray a little of this on your face and breathe deep."

Sarah did as she was told. "Wow, that smells great."

"Good, you take that home and spray a little on your pillow tonight and you should feel better tomorrow."

"Thanks, I'll give it a try."

"Now, how are ye really doing? Making some friends, are you?"

"No, not yet," Sarah answered. "I've been busy helping Mom get things unpacked and settled. I haven't had much time to cruise the town except when I go down to the store to see Dad. Where are Emma and Becky?"

"Oh, the wee tykes are out in the back painting rocks for the new garden we started.

"Ye know, the Ladyslipper Community and Activity Centre have asked me to hold some sessions for the young ladies on homemade herbal beauty products on Thursday afternoons. I've looked at the enrollment sheets and there are plenty of lasses your age signed up. Maybe you'd like to join us?"

"Hey, that sounds pretty cool. Will you be making stuff like that awesome hand and nail lotion you brought over for us?"

"Aye, that and more. Talk it over with your mum then just let me know. It would be grand if you could attend, and I think it would be good for you to get out and socialize a bit."

"That sounds awesome. Do you know any of the girls signed up? Are they nice?" Sarah sounded a little apprehensive.

"Well, now, girls will be girls, but most of the young ladies on the list I have taught at one time or another and they all were cordial in my presence. However, that has always been the rule with me. If you've not a nice thing to say, you say nothing at all. I'll tolerate not a thing else and they all know it."

"Well, I'll check with Mom, but I'm pretty sure you can sign me up."

"Grand, here's a form I'll be needing your mum to sign to make sure it's fine with her and that you do not have any allergies to speak of."

"Okay, I'll take it home, thanks." Sarah reached for the form and quickly glanced over it.

As she finished her tea, she looked at her watch and jumped up. "Oh, my gosh, I'd better get the girls and head home — Mom will be wondering where the heck we are. Thanks for everything, Tess." Sarah gave her a quick hug and headed out the back door.

"Hey guys, look at you!" Sarah called across the yard. "You sure look like you've been having fun."

Emma and Becky were draped in a couple of Tessy's old shirts, slathered with paint, talking and giggling up a storm. Emma ran over to show Sarah her latest creation, which happened to be a rock painted bright red with black spots and still very wet. Sarah jumped back so as not to get any of the paint from the rock or Emma on her new shorts.

"Wow, that's terrific. It looks exactly like a big, beautiful ladybug."

"That's because that's what it is, silly."

Sarah laughed. "Okay, but we really have to get going. Is there somewhere you guys can wash up?"

"Yep, over in that washtub over there. Tessy set it up just for us. She leaves it there just about all the time so Becky and I can get clean whenever we want. But sometimes Duke and Darby drink out of it, which we don't really care about, but I don't think I'd like to drink out of it. But Tessy says it won't hurt them as long as there isn't any paint in it . . . or when it gets really dirty, like probably today, then she empties it out and starts again. You know — "

"Emma . . . enough . . . please take your paint shirt off and you and Becky go over and get washed up. We really have to get going."

The two girls splashed and rubbed right up to their elbows trying to clean the day's project off, with considerable unnecessary splashing going on. Tessy could see that the PMS-struck Sarah was becoming impatient with the girls' antics so she picked up a big fluffy towel that had been lying on the lawn chair and went over to dry them off.

"Boy, Tessy, your towels always smell so good. What is that smell?" Emma asked slightly gasping for air from behind the towel as Tessy was wiping her face.

Tessy laughed and said, "Well, now, let's see . . . that would be a little mixture of baking soda, sun, and lavender."

"Can we get our towels to smell like that?"

"Of course ye can, dear. I'll whip up some lavender sachets for ye to take home and put in your closet next time you and Becky come to visit."

"Wow, thanks. I'll tell Mommy."

"Can I have some to take home, too?" Becky shyly asked.

"I'd never forget you, wee darling." Tessy wrapped the towel around her and gave her a big hug.

"Okay, guys, let's go. Thanks for everything, Tess. See you soon." Sarah was hurrying the girls along, reminding Tess of a mother goose flapping her wings over her chicks.

Tessy walked out to the front yard with them then watched and waved until they were out of sight. She always felt a little lonely when the girls left after being there for the afternoon. Duke and Darby seemed to sense her solitude and stayed very close to her. Darby picked up her Frisbee and nudged Tess's hand. Tess laughed, tugged it out of her mouth, and tossed it across the yard. "Ah, ye precious, wee darlins, where would I be without ye? You always know just what I need. Come now, I'll get ye a lovely treat." And with that, she tousled their furry heads and climbed the steps to the front porch.

Lemon Thyme Tea Loaf

2 cups (500 ml) all-purpose
    flour
2 tsp (10 ml) baking powder
1/4 tsp (1 ml) sea salt
1 package (225 g) soft cream
    cheese
1/2 cup (125 ml) softened
    butter
1 cup (250 ml) sugar

3 eggs
Juice of 1 lemon
1 tsp (5 ml) vanilla
1/2 cup (125 ml) milk
1 tsp (5 ml) grated lemon peel
1 tsp (5 ml) lemon balm or
    lemon thyme
1 tsp (5ml) thyme

Lemon Glaze

1/4 cup (50 ml) icing sugar

1 Tbsp (15 ml) lemon juice

Preheat oven to 350°F (180°C). Mix flour, baking powder, and salt in medium bowl and set aside. In separate bowl beat together cream cheese, sugar, and butter until light and fluffy. Add eggs one by one, beating after each addition. Add vanilla and lemon juice and mix well. Add flour; blend into creamed mixture, alternately adding milk. Beat until smooth. Stir in lemon balm, thyme, and lemon peel. Pour batter into greased and floured loaf pan. Bake for 60 to 75 minutes or until done. Drizzle the lemon glaze over the warm loaf and let cool before slicing.

Revitalizing Citrus Mint Tea Blend

Equal parts of (dried or fresh) orange geranium, lemon verbena, spearmint leaves, and calendula
Optional, to taste: cloves, peppercorns, dried lemon rind, and dried orange rind

Combine in teapot, pour boiling water over, and let steep for approximately 10 minutes. Add honey to taste or add pinch of stevia to herb mixture before adding hot water.

6

Recipe for Friendship

Tessy liked to do what she could to stay involved with her community. She volunteered and did charity work for organizations such as the SPCA, Food Bank, and the Christmas Bureau. This was Tuesday; and every Tuesday morning she liked to trek down to the seniors' complex to visit the shut-in and elderly. She would gather a group of them into the common area to do crafts; or they would sing old, familiar songs like, "Let Me Call You Sweetheart" or "Red Roses for a Blue Lady." Sometimes, she would get them to close their eyes and she would talk them through an imaginary journey to exotic places like Hawaii or maybe Rome; and although she might lose a few to slumber, the rest would sing tunes of that particular destination, such as "Tiny Bubbles," or "That's Amore." Then, before leaving, she performed some Reiki and handed out specific herbs or salves she'd made to help specific people; but she always checked with the head nurse first to make sure they would not interfere with their current medications.

Later that afternoon, Tessy was out on the front veranda thumbing through her favourite home remedy recipes, preparing for her class, when she heard whistling and looked up in time to see Roger opening her front gate. Duke and Darby both jumped up and bounded down the walk to greet him.

"Good morning, Roger."

"Good morning, Tess—a bit cloudy and cooler today. They say possible showers for the next day or two."

"Aye, a nice reprieve from what we've been having. Always nice when the garden gets a break from the suffering heat and the plants get a good drink."

"Yah, that's true. The clouds make it a bit more pleasant for me, too, but the rain, not so much!"

"Aye, don't be forgetting your Wellies. Ye don't want to be catchin' yourself a summer cold," Tessy chuckled.

Roger smiled. "That's for sure. By the way, I think I have all the invitations delivered for your Christmas in July celebration."

"Grand! Hard to believe that's arriving next week already. I've a few things yet to prepare; but, all in all, it's coming along quite snappy."

"Well, Connie and I are looking forward to it as always. Are you sure there's nothing extra we can bring or help you with?"

"No, no, but thank ye anyway. You're already doing a big service for me. Besides, I've been doing this for so many years now it's just like breathing in and out. Although, I must admit it was a mite easier when Dermot was here. Oh, how he loved his Christmas . . . and Christmas in July was as much fun for him as any. That twinkle in his eye was well worth any bother. But I've sure been letting my angels know I'll be needing fair weather before then."

"It's supposed to turn nice again, so it sounds like they've been listening. Better get going. See you tomorrow, Tess."

"Good day to ye, Roger. May your load be light and your shoulders stay dry."

Dermot was raised celebrating all the traditional Canadian holidays, while Tessy honoured more the Olde Celtic traditions. They learned to combine, respect, and enjoy each other's celebrations and beliefs unconditionally. Tessy and Dermot had been having "Christmas in July" for about five years before Dermot passed. It all started one year when they weren't able to fit in their annual December Yule Come and Go social due to busy schedules, illnesses, and weather. They tried time and again to reschedule the date, and before they knew it, it was July! Hence, "Christmas in July." It was such a hit that it became a new tradition for the McGuigans. The first year, after Dermot passed, Tessy just couldn't bring herself to host the event without him; but she and everyone else missed it so. She knew how disappointed Dermot would be, so since then, it has carried on with as much splash and merriment as ever.

Tessy gave her head a slight shake and focused back on her current task of getting the curriculum in order for her class this Thursday. "I am so glad Sarah has chosen to attend," Tessy smiled to herself. "It will do her a world of good to meet some of the lasses and move on with her new beginnings. The rest of the family has settled in quite nicely, but Sarah, the poor dear, seems to be hanging onto the bygone. Melancholy appears to be her only friend just now. Aye, we must fix that," she concluded out loud to Duke, who was paying close attention, while Darby was busily chewing on a big, succulent bone and not hearing a word (nor particularly caring). Duke, a very large, once orphaned, Heinz 57, was never far from Tessy's side and was most observant. Darby, being a golden retriever, had to stop and pick something up to have in her mouth; it didn't really matter what it was, just whatever happened to be in the vicinity: a stuffed animal, ball, rock, Frisbee, stick . . . anything would do.

Tess awoke the next morning to a good, old-fashioned, booming, prairie thunderstorm. The wind was up, pelting the driving rain across her windows. *Goodness gracious, I do hope I closed up all the windows tight last night!* was her first thought. She hopped out of bed like a woman half her age, slipped on her housecoat and slippers, and sprinted from room to room, making sure the house was securely buttoned up. After she was satisfied that everything was dry and in order, she flip-flopped her way down to the kitchen to put the kettle on.

Duke and Darby weren't quite sure what the game was that they were playing this morning, running through the house, but it certainly was outlandish fun. It did, however, get them bouncing and under Tessy's feet. "Okay, that's it, rain or no rain — it's outside with the two of ye. 'Way ye go, now." She opened the door, and they both bounded out to the back porch, where Tessy flew open the screen door, and they thundered down the steps out into the pouring rain. "Ugh!" she scrunched up her face. "You'll be smelling like a couple of wet, mangy rats when you're done, so count on spending some time drying out in the porch today."

She pulled her housecoat close up around her neck, turned, and stepped back into the kitchen, closing the door behind her. "Well, the good Lord knows we needed the rain, but ye can be turning down the power a wee mite, Father." She opened the cupboard, picked out her favourite cup, and poured hot water over a mesh ball filled with fragrant tea leaves. When she sat down at the kitchen table to watch the dogs romp and splash in the rain, the sprig of holly gently pricked the back of her hand. She carefully rubbed the shiny green leaf between her fingers and mused, "What is it you're trying to tell me, my green friend?" She soon turned her attention back to the dogs "Worse than a couple of kids, they are," she chuckled, looking down at Merlin and Cordelia snuggled in their cushioned basket. There was no doubt in Tessy's mind, or theirs, where they would remain for the duration of the storm.

Tessy puttered about the kitchen, fixing herself a bubbling pot of porridge. It just seemed like a porridge morning, and she served up a hefty helping. She got close to the bottom of the bowl and pushed it away, groaning, "My eyes have always been bigger than my stomach." She glanced toward the two snoozing felines and grinned. "Aye." She got up, reached into the fridge, opened up the carton of cream, and poured a generous amount over the remainder of her porridge. She then popped it into the microwave for a couple of seconds, pulled it out, stirred it, and placed it on the mat by the door. Their little heads sprang up and they raced over to the bowl, not even taking time for a good stretch. Tessy laughed as she could hear a combination of purring and their rough, pink tongues lapping the tasty goo as fast as they dared.

"Ah, now for those soggy pups. I'll be getting dressed before taking their towels and wrestling with them."

She ran upstairs, put on her jeans and a cozy sweatshirt, ran a brush through her hair and swept it up into a lazy ponytail, and grabbed a couple of old clean towels used just for the purpose she was about to perform. She got back down to the kitchen and pulled open the door. "'Tis not going to be a pleasant experience, I fear," she told the cats. She closed the inside door and went out to the porch and called the dogs. She opened the screened porch door as wide as it would go and stood back as far as she could behind it. The two drenched mutts came flying into the porch, slipping and sliding. Each stopped to have a great shake and then stood looking at her with tongues hanging. It took her about forty minutes, three more towels, and a change of clothing; but after all was said and done, the dogs were somewhat dry, and the floors, walls, and deck furnishings were all wiped down.

The downpour had diminished to a drizzle by mid-morning, and Tess was on the computer finishing up her lessons for tomorrow. It had taken her a little longer to prepare than she had anticipated but she wanted some unique combinations for the girls to try. After all, they were maturing into beautiful young ladies, and she thought a wider range of products would be in order. She had quite a list of recipes and was wondering if they could fit them all in during the allotted time frame. She put the finishing touches on the page she was working on and hit "PRINT." "There," she said. "Finished at last, and the wee computer goblins steered clear for me, bless their souls." She reached down and stroked Merlin as he wound himself in, out, and around her chair, dragging his massive tail over her legs. She pulled the page off the printer and read its contents, which happened to be the outline for the course projects. My, there did seem to be a goodly number of them. *Ah well, better too many than not enough.* She wanted to make sure there was a little of everything, for hair, face, hands, body care, even insect repellent for the outdoorsy types, if there was time. And then there were the lip balms and bath salts she was hoping to squeeze in. It was a good thing that the Community Centre had her agree to three consecutive Thursdays, as it was going to take at least that amount of time to complete what she had organized.

Thursday morning proved to be a much brighter start. The sky was clear, with fluffy white clouds that slowly billowed past Tessy's bedroom window. Tessy lay in bed feeling relaxed and preparing her day in her mind. She was so blessed. She took in a few deep breaths, thanking God and her angels for all the blessings bestowed on her and asked that they stay close during her endeavours today, especially since a room full of hormonal teenage girls was on the agenda!

As she asked for that particular blessing, she chuckled and hopped out of bed. "There, now, my day has begun!" she said out loud. Downstairs, she found both dogs, tails wagging, waiting at the door for her to let them out. "Good morning to ye. Ready to go out now, are ye?" She lovingly gave them each a pet before opening the door and quickly dodging out of the way. "It's no wonder some mornings I feel we barely escape with our lives when those two brutes bolt out the door like that!" She looked over at Merlin and Cordelia, who had just come in from a night of prowling and were now ready for a well-deserved nap.

Tessy arrived at the Community Centre at around twelve thirty to set up and found Sarah already there, waiting outside for her.

"Hey," Sarah called out, running over to meet Tessy, looking very relieved to see her.

"Hey, yourself," Tessy smiled. "I'm so glad ye came."

"Well, me too, I hope! Here, can I help you with some of that stuff?" Sarah reached for the bags in Tessy's arms.

"Oh, thank ye. I couldn't get everything in the wagon so had to carry a few parcels." Tessy gave her arms a shake as they became free.

They entered the Centre, and Tessy led the way to the classroom. She flicked on the lights and wandered about, opening up the blinds and preparing the room with ease, as she had done hundreds of times in the past. All of a sudden, Sarah noticed the room was full of light and took on Tessy's aura of energy. She had explained to her mother it was one of the reasons she loved just hanging out with her — the energy she exudes is so amazing, and the wonderful part is that it's contagious!

Tessy handed Sarah some folders, homemade booklets, and pens and asked her to distribute them on the tables that were set up in an open "U" shape as per Tessy's instructions. It was a particularly large room with a kitchenette off to one side. A stove was an absolute must when the arrangements were being drawn up for this class. Tess was busy pulling a double boiler out of one of her boxes when she heard some movement by the door.

"Well, Cherokee, dear, come in, come in. So good to see ye again. How is your mum?" Tessy hurried over to the door to hug one of the most beautiful girls Sarah had ever seen.

"Hi, Tessy. It's so good to see you, too. Mom is doing great. She said to say hi."

"Come in," Tessy repeated. "This is Sarah Tucker. I've been wantin' the two of ye to meet. Sarah, this is Cherokee Amiotte. Her mother, Skye, and I taught together; and her father is a special constable here in the area."

"Hi, nice to meet you," they echoed together, then laughed.

"Cherokee is one of my star students, not just in history but more in the way of a budding herbalist. She belongs to an ancestral line of shamans, and I can see her venturing into somewhat similar footsteps."

"Oh, Tessy, I don't know about that. I love learning about nature and my ancestry but I can't see a profitable future in shamanism," she joked.

"Aye, perhaps, but ye could have a wonderful future in herbalism, homeopathy, or maybe as a naturopathic physician," Tessy remarked as she continued to unpack pots and bowls from her boxes. "Ye can help Sarah pass out those stacks of papers — recipes, mostly — if you'd like."

"I understand you've just moved to town, Sarah. How do you like it?" asked Cherokee.

"Good so far. Haven't really done anything or met anyone other than Tessy but I think I'm going to like it here. I'm really glad I came today. I think this is going to be so cool."

"Oh, you are going to love Tessy's classes. They are always something out of the ordinary. I had Tessy as my history teacher for a couple of years and even that she made fun and interesting. How often does that happen?" she added.

"No kidding," Sarah agreed.

Soon the rest of the girls arrived, and Tessy announced for them to take a seat. After giving the girls a brief overview of what the class would entail, she had each of them introduce themselves and say which of the treatments they were most interested in.

"Now, before we go any further, as some of ye know, I like to begin my classes with a song that I feel particularly passionate about. I share it in hopes of its message radiating throughout the world. The name of it is "Desiderata." There are many theories as to where it came from but most believe it was originally a poem written by a chap named Max Ehrmann, and first copyrighted in 1927. The song, however, was performed by Les Crane in 1971 and was very popular when I was about your age. After it's over, I'd like to spend a minute or two discussing it. Ye all have a copy of the words in your folder, and I'd like ye to follow along. Please feel free to sing if ye wish. Okay now, here we go," and Tessy hit the "PLAY" button on the CD player.

> Go placidly amid the noise and haste, and remember what
> peace there may be in silence.

> As far as possible without surrender, be on good terms
> with all persons.

> Speak your truth quietly and clearly, and listen to others,
> even the dull and ignorant; they, too, have their story.

> Avoid loud and aggressive persons; they are vexations to
> the spirit. If you compare yourself with others, you may
> become vain and bitter; for always there will be greater and
> lesser persons than yourself. Enjoy your achievements as
> well as your plans.

> Keep interested in your own career, however humble; it is
> a real possession in the changing fortunes of time. Exercise
> caution in your business affairs, for the world is full of

trickery. But let this not blind you to what virtue there is; many persons strive for high ideals; and everywhere life is full of heroism.

Be yourself. Especially, do not feign affection. Neither be cynical about love; for in the face of all aridity and disenchantment, it is as perennial as the grass.

Take kindly the counsel of the years, gracefully surrendering the things of youth. Nurture strength of spirit to shield you in sudden misfortune. But do not distress yourself with dark imaginings. Many fears are born of fatigue and loneliness. Beyond a wholesome discipline, be gentle with yourself.

You are a child of the universe, no less than the trees and the stars; you have a right to be here. And whether or not it is clear to you, no doubt the universe is unfolding as it should.

Therefore be at peace with God, whatever you conceive Him to be; and whatever your labours and aspirations, in the noisy confusion of life, keep peace with your soul.

With all its sham, drudgery, and broken dreams, it is still a beautiful world. Be cheerful. Strive to be happy.

Tessy hit the "STOP" button and remained silent for a moment. She looked up and scanned the room. It was reverently quiet. She stepped forward and smiled at the girls. She knew the intended message had been received. "Now, who would like to share their thoughts on this wonderful piece? Aye, Jodi?"

"I think it's saying be kind to people and be thankful for what we have."

"Aye, that's definitely in there." Tessy nodded her head up and down. "Who else? Cherokee?"

She was silent in thought, then she said, "Look inside yourself; be true to who you are. That we all belong here and are here for a reason.

Listen to what's going on within us and stay at peace even in the hustle and bustle of our day-to-day lives."

"Aye, good. I think ye got the message and I'm wantin' you all to take that poem out of your folders and put it up at home. Maybe in your room or on the fridge or even in your bathroom — just put it where you'll read it often and think about it. Now, let's carry on." She changed the CD to some soothing Zen music and asked all the girls to join her in the kitchen area.

"We'll be starting with a light Magick Mist that may be used on all skin types and is also good for sunburned or windburned skin. Teresa, I believe that this was your favourite pick, was it not?"

Teresa nodded her head up and down and quietly clapped her hands together, smiling and slightly gloating. The other girls laughed and groaned.

Tessy continued, "This recipe is extremely easy to prepare and you won't need much else than a storage container. It makes a wee more than one-half cup, so we'll use a container such as this and start adding the ingredients — distilled water, aloe vera juice, vegetable glycerin, and about five drops of mandarin essential oil. Now, you may use geranium, grapefruit, or lavender oil if ye do not fancy the mandarin. Ye then pop the top on the bottle, give it a mighty shake, and it's ready to use. You must always label what you've made, including all the ingredients, and it's a good idea to put the date on it, as well. Make sure ye shake it every time you wish to use it. Here, Teresa, spray a bit on the back of your hand. Isn't it nice? Here, now, the rest of you try some."

They sprayed a little on to try and all agreed that is was so refreshing and so easy to make! The question of whether it needed to be stored in the refrigerator came up. Tessy replied, "No refrigeration is necessary, but for maximum freshness, it should be used up within six months." The girls all laughed and said that would not be a problem!

"The next recipe we are concocting today is the Hand and Nail Repair, which I believe was Sarah's favourite pick — correct, Sarah?" She, too, rubbed and clapped her hands together looking rather smug. Again, the girls laughed and groaned.

"Where do we get all this stuff, and how expensive is it?" asked Robyne.

"Good question, dear. Some of the essential oils can be a bit dear but quite worth it in the end and most everything can be purchased at the health food store or some craft stores; or the pharmacy will have a good deal of the ingredients. Is that correct, Sarah?" Tessy inquired.

"Some items I recognize but some not—but I'm sure going to talk to my dad and see if we can order in all this stuff," Sarah assured her.

"My, that would be wonderful, and very welcome, to be sure. Well, looks like I should be giving our brew a wee stir and moving it off the heat. We'll add about 35 drops of our essential oils, stir it again, and pour it into our containers. Now, the choices of essential oils I brought along today are mandarin, peppermint, geranium, rosemary, grapefruit, and lavender; or ye can have a combination of a couple, if you like. What will it be?"

After much sniffing and calling out, the decision was to add lavender and rosemary. Tessy had the girls lay out their tins and jars and she filled each one.

"It takes some time for it to set, so we'll cover the containers with a tea towel for now and leave them here in one of the cupboards until tomorrow. I'll come and seal them up, and they will be all ready for you to take home next week. Again, ye need not refrigerate your salve but you will need to use it up within a year. Now, our last project for today is a microdermabrasion."

"A *what?*" echoed throughout the room.

"Micro-derm-abrasion," repeated Tessy, giggling. "But you must use extreme caution when applying it to your skin. It's an exfoliant that is good for all skin types but NOT to be used on sunburnt, windburnt, or sensitive skin; and only to be done once a week. You make up only one treatment at a time, and it is very easy to do."

She reached for a small bowl and called out the ingredients as she put them in: "Baking soda, sugar, distilled water, and a couple of drops of lavender essential oil. Take a spoon and mix into a watery paste, like so. Shelley, dear, come dip your fingers into this and rub VERY GENTLY onto the back of your hand. Don't use much pressure—let the baking soda and sugar do the exfoliating for you.

"Normally, ye would lightly massage your face and throat using small circular motions. After about five to ten minutes, thoroughly rinse, and that is when you'd apply your Magick Mist Moisturizer that ye blended today over your face and throat area. There will always be CAUTION in big red letters when caution is needed with any of these products. Which I'll be expecting ye all to mind.

"Do ye have any questions, now? Okay, that'll be all for today, then.

Thank ye all for coming. Ye can take your booklets home but please don't be trying the recipes that we haven't prepared in class yet. You'll find an ingredient dictionary in the back of your booklets, which will help you with the properties and components. Enjoy your new products. I'll be here at the hall tomorrow around one p.m. if ye wish to come by and collect your salves; if not, they'll be here for you next Thursday."

Sarah, Cherokee, and a couple of the other girls stayed and helped Tessy clean up and get things put away before dispersing. Tessy, Sarah, and Cherokee were all headed in the same direction and set off together, each taking a turn at pulling Tessy's wagon, although it was much lighter than when she arrived at the Community Centre. The girls were busy discussing the afternoon's creations, with Tessy occasionally being able to squeeze in the odd question and answer. When they got to Tessy's corner, Cherokee handed the wagon over to her, and they said their goodbyes. The girls stood and watched her off then turned to one another. There was an awkward moment of silence then Sarah asked, "Would you like to come over to my house for a while?"

"Sure, that would be great — if your parents won't mind."

"Mind? Of course not! They'd love to meet you. Come on, it's just down this street a couple of blocks," Sarah blurted.

"Okay, but I should probably call my mom as soon as I get there and let her know where I am."

"No problem!"

And another treasured friendship was crystallized with a sprinkling of assistance from a very wise woman.

Hand and Nail Repair

4 Tbsp (60 ml) sweet almond oil
3 Tbsp (45 ml) beeswax
2 Tbsp (30 ml) refined coconut oil
1 Tbsp (15 ml) anhydrous lanolin
25 drops lavender
10 drops rosemary
(Or whatever combination of essential oils you wish)

In a double boiler or in a glass bowl set over a saucepan of hot water, combine all ingredients except essential oils until melted. Remove from heat, add essential oils, and mix. Pour into containers and cover with paper towels until cool and well set.

Screaming Headache Salve

3 Tbsp (45 ml) beeswax
1 Tbsp (15 ml) refined coconut oil
1 Tbsp (15 ml) sweet almond oil
15 drops each of rosemary, chamomile, and peppermint
    essential oils
10 drops lavender essential oil
8 drops sweet marjoram essential oil

In a double boiler or saucepan over low heat, combine all ingredients except essential oils until melted. Remove from heat and cool for approximately 10 minutes, stirring occasionally. Drop in essential oils and stir. Pour into containers, cap, and refrigerate for 12 hours.

7

Blooming Yule

The next project on Tessy's busy calendar was "Christmas in July," which is always held on the last Sunday of July. Having it near the end of July coincided perfectly with her Celtic celebration of Lammas, the festival of the first harvest: The feast of Lugh and the Sacrificial King, who is most often, in this day and age, represented by a gingerbread man. She always considers this one of her favourite undertakings and tackles it with great gusto. The yard was in full bloom, the invitations had all been sent out informing everyone of the day's festive shenanigans, and her excitement was mounting. The whole time Tessy works on the arrangements for this occasion, she goes about with a huge smile on her face, remembering the anticipatory twinkle in Dermot's eyes.

Tessy decided to leave the menu pretty much as it always had been: cold turkey and ham to have with her homemade grain loaves, lots of homemade cranberry sauce, potato salad, bean salad, and fresh, cut-up vegetables. To drink there was plenty of her Berry Blessed Lemonade and, of course, Iced Spiced Apple Cider. Whenever available, a large bowl of mandarin oranges will adorn the middle of the table. For dessert, there is cherry, apple, and pumpkin pie, along with mincemeat tarts and plenty of decorated gingerbread men. Some of the cookies will be wrapped in cellophane and hung in the trees for the children to collect on their yearly treasure hunt.

Preparations for this event take Tessy almost the whole year to pull off, but she wouldn't change a thing. Weeks ahead, she bakes the festive loaves, cookies, and pies, a few at a time; and buys the turkeys and ham from a neighbour who raises them organically and freezes everything. This way, the expense is spread out and never becomes an issue.

This year, the July heat has been way too extreme to even consider cooking the turkeys and ham herself so she arranged for the local caterer to cook and carve them for her. Besides, this had always been one of Dermot's contributions to the day (in part, she knew, so he could secretly snack on his favourite morsels, the turkey wings, but nevertheless, she hadn't wanted to take that away from him). She had taken the meat to the caterer about a week ago and was scheduled to pick them up on Saturday morning, as Sunday they were closed. She was in the process of planning her day with a cup of tea in one hand and pen and paper in the other when the phone rang.

"Good mornin' to ye," she answered.

"Good morning, Tess. It's Roger, here. I was wondering if you had the Santa suit ready yet."

"Aye, Roger. I was about to head on up to the attic just now and fetch it out of my trunk. I'd be having it ready in a shake of a leg but I'd like to hang it out on the line for a wee while as to get the must out of it."

"Well, Connie and I are on our way out to pick up a few things downtown so we could probably come by in a couple of hours, if that's okay?"

"That would be just grand. I'll fetch it straightaway and put it out on the line."

"Okay, we'll see you then, Tess."

"Grand, and Roger, thank ye for being Santa for the wee ones again this year."

"Oh, my pleasure. I always have a great time playing Santa. See you in a bit. 'Bye."

"'Bye for now, Roger."

Tessy left her tea and list and headed upstairs. The stairs to the attic were disguised behind a small door in the hallway that could very easily be mistaken for a linen closet. The door stuck slightly from moisture and lack of use. The stairs were steep and narrow and they creaked as Tessy ascended. There was a comfortable, musty smell of past decades, with packed treasures, boxed vintage china, bundles of heirloom fabric, and old photographs. The oiled floorboards also creaked as Tessy made her way over to the far side of the attic where the oval stained glass window cast a colourful aura about the room. With suspended dust particles dancing through the multicoloured rays, she spotted the particular trunk she was after, which sat just under that window. She pulled over a wooden crate that was nearby, sat down, and opened the trunk lid. The sweet smell of cedar immediately struck her senses and she smiled. She moved aside a couple of winter sweaters she had placed in the trunk earlier that spring, not really knowing what else to do with them, and there it was, the Santa suit. She paused then placed her hand on the fuzzy red garment. She slowly picked it up and softly caressed her cheek with it. Playing Santa was Dermot's favourite Christmas task. Whether it be winter or summer, when Dermot put that suit on and transformed himself into that jolly role, he could persuade even the staunchest of skeptics.

She peeked over the edge of the trunk and picked up the old hat that Dermot had worn so many times. She brought it up to her nose and took in a deep breath. Ahh . . . the aroma of "Old Spice" whisked her back to when she would watch Dermot carefully splash it onto his face and around the back of his neck when he finished shaving. Tessy never let Roger or anyone else ever wear this hat or the beard. She had purchased new ones to go with the costume. The old ones stayed right where they were, in the trunk. No one was allowed to take these small, pleasurable moments away from her.

She sat for a little while, eyes closed, breathing in memories until she felt a little light-headed and slightly intoxicated. She let out a deep sigh and gently placed the cherished memento back into the trunk. She leaned deep into the contents, dug around until she found a large feather pillow, gathered up the rest of the costume, then closed the lid. She patted the curved top of the old chest and, as she turned to leave, said, "Well, my love, I'm sure Roger will do ye proud again this year. He's not quite the Kris Kringle ye were but he does a fine job, bless his heart."

With her arms full, Tessy took extra precautions descending the steep stairs, as she had no time for injuries nor any other mishaps to occur. As she was bumping her hip up against the attic door to get it closed and latched tight, she heard someone tapping at the front entryway. "My stars, I hope that's not Roger already," she thought out loud. "I didn't hear the dogs making a fuss so it has to be someone they know." She hurried her step a little but was still extremely careful going down the main staircase. Reaching the landing, she could see through the screen door that it was Sarah and Cherokee. "Oh, girls, come on in. I forgot ye were coming to help me wrap cookies. Come. Come." She continued down the stairs and, reaching the foyer, motioned with her elbow for the girls to follow her into the kitchen.

She plunked the pillow down on one of the kitchen chairs and laid the costume over the back of it so she could give the girls each a generous hug. "Thank ye so much for coming and giving me a hand. It's awfully kind of ye."

"Hey, no problem. This party is going to be so much fun! I've never heard of an actual Christmas in July before. Cherokee has been telling me all about it, the candy cane and cookie hunt for the kids, Santa, the Chinese gift exchange and then a bonfire. It sounds incredible!" Sarah was so excited she had to gasp for air.

Tessy chuckled. "Well, I'm hoping everyone has a real grand time."

"How could they not?" continued Sarah. "Emma and Becky had a great time over here the other day making the cranberry and popcorn garland with you. They haven't stopped talking about it yet. So what would you like us to do?"

"Well, now, let's see . . . The cookies are in tins in the back kitchen fridge, and you'll find the Christmas cello and bags for the candies on the prep table in there, as well. I've already cut the cello to fit around the cookies and the ribbons for tying them. The bulk candy and candy canes are here in the pantry, and there is a bag of trinkets in the hall. Each candy bag that Santa gives out must have a wee prize in it. If ye could get things all set up here on the kitchen table, I'll be back in the shake of a leg to help you. I've got to get this suit hung over the line and airing before Roger arrives to pick it up."

Just off Tessy's main kitchen is a small room, which in its day was called the prep kitchen. That is where she stores and prepares all of her herbal concoctions. It has a beautiful, old, yet still quite functional wood cookstove that includes a water reservoir and warming oven. Beside it is the woodbox. A number of hutches and cabinets line the room's perimeter. One unique cupboard, which Tessy designed and constructed herself, has a screen mesh door with removable wood-framed screen shelves used solely for the purpose of drying herbs. Then, there is her apothecary, which spans the whole length of one wall and houses all her herbal treasures. There is an antique icebox in the corner used only for storage now, although she does have a small fridge in this backroom for any formulas needing to be kept cool. Finally, down the middle of the room, is a long, narrow work table, cut just the right height for Tessy.

The girls headed for the prep kitchen and proceeded to find everything just as Tessy had said. "Wow, this place is really cool. I've never actually been in here before. Look at all this neat stuff." Sarah glanced around the dusky room at all the shelves lined with jars and containers filled with dried vegetation and bits of odds and ends.

"Yah, one summer I helped Tessy pick and dry herbs, and we spent a lot of time back here. She taught me some amazing things about herbs and vegetables and flowers. She is so knowledgeable about all that kind of stuff, and it just seems to come so naturally to her. I love just hanging out with her," said Cherokee. "Well, we better get this stuff out to the main kitchen and get started. If you get the tins, I'll take the cello, bags, and ribbons . . . Great, let's go."

By the time Tessy returned to the kitchen, the girls had everything out, and the "working bee" was well under way. They soon had a system going, and before they knew it they had gaily talked and shared and nibbled and giggled the morning away. Each group of treats was set in a separate basket for easy distribution on Sunday morning, which the girls said they would gladly come and help out with.

"About how many little kids do you expect?" Sarah asked.

"Oh, I usually end up with close to thirty wee ones, I'd say."

"Wow, you'll have plenty of candy, then. There has got to be enough here for at least fifty."

"Well, better too much than not enough. Besides, that leaves a bit more for you bigger ones, now, doesn't it!" Tessy teased.

"True!" the girls echoed as they high-fived.

"Oh, Tessy—I almost forgot," Sarah said. "My Grandpa Tayse is coming to visit for a couple of weeks and he is arriving tonight. We were wondering if he could come to the party with us."

"Aye, of course he's invited. More the merrier. Your mum's father, I'm presuming."

"Yep, can't wait to see him. He lives in Winnipeg, and we haven't seen him since Easter break. Matt and I got to go and spend the week with him and he took us all over the place. You wouldn't think there'd be that much to do in Winnipeg but you'd be surprised."

"Winnipeg, is it?" Tessy piped. "I lived and schooled in Winnipeg for a time when I was a young lass. Winnipeg is a very interesting city; some parts are very old—at least considered old in this part of the world. It's a city rich in culture, with many ethnic groups of all kinds. Very strong French Canadian population, and they have a wonderful winter carnival called Le Festival du Voyageur. Well, now listen to me go on and on. Aye, brings back some fine memories for me."

"Tessy, you know something about everything," Cherokee said, shaking her head. "I don't know why I should find that surprising, though. You never cease to amaze me."

"I've lived a fair, long life. You'll eventually see that many things just come with age and experience, my dears." Tessy laughed. "Now, I thank ye kindly for your help but I must be heading off to the Centre right quick, as I promised I'd be there around one o'clock. Will ye girls be wanting your nail salve today? I could bring yours home here if ye like, as you'll be back tomorrow."

"That would be great, if you don't mind. Sarah and I are on our way to the lake right now. I promised I would take her out to Baker's Beach and show her where we play beach volleyball and meet some of the gang. Most of them will be out there this afternoon, so I'm sure there'll be at least one or two good matches scheduled," Cherokee surmised.

"It's a grand afternoon for the beach. I'm sure you'll have a dandy time. And I don't mind a lick about bringing your lotion home."

Just as they reached the foyer, Roger knocked on the screen door and stepped in. "Hello, there. Sorry, Tessy — Connie and I are running a little late. Hi, girls."

"Not a problem, to be sure. I'll just run out back and gather the suit up off the line. 'Bye, 'bye, girls. Enjoy your afternoon. Thanks again." And off scurried Tessy to the back to retrieve the suit.

The next couple of days were a flurry of activity. There were decorations to put up, music to select, food to prepare, and small gifts to wrap. Tessy took it all in stride and relished every minute. Sarah and Cherokee were back on Saturday and brought Emma and Becky to help put up the decorations and they giggled and laughed and played with the dogs all morning.

"How much fun is this?" Sarah grinned.

"I know, putting up bows, lights, and these really cool, huge tree decorations in July!" beamed Cherokee.

It was Emma's and Becky's job to string their homemade garland all along the fence and around some of the smaller shrubs for the birds to enjoy but hopefully leave alone for a day or two. Duke and Darby never left their sides, waiting for any handouts along with pets and hugs. Tessy watched with great delight from the kitchen window as to how the backyard was being transformed into a Christmas wonderland. She thought it was time for the girls to take a break so she took out a sample pitcher of the chilled spiced apple cider she had been mixing up.

"Aye, girls, I'd like ye to have a taste of my mulled cider and see what ye think."

The girls all dropped what they were doing and came running over to the picnic table. Tessy had also brought out a "sampler" plate of gingerbread man cookies.

"Well, I guess the way they're disappearing, everything must be consumable!" Tessy laughed.

"Oh, Tessy, these cookies are so good, and the apple cider is delicious. I can't wait till tomorrow." Sarah covered her mouth as she munched. "Excuse me," she blushed.

"Speaking of tomorrow, did your grandfather arrive?" asked Tessy

"Yes, it's so good to see him. He and Mom are catching up this morning, and after lunch we're all going for a drive to show him around town and where Dad's store is, and our schools, and probably the beach, and wherever else we can think of."

"Well, that sounds like a grand idea. I'm sure he'll enjoy that. Oh, my, I hope I haven't spoiled your lunch with our goodies, here."

"Heck no, we just had our dessert ahead of time, that's all. But if we're almost done here, we should probably be heading home, right, Emma?"

Emma, licking off the remaining icing from her gingerbread man, looked up and nodded. "I'll take the rest of my gingerbread man home and have it later, okay?"

"That's just fine, my dear." Tessy leaned over and kissed the top of her head. "Well, again I thank ye kindly for all your help here and I'll be looking forward to seeing you all tomorrow."

Cherokee waited for Sarah and the girls to reach the far side of the yard to quietly tell Tessy that she and Sarah would be over early in the morning to help place the cookies and candy canes in the trees. Tessy gestured her appreciation by patting Cherokee on the arm and then earnestly hugging her. As she watched them clamour off all abuzz, she once again felt truly blessed.

Lemon Lavender Shortbread Cookies

1 1/4 cups (300 ml) all-purpose flour
3 Tbsp (45 ml) sugar
1/2 cup (125 ml) butter
2 tsp (10 ml) finely shredded lemon peel
1 tsp (5 ml) dried lavender buds

In a medium mixing bowl, combine flour, sugar, and lavender buds. In a small mixing bowl, add the lemon peel to the butter. Cut the lemon butter into the flour mixture until it resembles fine crumbs. Form into a large ball and knead until smooth. To make shortbread strips, roll dough on a lightly floured surface to approximately 1/2 inch (1 cm) thick. Use sharp knife or pizza cutter to cut into 24 strips about 2 inches (5 cm) long by 1 inch (2.5 cm) wide. Place one inch apart on ungreased cookie sheet. Bake at 325°F (160°C) for 20 to 25 minutes. Yield: 24 cookies.

PMS/Menopausal Spray

1 1/4 cups (300 ml) distilled water
1/2 cup (125 ml) witch hazel
20 drops lavender essential oil
15 drops clary sage essential oil
10 drops geranium essential oil
6 drops grapefruit essential oil
6 drops peppermint essential oil

Combine all ingredients into sealer jar, shake well, and transfer into spray bottles. Shake well before use. When experiencing a hot flash, lightly mist your face and any exposed skin. Repeat as needed up to three or four times daily. May also be applied as a pillow mist to help with night sweats and relaxing sleep.

8

Humbug

When the girls arrived home, lunch wasn't quite ready, so Sarah asked if she and Cherokee could go check out the new computer, which had finally arrived.

"I suppose that would be fine. I haven't downloaded all the programs yet, but your email should be up and running."

"Fantastic, let's go!" Sarah squealed as they made their way to the den. "I have been waiting to see if Jen has emailed me. I know you two would get along great. I'm hoping she can come and visit next month. Something back there is not quite right, and she hasn't explained what it is yet. It's driving me crazy. So, hopefully, today I can get an answer.

"Okay, let's see . . . Here we go . . . Yep, there it is. Sit and read it with me."

"Are you sure? I don't want to intrude on your privacy."

"Privacy? Heck, no. I want you two to really get to know one another. Come sit."

Sarah read aloud:

Hey Sarah

Sure glad you've FINALLY got your computer hooked up. Handwriting a letter, having to mail it then wait for a reply, is a real drag!! Hard to believe that's how people actually had to communicate in the old days!! How are you doing? Cherokee sounds really cool and I love her name but I hope she isn't as cool as me!! Seriously, I am glad you've made a friend but I'll always be your best friend right? I know you keep asking about "you know who" so I guess I'd better come clean and let you know what I know. Please, please, please don't shoot the messenger or be mad at me. Sarah, you need to forget about him, he is not worth your while. He thinks he's such a jock but with him it's

57

pronounced JERK! He has been seeing Sharon and he even took her out once while you were still here. I found out that's actually why Sharon and Peter broke up. I honestly didn't know until after you left that that's what was going on. I was sure something fishy was going on but I didn't know exactly just what. I always knew he was never good enough for you. Don't give him another thought, you'll meet someone a thousand times better. Sorry, I wish I could be there for you. If you like, give Cherokee my email address and I can tell her all about your favourite things to eat and do and wear so she can help make you feel better. Sorry, gotta go, my EXTREMELY bratty brother is coming and I don't need him reading this.

> We need to plan a date when I can come visit......
> soon........

> Luv ya lots.....talk to you soon......say hi to
> Cherokee for me........
> Your very "bestest" friend,
> Jen #1

Sarah, in a slight state of shock, read the email over again before she started to cry. Cherokee put her arm around her new friend and just sat and let her cry for a few minutes before saying anything.

"I'm so sorry, Sarah. That must have been so difficult to hear. You said you knew something wasn't quite right. Did you have any idea this is what it could have been?" Cherokee handed Sarah a tissue.

Sarah lifted her head, dabbed her nose, and slowly nodded up and down. "All my close girlfriends said he was a conceited jerk, but he was the captain of the volleyball team and he liked me; but apparently he liked a lot of other girls, too." Sarah buried her head in Cherokee's shoulder and got one more good cry out of her system.

"I'm such a fool. How could have I been so stupid?" sniffed Sarah.

"Hey, don't beat yourself up over this. As Tessy once told me — the heart isn't always the best judge of character. I have found that out myself a few times," Cherokee offered.

Sarah dried her eyes and turned off the computer, and she and Cherokee went up to her room. Sarah marched over to Eric's picture, opened up the frame, and yanked it out. She proceeded to rip it up into a dozen pieces, placed them in an envelope, and addressed it to Eric along with her return address. "I want him to know exactly where this came from," she told Cherokee.

"I don't think Roger has been here with the mail, yet. I'll just make sure he takes this today. The sooner THAT JERK gets this, the better! By the way, how well do you know that guy Ryan who was playing beach volleyball the other day?" Sarah asked holding her head up high.

"Well, as a matter of fact, quite well, my dear friend, quite well." Cherokee smirked.

Sarah completely dried her eyes and applied a little makeup before she and Cherokee went downstairs to wait for Roger.

Cherokee and Becky were invited to stay and join them for lunch. Matt had been in the backyard playing with Jason and Brendon, so they, too, were invited. It was quite a congested scene with everyone dishing up at the kitchen island, along with the non-stop chattering about the Christmas party tomorrow. Soon the kids dispersed to their self-appointed eating destinations, leaving Penny and her father at the kitchen table to quietly continue their visit. Marshall Tayse was a semi-retired general practitioner, widowed, and, although easygoing, was not afraid to speak his mind. "What kind of a person has a Christmas party in July?" sniffed Marshall.

"Tessy would be that kind of person, Dad." Penny smiled. "You have to meet her to know this would not be out of the ordinary for her. She is a wonderful person and she is so good to all the kids. She's fun, full of life, and really one of a kind."

"I will certainly agree she's one of a kind. I think it's a hair-brained idea. Christmas in July!" Marshall continued, shaking his head.

"Oh, Dad, just come with us tomorrow. You'll have fun. If nothing else, you can watch the kids have a great time."

"Oh, all right. I'll go. But you say I have to bring a ten-dollar gift and wrap it? What the heck do you buy for a Christmas party in the middle of summer?"

Penny laughed. "We'll stop this afternoon and pick something up and I'll wrap it for you. Oh, and don't let me forget, we all have to bring lawn chairs."

With that, she got up, hugged her father around the neck, and proceeded to clean up the kitchen.

Penny called, and the troops came running. After they had all set their dishes in the dishwasher and lined up, she announced, "All right, who is coming along for the ride? We can't all fit in the SUV but let's count and see who really wants to go."

It turned out that Matt and the boys had decided to ride their bikes out to the beach and they would meet them out there later. Cherokee had promised her mother she would spend the afternoon shopping with her so she was on her way out anyway. Which left Sarah, Emma, and Becky to tag along with Mom and Grandpa for the day.

They had a wonderful time showing him all around and they even found a few hidden spots they hadn't discovered yet. They stopped in at the drugstore to say hi to Dad and whisked him away for a quick coffee at Sheree's Sidewalk Café next door. Grandpa bought each of the girls an orange float, which was one of the highlights of the afternoon, especially for the little ones. Then came the unpleasant task of finding a pointless ten-dollar "something" for a Christmas gift exchange in the middle of summer. Penny and Sarah were chuckling, despite the opinion of their disgruntled, complaining guest.

"Come on, Grandpa, lighten up. It's going to be so much fun. How about this pretty calendar?"

"The year's almost over. Who would want a calendar now?" he huffed.

"Well, let's see . . . then how about this beautiful scented candle or maybe this, or this . . ." Sarah walked up and down the aisle picking up item after item, not having much luck with her grandfather. Finally, after what seemed forever, her grandfather, being the practical man he is, chose a very nice pen and pencil set that was just slightly over the allotted amount. He handed it to the cashier and paid her. As they made their way out of the store, Penny impishly grinned, "There, that wasn't so bad, now, was it?"

Both Sarah and her grandfather cast her a look that would have moulded her to salt if she had ventured to turn around.

Their next stop was the beach to meet the boys and let the girls splash around in the water for a while. Penny and her father spread a blanket under a grove of willows and sat to watch the kids play on the beach. Marshall had forgotten how wonderful it was to just sit and watch children at play. He realized just how much he was missing by being so far from Penny, Jim, and the kids. "I'm sorry I haven't been around more," he blurted, which caught both him and Penny by surprise.

"Oh, Dad," Penny said, touching his hand. "I know it's not been easy since Mom passed, but now that we live a bit closer, we'll hopefully be able to spend a little more time together — okay?"

"That would be nice. I'd like that." And nothing more was said about it.

Everyone had had enough sun and was ready to head home. Matt jumped on his bike and was gone before the rest had even reached the SUV.

"Jim said he was picking up steaks for supper, so I'd better get home and make up some salads. Sarah, you can wrap the potatoes and cut up the garlic bread. It's nice enough for us to eat outside, so Emma, you can wash off the picnic table."

"What's Matt gonna do?" pouted Emma.

"He cut the grass this morning, but I suppose he could carry out the plates for us. Does that sound fair, little Miss Pouty-pants?" Penny raised her eyebrows and flashed a look in Emma's direction.

"Sorry. Yah, I guess that's okay," Emma sulked.

All the extra kids dispersed, leaving the Tuckers to gather for an evening of family fun. The food was great, the conversation was light and easy, while the joking and reminiscing was comfortable and loving. They played a fierce tournament of bocce ball then sat out by the fire until it got dark and the bats began to swoop and dive. The kids were tired from their busy day and were looking forward to tomorrow's festivities; so it was off to bed for them all — without even one complaint! After giving Mom and Dad a hug and kiss goodnight, they got a special tuck-in from Grandpa. His favourite goodnight phrase was the one he stole from his Grandma Tayse, "Snug as a bug in a rug." And as he said it he tucked in the blankets so tightly there was no room for any wiggling or giggling.

Jim stoked the fire while he and Penny waited for Marshall to return. Jim had poured them each a glass of red wine, and they sat out under the stars to enjoy some quiet adult time.

Marshall raised his wine in a toast. "Those are terrific kids." After tapping glasses, they each drew in a long, savouring sip.

Magick Mist Moisturizing Spray

1/2 cup (125 ml) distilled water
1 Tbsp (15 ml) aloe vera juice
2 tsp (10 ml) vegetable glycerin
5 drops mandarin essential oil

Pour all ingredients into a spray bottle and shake well. May be applied with cotton pad or by spraying directly onto face and throat.

Berry Blessed Lemonade

1/2 cup (125 ml) honey
1 1/2 cups (375 ml) lemon juice
2 tsp (10 ml) grated lemon zest
4 chamomile tea bags
2 cups (500 ml) blueberries
6 cups (1.5 L) water

In a saucepan over low heat, dissolve honey in lemon juice. Add tea bags and lemon zest and let steep for 10 minutes. Remove tea bags and pour mixture into blender. Add blueberries and water to blender mixture and purée until well blended. Refrigerate for 2–4 hours. Serve over ice.

9

Joy to the World

Sunday morning started out bright but overcast. The forecast called for sunny periods with cooler temperatures, which wasn't all bad, as it had been extremely hot the past few days. Tessy was up early and busily pulling out platters and punch bowls, preparing for the day's culinary delights. She was standing in the kitchen surveying the table when she remembered she hadn't selected the music yet. Her stereo was wired with outdoor speakers, and she always enjoyed having music in the background when she was entertaining. Of course, today's preferences would be nothing but a collection of Christmas medleys. She smiled with amusement while deciding on her CD choices. *How fun, let's see . . . we must have a little something for everyone. There has to be a mix with Bing Crosby and the gang for all the crooners; Kenny, Dolly, and Alabama for the country fans; oh and here's Anne Murray, Celine Dion, Kenny G, Boney M, and aye, it wouldn't be Christmas without Elvis. Now for the wee ones . . . Mickey's Christmas and the Chipmunks will do just fine. And for me: a little Celtic to bring in the Yule of Olde. There, that looks like a pretty diverse assortment to start things off, and if we run out, I have a few more Christmas mixes.* Tessy popped her selections into the CD player and hit RANDOM, just to get her in the mood as she danced back into the kitchen, singing a duet with Celine.

An hour later, Sarah and Cherokee were at the door, both amazed to hear Christmas music playing.

"Hey, good morning, Tessy!" they echoed.

Cherokee added, "Great tunes! Didn't think you'd really be into Boney M, though."

"And why wouldn't I be, now? I don't live in the Dark Ages all the time, ye know," Tessy replied, slightly wounded but still good natured.

"Sorry. Guess we shouldn't be surprised, considering," Cherokee piped.

"Yeah," Sarah agreed. "Well, we're here to get hanging. Are the baskets in the back kitchen?"

"Aye, my dears. If ye don't mind going to fetch them yourselves." Tessy was busy measuring out cups of mulled apple juice for her cider into the punch bowl and didn't want to lose count.

"Okay, we'll just take them right outside and get started, then," Cherokee called from the back.

"That would be grand. Just like Santa's wee helpers, ye are!" teased Tessy, still counting.

It didn't take the girls long to hang the cookies and candy canes. Tessy went out to inspect the finished project.

"My, ye girls have done such a fine, beautiful job. I don't know how I'll ever be able to thank ye. You've done so much for me! Wait here. I picked ye each up a little something for all your troubles." Tessy came back with two sets of Christmas tree dangle earrings that lit up, and a couple of Santa hats. "Thought ye might have fun wearing these this afternoon at the party."

"Tessy, these are great! Thank you so much. Where on earth did you get them, especially at this time of the year?"

"Well now, an old woman from the Dark Ages such as meself has her ways, ye know," chuckled Tessy.

"These are too cool. I love them. Can't wait to wear them!" Sarah bubbled.

"I'm glad ye like them," smiled Tessy.

The girls spent another hour laying out tablecloths on the picnic tables, hauling out galvanized tubs for ice, labelling large bins for cans and bottles and garbage and placing them accordingly. After they left, Tessy kept herself occupied for a time then decided she was ready for a well-deserved break. She made herself a cup of strong coffee, as she felt she would need the caffeine rush to keep up her pace. She took it outside and sat down at one of the picnic tables and was astounded at the way the backyard had been so beautifully transformed. She was sure it had never looked this festive before. She was thrilled.

Guests were to start arriving at around two p.m., so at twelve thirty, Tessy went upstairs to shower and get ready. She had decided to wear a beautiful, long patchwork skirt with a crisp cotton blouse in the loveliest shade of fawn. It had a lace inlay with a high neck collar and a ruffle just under her chin. She swept her hair up in a loose bun with wispy curls falling from the base of her hairline and a couple just off her temples. To accessorize, she wore a pair of stunning moonstone drop earrings with a bracelet to match. For shoes, she reached for her cream kid leather ballerina slippers and stepped into them. She stood in front of her oval mirror and was pleased with the outcome. "There, I think that will work just fine for today," she said to herself as she wiped a small stray smear of lipstick from the corner of her lip. She stood back and took one more look just to make sure her ensemble was perfect for the day but did not notice the beautiful angelic aura that encircled her. Once she was satisfied, she turned, closed her bedroom door, and lightly skipped down the stairs to the kitchen.

Tessy grabbed a Christmas apron that was hanging in the pantry and wrapped it around her so that her outfit would remain unscathed until her guests arrived. Skye and Cherokee were usually the first on the scene, as they liked to come early to help out with last-minute preparations. This year was no exception. Tessy was standing at the sink when she noticed Skye and Cherokee gazing about the yard as they walked past the window and up to the back door.

"Come in, come in! Merry Yule!" she called out.

"Hello — Merry Christmas!" Skye reciprocated, giving Tessy a big hug. "Oh, Tessy, you look so lovely."

"Thank ye. You two are as beautiful as ever, yourselves," Tessy replied.

"Hey, Tessy. Merry Christmas!" Cherokee added, hat perched on her head and earrings flashing. "Want me to put Duke and Darby in their kennel?"

"Aye, that would be a fine idea. I've a couple of nice smoked ham bones here to help things along. They don't mind going in their pen, but this always makes it a bit sweeter for them." Tessy pulled the bag of bones out of the fridge and handed them to Cherokee.

"I don't know why they would not like going in their kennel — it's bigger than most other dogs have for their entire yard. Do they have water and food and stuff?"

"Aye, I took care of that earlier today. Thank ye."

"My, Tessy, everything looks fantastic," Skye remarked.

"Well, with great thanks to your daughter and Sarah. The pair of them were a wonder and they did a beautiful job."

"That's good. It certainly didn't hurt them any, and I think they really had fun doing it. Now, what is there left to do?"

Everyone started arriving as scheduled, and the yard was filling up nicely. Some people had the yard games out already, others were mingling, and more were wandering about the gardens. About half were in attendance when the Tuckers arrived. Emma came running over to give Tessy a big bear hug as soon as she spotted her.

"How's my wee darling today? Merry Christmas." She leaned down and kissed the child.

"Merry Christmas, Tessy. Is Becky here yet?" Emma was wildly glancing around.

"Aye, darling, they are. I think I last saw her and her mum over there by the ring-toss game." She pointed to the far side of the yard.

By now, the rest of the Tuckers had caught up to Emma and were all merrily greeting Tessy.

"Aye, greetings, greetings. Welcome. Merry Christmas," returned Tessy.

Penny stepped closer and said, "Tessy, this is my father, Marshall Tayse. Dad, this is Tessy McGuigan." They each stretched out their hands and exchanged a hearty handshake.

"Welcome, Mr. Tayse, thank ye so much for coming to my Christmas shenanigans," Tessy smiled.

"Oh, please call me Marshall, and it's my pleasure. Thank you for allowing me to attend. I must say I've never been to a Christmas in July, but there's a first time for everything. I'm quite looking forward to it."

Penny, a little puzzled, threw Jim a look and noticed her father hadn't let go of Tessy's hand yet. And she noticed Tessy was beginning to look a little uncomfortable.

Sensing the awkwardness, Penny intervened. "Dad, we should let Tessy move on to some of her other guests while we go and put these gifts over with the others. And I'd like to introduce you to Susan, Becky's mother, and Cherokee's mom and dad, Skye and Cache."

"And Becky, but you already know her," Emma blurted.

"Oh, of course. Well, then, I guess we'll catch up with you a little later . . . then. 'Bye for now." And with that, Marshall finally let go of Tessy's hand, slightly bowed and backed away. Once out of earshot, he turned to Penny and said, "THAT is Tessy McGuigan? You didn't tell me she was absolutely charming. Did you see her hair and those eyes?"

"Well, well. If I didn't know better I'd say you were slightly smitten with our Ms. Tessy. Maybe Christmas in July is not such a hair-brained idea after all, aye, Dad?"

"Oh, now, let's not get carried away. Really. Smitten. I just mentioned she was charming. And I don't think I put it exactly as hair-brained, did I?"

Penny didn't even bother to try and hide a hearty laugh.

The afternoon was going even more splendidly than Tessy had anticipated. Santa had just arrived, and the children were lining up to sit on his knee and receive their bag of goodies. Roger had done a fine jovial job of ho, ho, hoing and jiggling his belly like a bowl full of jelly. The children were jumping up and down with excitement. Parents were busy taking pictures, and everyone seemed to be enjoying the magical appearance of jolly old St. Nick. Tessy was standing off to the side taking in Roger's performance when Marshall came up behind her and touched her shoulder. Startled, she gasped, leaped back, and her hand automatically went to her chest.

"Oh, I'm so sorry I frightened you," apologized Marshall.

"My," puffed Tessy. "No, no, it's fine. I guess I was concentrating a little too hard on the wee ones."

"Are you all right? Would you like to sit down?" asked the concerned Marshall.

"No, no. I'm just as fine as frog's fur," chuckled Tessy. "Oh, there's Danny Baker coming up the lane. I must go off to meet him — excuse me." Tessy turned and quickly headed toward the lane with Marshall hot on her heels. In mid-trot, Marshall was still trying to initiate a conversation with this striking woman.

"Danny Baker? A close friend of yours?" questioned Marshall.

"Well, a friend, to be sure; don't know about close, but a fine neighbour, for certain," answered Tessy still in full stride. "I've asked him to bring over his wagon and a team of horses for a surprise hayride for the children before supper, but he's a mite early, and I must catch him before he spoils the surprise."

Tessy was able to head Danny off at the end of the lane, and luckily everyone was too engrossed with Santa to notice the sound of the bells on the horses' bridles. She, Marshall, and Danny stayed with the team and chatted for a while until Tessy was sure it was time for Santa to leave. She snuck up to where she could see Santa standing and waving goodbye to the children, while heading in her direction. Yes, it was time for the wagon to make its appearance. She waved her hand for Danny to continue on up the lane, with the horse bells merrily jingling. As soon as the children spotted the wagon, their attention immediately switched, and Santa was able to make a clean getaway.

Marshall caught up with Tessy and walked her back to the yard. He was trying his darndest to spend a few quality moments with her, but it was proving a nearly impossible undertaking. He hated to admit it but he really was enjoying himself at this outlandish event. Christmas music, Santa, hayrides — all in July. What next? How on earth was he going to attract the attention of this amazing creature? Up until now, all he had seemed to accomplish was to stammer and stumble over himself the entire time he was in her presence. He promised himself that today, somehow, someway, he was going to make a positive impression on this elusive woman!

Earlier in the week, Tessy and Danny had agreed that pulling the team up to the clothesline platform would be the easiest way for the children to step into the wagon. As the children lined up, each taking their turn to get in, Tessy stood back, revelling in their excitement, while Marshall stood back and revelled at Tessy. However, it wasn't long before Tessy was on the move again, this time, delegating preparations for dinner.

The meal and the rest of the day sailed playfully by without a hitch. The sun had popped in and out all day but was now getting low in the sky, and it was time for the bonfire to be lit. This also meant it was time for the adults, age fifteen and over, to sit around the fire and begin the Chinese gift exchange. Earlier in the day, once Tessy knew how many were participating, she'd had the girls write out the numbers on a piece of paper and cut, fold, and place them in a Christmas cookie tin. All the presents were arranged in a pile, and it was Matt's job to take around the cookie tin for guests to pick out their number. The rules were announced and the game commenced.

As the gifts were opened one by one, there was plenty of stealing and even more laughter. It was Tessy's turn and she spied a lovely little gift, wrapped in the most tantalizing blue foil, topped with a crisp white bow and oddly enough, with a little sprig of fresh holly tucked in it. She brought it up to her lap and with all eyes upon her she announced, "Nice things do come in wee packages." Immediately Marshall recognized it as the gift he had brought and Penny had wrapped. He now was wishing, with all his might, he had taken a little more time to pick out just the right thing. Maybe those scented candles would have been better or maybe a beautiful bottle of perfume . . . something, anything but a plain old practical pen and pencil set . . . something, anything more fitting for the lovely Ms. Tessy.

Tessy took her time opening it, as she knew it was always the anticipation that makes the game most fun. While Marshall held his breath, she drew out the unwrapping process as long as she could before she lifted the lid to reveal its contents. She was quite impressed with the set and, much to Marshall's delight, decided she would keep it. The game carried on and when it was finally over, everyone clapped and had a good laugh. Tessy bundled up her pen set and took it to the kitchen to put it away along with the little sprig of holly, which she added to her sprig that had appeared so mysteriously. She returned outside to settle in for some more visiting while winding down and enjoying the evening fire.

The festivities were drawing to a close, and the children were getting tired. Guests were picking up their lawn chairs and hunting down Tessy to say thank you and good night. It had been a very long day, and Tessy was getting a little weary, too, but she graciously bid farewell to each and every guest. The Tuckers were among the last to leave. Penny hugged Tessy while Jim held a very sleepy Emma in his arms. Emma barely lifted her head to say good night and to reach for a faint hug. Tessy kissed her softly on the cheek and laid her hand gently on her little head. "Good night, my wee darling. See ye soon."

Jim smiled down at his youngest sleepyhead then looked at Tessy and thanked her for a wonderful family day. He also mentioned he had been wanting to speak to her about the possibility of helping him with something but that he would catch up with her at a later date.

Next was Matt. With a hearty handshake, he said, "Thanks. I had a good time. And thanks for letting me help out with that Chinese gift thing. Why do they call it that, anyway?"

"Well, now, good question. I really don't know the answer to that. I guess I'll have to be looking that up. But thank ye for helping me with such an important task. Good night to ye, young sir."

Sarah and Cherokee, with their Santa hats still placed firmly on their heads and earrings blinking in the dark, ran over to say good night to everyone and to give Tessy a huge hug. They were on their way to Cherokee's for a sleepover, but it certainly did not seem like they were ready to settle down any time soon.

"Thank ye girls so much for all your help over the past few days. I'm not sure what I would have done without ye."

"Hey, no problem, we had a great time," the girls said. "We can come by tomorrow and give you a hand cleaning up, if you like."

"No, thank ye. You've done enough; and besides, everyone pitched in today, and there's not a whole bunch left to do. But don't forget about our class on Thursday — I'll be expecting ye." Tessy had an arm around each girl and gave them another hug and a kiss on the cheek.

They all started off down the lane, leaving Marshall to bid Tessy farewell and to hopefully make a lasting impression.

Tessy held out her hand, smiling. "Well, now, Marshall, thank ye for joining us today. I'm hoping ye enjoyed a wee taste of Yule in July."

"It was my extreme pleasure to be here. Thank you very much for including me in the festivities," Marshall said as he held Tessy's hand.

"Marshall, if ye don't mind, I have a question."

"Not at all — please."

"The pen and pencil set was from you, was it not?"

"Why, yes. How did you know?"

"Just a hunch. How did the holly come to be on it?"

"Well, that's a funny story, actually. When we were leaving the house to come here today, Penny and I were waiting outside for the rest to join us. We happened to look down, and there it was just lying at the end of the walk. Penny reached down and stuck it in the bow on the gift. We figured it must have fallen off a floral delivery truck or something. Quite a coincidence, though, wasn't it?" Marshall mused.

"Aye, quite," Tessy replied, throwing a glance upwards. She now knew for sure the holly held a special meaning specifically for her.

"Well, Tessy, I must admit I really wasn't sure what to expect today. Certainly nothing like this," and with that, he raised Tessy's hand to his lips, kissed it gently, said "Good night," and stepped back into the shadows.

Tessy, slightly taken aback, pulled her hand up to her chest and held it there, not quite knowing what to do next. Thankfully, there were a few more people to say good night to. This gave her time to clear her head and brush off what had just happened as surely nothing more than a pleasant, gentlemanly gesture.

After everyone had left, Tessy walked over to the kennel and let Duke and Darby out into the yard. They were overjoyed at their new-found freedom. Tails wagging frantically, they ran all over, darting from side to side and sniffing to find any minute morsel left behind. Tessy watched their excitement over the new smells like they were off on a wild adventure. She smiled to herself. *They just enjoy and live for the moment. Oh, how wonderful that is to witness!* Tessy always tried her best to live that way, too, but sometimes memories just got in the way. *Now is not the time to start over-thinking things,* she told herself. Instead, she looked up at the bright, shining Mother in the sky and began her solitary Lammas ritual.

She went to the kitchen and filled a basket with the tools and ingredients she required and headed back outside. She set the basket down on a picnic table close to a small, empty garden plot. She reached in and pulled out a yellow beeswax candle and a bowl of Lammas incense consisting of frankincense, jasmine, sandalwood, hops, and dried apple blossoms. She lit them and quieted herself. After a moment, she poured some wine into a beautifully adorned goblet, set one of her small grain loaves on a matching plate, and left them on the table. She walked over to the garden plot and began to carefully clear and weed it while thinking of areas of her life she, too, would like to clear and to make room for future growth. After she was satisfied with this clearing, she planted four ferns, one for each of the elements — for protection, and because faeries are especially attracted to them. She returned to the table, took a bite of the loaf and a drink of wine, and chanted:

> Lord and Lady full of grace,
> Thank you for this sacred place.
>
> I celebrate this first harvest of plenty
> In my garden filled with wee Gentry.
>
> The days grow shorter and the nights long
> While the birds still swoop and sing their song.
>
> Though prosperity and blessings I thank you for,
> I ask that it is love and peace on earth you pour.
>
> This will I gently plea.
> So mote it be.

She took another small bite of bread and sip of wine then returned to the garden and gave the last bits as an offering to Mother Earth. Once she had finished giving thanks, she snuffed out the candle and poured the incense into the ashes of the waning bonfire. She called the dogs to her side, switched off the lights, and they all turned in for a good night's sleep.

Iced Spiced Apple Cider

Peel of one large orange
4 quarts (4 L) apple cider
1/4 cup (50 ml) brown sugar
3 Tbsp (45 ml) fresh lemon juice
15 whole cloves
10 whole allspice
6 cinnamon sticks, broken in half

Peel orange in long strips and place peels only in large pot or Dutch oven. Add remaining ingredients and bring to the boil, stirring constantly until sugar is dissolved. Reduce heat to medium low and simmer until mixture reduces to approximately 8 cups (2 L) (about 45 minutes). Strain and refrigerate until cold. Serve over ice or reheat to enjoy hot.

Foot and Body Scrub

3/4 cup (175 ml) Epsom salts
1/2 cup (125 ml) sea salt
1/4 cup (50 ml) sweet almond oil
1 tsp (5 ml) Castile soap (optional)
1/2 tsp (2 ml) vegetable glycerin
10–15 drops essential oil(s) of choice

In a small mixing bowl combine the salts, stir, and slowly add almond oil to make a paste-like texture, remembering that the Castile soap, glycerin, and essential oils will also add moisture.

10

Plain Out of Sorts

As tired as Tessy was, she did not have a good night's sleep. The next morning, she awoke feeling not nearly as refreshed as she hoped to be. She had tossed and turned all night and couldn't quite figure out why. She chalked it up to indigestion and rolled herself out of bed. She dressed and headed downstairs to let the dogs out. Looking about the kitchen, she became brutally aware that there was a little more to be done than she had expected. "Oh, well, if I keep busy, it'll take my mind off whatever it is that's plaguing it," she told Merlin and Cordelia.

A couple of hours into her cleaning frenzy, she realized just how much she had actually accomplished. The house and yard were pretty much back to normal, and she felt that a congratulatory cup of tea was in order. She headed into the back kitchen to retrieve her tin of favourite revitalizing tea blend—her special Revitalizing Citrus Mint Tea, made with spearmint, lemon verbena, orange geranium, calendula petals, mostly for colour, dried lemon and orange rind with cloves and a couple of peppercorns for some extra kick. *Just what the doctor ordered,* she thought. She poured the boiling water over the infusion and took in a deep breath. The heavenly aroma instantly slowed down her whole world. She let it steep for a few minutes, removed the mesh ball, and then sat down to enjoy the enhanced flavours in her very clean kitchen.

Now, relaxed and gently sipping her tea, her mind wandered back to the evening before, and, oddly enough, Marshall Tayse. Suddenly her eyes flew wide open and she quietly gasped "Oh, dear . . . oh, Father in heaven . . . surely not." She finally realized why she had not slept and had had such a murky aura all morning. How could she have been so blind? "Oh, dear . . . oh dear . . . no, that's silly . . . a woman my age. Well, I *am* just barely in my fifties. I'm not exactly in the Dark Ages, as the kids presume . . . but still . . ." She was muttering to herself or to the cats; she wasn't sure which. Somehow, her tea was no longer soothing her.

She glanced over at the holly sprigs, and all of a sudden, it all fell into place. She grabbed them up, pounced out of her chair and announced, very loudly: "Dermot Patrick James McGuigan, I need to speak to you in the library—NOW!" She stormed down the hall and entered the library at lightning speed. "I know you're here, Dermot McGuigan. I might not be able to see ye but I can sense that you're here and I also know ye have your hand in all this. It was ye who put this holly in the tree for me to find; and then again on the wee package. You and your sentimental feelings about Christmas. I'll have ye know, I'm just fine with the way things are and always have been. If you're thinking 'tis a man I need to take care of me, you're mistaken. Now, I trust this shall be the end of these shenanigans of yours, or ye and I'll be having another wee talk. I'll say good day to ye now before I say something I may regret!" And with that, she turned and marched out.

She decided to go out into the garden to get grounded and hopefully to dissipate her anger and the murkiness she was experiencing. If she was correct, what was the worst that could happen? Marshall Tayse was just here for two weeks. What could happen in two weeks?

Tessy settled into her favourite meditative pose and closed her eyes. She began to pray out loud. "Oh, dear . . . well . . . Lord, I'll be giving this wee conundrum to ye and my angels to be finding an amicable solution. Who knows, maybe I'm blowing matters way out of hand." Tessy then quietened, taking her time to focus on her peaceful quest. She opened her eyes about ten minutes later, feeling much calmer. "There. Thank ye, Lord. Feeling lighter already. You are truly amazing." Tessy unravelled herself and began a therapeutic walk around her gardens. She even managed to chuckle about the situation. "Aye, doesn't life just throw ye a wee curve when ye least expect it? Oh, and Dermot—what a scallywag he is. Bless his heart for worrying about me." She placed her hand on Duke's soft, understanding head and, feeling the healing energy of his unconditional love, stroked him.

Over at the Tuckers, thoughts were not too dissimilar.

Marshall, too, had had a restless night. Still in bed, he kept replaying the previous day over and over in his head. *How could I have been such a bumbling idiot the whole time? And besides, what is it about HER? Well, she is extremely attractive and a character for sure. Smart, kind, energetic . . . Oh, face it, Marshall, she is absolutely amazing!* Marshall rolled over and gently punched the spare pillow to bury his head in. Realizing he wasn't going to get any more sleep, he groaned, threw off the covers, and got up. He walked over to the mirror and groaned again. His greying whiskers, along with the bags under his eyes, were not the most flattering reflection. He was sure a shower and a cup of good strong coffee would definitely make all the difference in the world.

Dressed for the day and feeling somewhat refreshed, Marshall made his way downstairs to the kitchen. Jim was already off to work, and Penny was enjoying a quiet cup of coffee and the morning paper.

"Good morning, sleepyhead," Penny teased. "Oooh, looks like you should maybe have stayed in bed a bit longer."

"Thanks a lot. Do I really look that bad?" asked her father.

Penny laughed. "Sit down, and I'll get you a cup of coffee. Didn't you sleep well?"

"Not worth a damn. Sorry."

"Well, well, we did get out of the wrong side of the bed this morning," Penny said as she handed her dad his coffee. "It wouldn't have anything to do with a certain Irish lass, would it?"

"Is it that evident? What is *wrong* with me? I haven't even noticed another woman since your mother passed. Why now, and why HER?"

"Well, Dad, maybe it's time. With Mom having been as sick as she was for so long and then her passing, you've been alone for a long time. And why Tessy? Why not? She's fascinating . . . everyone loves her! I think you should ask her out on a date."

"What? A date? Are you crazy? I haven't been on a date in almost forty years!"

"It's like riding a bike, Dad. I don't think dating has changed that much."

"Are you kidding? I'm a doctor. I know *exactly* how much dating has changed in forty years!"

"Father! I'm not suggesting anything like *that!* A nice, quiet dinner and maybe a walk along the lake is a little more what I had in mind. Besides, I have a feeling if anyone tried anything with Tessy, she would flip him like a pancake! She's pretty feisty!"

"I can't believe I'm having this conversation with my daughter . . . and especially this early in the day!" Shaking his head, Marshall covered his embarrassed face with his hands.

Much to Marshall's relief, little Emma came running into the kitchen.

"Mommy, are you making us pancakes?"

Both Penny and Marshall laughed.

"Yes, honey. Mommy will make pancakes, if you'd like."

"Yeah!" Emma clapped her hands. "Can I help?"

After everyone had had their fill of pancakes and the dishes were done, Marshall and Penny found themselves alone again.

"IF I were to ask Tessy out to dinner—and I said IF—where would you suggest we go?" Marshall sheepishly asked.

"There's actually about three really good spots that Jim and I have discovered, so far. Remember where we went for coffee and ice cream the other day—Sheree's Sidewalk Café? Well, they stay open late on Thursday, Friday, and Saturday evenings. Jim and I had a lovely evening there last week. They offer a couple of entrees to choose from; and they're licenced for those evenings, so you can order a nice bottle of wine. They put checkered tablecloths, flowers, and candles on the tables outside and play soft music. It's very romantic. Reminds me of France."

"Your mother and I loved France. I have wonderful memories of those days."

"Dad, it's time for you to make some new memories."

"I guess, maybe. What are the other choices in town?"

"Well, there's the Lotus Garden Café if you want oriental. Oh, and the Inner Peace Bistro is so cool. The food is quite unique and absolutely delicious. It features authentic Native cuisine, like buffalo, bannock, lots of local fresh fish and vegetables. Cherokee's aunt owns and manages it. Jim and I went there one night with Skye and Cache . . . had a wonderful time. It's a beautiful log chalet just outside of town overlooking the far side of the lake. Gorgeous spot."

"I'm actually quite surprised and impressed with the selection of restaurants for a town this size."

"Then of course, we have all those fast food joints if you want to show her your frugal side," Penny quipped.

"Very funny. You should be extremely proud of your Scottish heritage, young lady! Your grandmother will be turning over in her grave if she hears you talk like that! Well, I guess that gives me some idea as to where to start. This little conversation never happened and it will stay between us—right, dear?" Marshall raised his eyebrows in Penny's direction.

"Oh, no. You HAVE to let me share this with Jim. Please," begged

Penny. "Please."

"I suppose. I could probably use a man's opinion on all this, anyway."

"Who said anything about giving him an opinion? No, no, no. This is definitely a go!"

"And here I am thinking of getting involved with a woman. I need my head examined!" Once again, Marshall buried his face in his hands.

Penny just laughed and gave him two thumbs up.

Foot Refresher Spray

1/2 cup (125 ml) distilled water
1/2 cup (125 ml) distilled alcohol (vodka)
1/2 tsp (2 ml) vegetable glycerin
25 drops peppermint essential oil
20 drops tea tree essential oil

Combine ingredients in spray bottle and shake well.

White Musk and Ginger Scent

4 parts white musk oil (plant derived)
2 parts vanilla essential oil
1 part white ginger essential oil

Chewy Peanut Butter-Chocolate Macaroons

2 cups (500 ml) sugar
6 Tbsp (90 ml) cocoa
1/2 cup (125 ml) butter
1/2 cup (125 ml) milk
1/2 tsp (2 ml) vanilla
1 cup (250 ml) shredded (unsweetened) coconut
3/4 cup (175 ml) peanut butter
3 cups (750 ml) quick rolled oats

Combine sugar, cocoa, butter, and milk in a saucepan. Bring to a boil. Remove from heat and stir in vanilla, peanut butter, coconut, and rolled oats. Drop by the spoonful on wax paper and chill. Yield: approximately 48 macaroons.

11

Grandpa Comes A-Courtin'

Except for her Tuesday morning with the seniors, it had been a quiet few days for Tessy, which gave her time to catch her breath and prepare for her Thursday class. She was in the kitchen sorting containers of herbs and oils into one of her baskets when the phone rang.

"Good mornin' to ye!" was her gleeful salutation.

Surprised at the unusual greeting, there was a moment of silence. Marshall finally cleared his throat, apologized, then said, "Good morning, Tessy. This is Marshall Tayse."

Equally surprised, Tessy just said, "Oh, so it is," as she plunked herself down on the closest kitchen chair.

"I just wanted to thank you again for your wonderful hospitality last weekend and to see if I could return it this Saturday evening by taking you to dinner." Marshall was so thankful that he actually got the words out without stammering as he read them off the piece of paper he had rehearsed over and over again.

It was Tessy's turn for a moment of silence. What on earth could she say? Her mind was reeling. "Oh, oh, oh," was all that seemed to want to come out. She finally collected herself enough to say, "Oh, that really isn't necessary, Mr. Tayse . . . em . . . Marshall. I was so happy to have ye join us."

Marshall anticipated and rehearsed for almost any answer Tessy might deliver. Luckily this was one of them. "Yes, and I appreciate that; but it would be my extreme pleasure to have you join me for dinner on Saturday evening. I could come pick you up, say, around seven p.m." He was not leaving any room for debate.

"Well, now, I suppose seven p.m. would be as good a time as any. If you're sure this is what you want?"

"Yes, I would like it very much. Good. I'll look forward to seeing you on Saturday, then. Thank you. Goodbye, Tessy." Marshall decided to keep the conversation short for fear of any rebuttals Tessy might render.

Tessy could not believe what she had just agreed to. *Oh, Dermot, my love, what have ye done? What have I done? Am I really going on a date?* Shaking her head, she sat for a moment and let it sink in. Collecting herself again, she walked to the kitchen window to look out over her gardens. They always soothed her and made her feel safe. She was experiencing uncomfortable, foreign feelings and she wasn't quite sure what they were. There was a mixture of shock, panic, and even betrayal of her Dermot . . . yet still a sense of excitement. "Oh, this is ridiculous. It's just a nice dinner out with a new friend. That's it. There, be gone with ye now." Scolding herself, she went back to her task of sorting herbs.

In view of Tessy's present mental state she opted for some easier projects than originally scheduled and a bit shorter class today. She decided to concoct a simple Foot and Body Scrub, Refreshing Foot Bath, and a Foot Refresher Spray. Thus, the girls could interact a little more by soaking their feet then massaging them with some of the nail butter from last week.

The afternoon came and went in a bit of a haze for Tessy, but the girls didn't seem to notice anything out of the ordinary, much to Tessy's relief. When it was over and Tessy was tidying up, she gave herself another scolding. "You silly, silly woman. Why would ye be letting something like this upset your life so? Now ye stop *right now*. It's just a little dinner with a new friend, that's all." She was muttering out loud and didn't notice that Sarah and Cherokee had returned.

"Tessy, are you okay?" Sarah asked.

"Oh, girls, I didn't see ye come in," Tessy replied, a little embarrassed.

"Tessy, are you worried about going to dinner with Grandpa?"

"Oh, you know about that, do ye?" Tessy blushed even more with embarrassment.

"Sorry. I don't think I'm supposed to know but I overheard Mom and Grandpa talking. I am so excited! I think it's wonderful. Please don't be worried—he's really very nice," Sarah urged.

"If you like, Sarah and I could come help you get ready for your big date," offered Cherokee.

Sarah scowled at her friend, knocking up against her.

"Ooops, sorry!" Cherokee winced.

"Now, girls, it's not a date. Your grandfather just invited me out to thank me for last weekend. That's all there is to it. It's not a date, not at all."

"We know that but we could at least come over for some girl time with you Saturday afternoon," Sarah volunteered.

"Well, I suppose that would help pass the day along. That would be lovely; thank ye, girls. I appreciate your kind offer."

"Great. Now, what can we do to help you clean up here?" asked Cherokee, hoping to change the subject.

Saturday came all too quickly for Tessy. She tried as hard as she could to go about her regular routine. It was a beautiful morning, so she headed out to her gardens for her daily meditation and yoga. She settled in her favourite spot but found it difficult to quiet her mind and properly focus. She eventually succeeded enough to feel refreshed and calm when she was done. Ready to take on the day, she spent the next hour dead-heading, then the latter part of the morning harvesting some of her herbs. The girls had arranged to come over around four thirty p.m., so she had plenty of time to spend doing what she loved best. The animals were all close by; well, except for when it was time for Merlin and Cordelia to have their mid-morning nap.

While in the garden, she decided to go out into the greenhouse to have a wee chat with Dermot and clear the air between them. "Dermot, my dear, I know what ye are doing is out of love for me and I bless your heart for it. When ye were lying in your bed before ye passed on, ye told me time marches on and so must I. Well . . . I'll go on this wee outing to see how it goes, but don't be getting any fancy ideas in your head." She sternly looked up and wagged her finger back and forth. She then smiled, shook her head, and said, "God love ye, my darlin'," and stepped back outside, quietly closing the door behind her.

Marshall, on the other hand, spent the morning mostly pacing.

"Father, you are going to wear a hole in my new carpet. Come sit. Relax," Penny begged.

"I *am* relaxed. I just had a bit too much coffee this morning."

"Really? You have had the same number of cups of coffee every morning since you've been here. You are going to do just fine tonight, Dad. You'll have a great time. Now, please come and sit down for a while." Penny reached up and grabbed her father's hand.

"Thanks, honey. I guess I am a little nervous. But I think—if you don't mind—I'm going to take a walk down to the park and watch the boys play baseball."

"That sounds like a great idea. Do you want some company?"

"Sure. You're still my favourite date."

"Oh, yah, you say that now — we'll see what you say tomorrow!"

Shaking his head, Marshall took his daughter's hand, pulled her off the couch, and they marched out the front door arm in arm.

Tessy peeked into the kitchen window to check the time and was amazed to see that it was four o'clock already. "My stars. I'd best be getting into the shower straightaway," she said to Darby, who was lying under the window chewing on a treasured ham knuckle. Tessy poured the remains of her watering can onto the scented stocks by the back door and ran into the house, leaving the can on the back step.

The girls arrived precisely on time to find Tessy in her housecoat, damp-haired and a bit unsettled.

"Maybe I should call your grandfather and tell him I've changed my mind," Tessy said, wringing her hands.

"Tessy, you'll be just fine. Come on, let's go upstairs and start getting you ready," Sarah said, grabbing Tessy by the hand and leading her toward the stairs.

"You two go on up and start while I make Tessy a cup of her favourite calming tea," Cherokee offered.

"Aye, thank ye, dear, that would be lovely," Tessy thankfully replied.

They made their way up to Tessy's bedroom, and Sarah sat her down in front of her wing-mirrored dressing bureau.

"Now, what shall we do with your hair?" Sarah thought out loud, while running her fingers through it. She gathered it all up around Tessy's face then she let it fall down around her shoulders and ran her fingers through it again.

"I didn't realize your hair was quite so long," she said. "You always wear it up. Would you consider wearing it down tonight?"

"Oh no, I haven't worn it down for years. I fear I'm too old for that now."

Just then, Cherokee arrived and handed Tessy her tea.

"Cherokee, what do you think? Up or down?" Sarah asked, ignoring Tessy's last comment.

"Humm . . . to be perfectly honest, I'd say up."

"Yah, I think you're right," Sarah concluded. "Well, let's get started. Tessy, do you have a blow dryer?"

"Aye, I do but I don't use it often." Tessy leaned down and pulled a hair dryer out of one of the side cupboards and handed the large, cumbersome relic to Sarah.

Sarah looked at it and blurted out without thinking, "What on earth is this? I've never seen anything like it before."

"Well, as I said, dear, I don't use it often. I let Mother Nature dry my hair."

"That's probably why your hair is so soft and healthy." Cherokee came to Tessy's defence while throwing Sarah a glare.

"Oh, I'm sorry, Tessy. I didn't mean to be so blunt and rude," Sarah apologized.

"No harm done, my dear. I suppose it *is* a bit of an antique," Tessy chuckled.

"Well, it's a good thing I came prepared and brought my backpack full of necessities. I'll just run downstairs and get it."

Sarah was back in a minute, and soon the girls began to work their magic. There was blow drying, curling, fussing, and primping. Once they were satisfied with what they called "her do," they moved on to her makeup, at which point Tessy promptly announced: "Now, ye won't be making me look like a painted harlot, will ye?"

Both girls laughed and promised to give her a soft, natural look. The two girls busily pulled out pallets in an array of colours, holding them close to Tessy's face and discussing which tones would best work. Then came packets of eye shadow, liner pencils, tubes of mascara . . .

"My stars," Tessy mused. "How on earth do ye girls get anywhere on time if ye go through this every day?"

Both girls laughed again and kept on with their artistry. Tessy was not allowed to peek until the girls had finished. When they agreed that they had put the final touches on their masterpiece, they turned to one another, smiled, gave a thumbs-up, and turned Tessy toward the mirror.

Tessy gazed at the reflection staring back at her.

"Oh, my, what a fine job ye girls have done." Tessy gently touched her face, amazed at the transformation. "It still looks like me, but a bit defined is all."

"Do you really like it?" the girls echoed.

"Oh, aye. Thank ye so much. I've never quite looked this way before."

"You look so beautiful, Tessy." Cherokee smiled. "You are going to knock Grandpa Tayse's socks off."

"Now, now, there'll be none of that." Tessy blushed. "Grandpa Tayse?"

"Oh, all of our friends are calling Grandpa that now; and you do look fantastic, Tessy. I'm quite sure Grandpa will not be able to take his eyes off you," Sarah boasted.

"Oh you girls! Stop your nonsense . . . but thank ye very much." Tessy blushed again.

"Tessy, what do you plan on wearing?" Cherokee asked.

"Well, I had a couple of choices in mind. Come look. See what ye think?" Tessy walked into her closet and brought out three cotton dresses and held them up for the girls to see. They were all a definite NO. Tessy went back in, rummaged around, and pulled out a fourth one. It was a cream muslin with large, pale pink flowers and soft sage green splashed throughout the fabric. It was above mid-calf, yet full enough to gracefully flow as she walked.

"This is the one," the girls agreed. "Put it on so we can see before we go." They gathered up their things and went down to the kitchen, leaving Tessy to get dressed.

Tessy flung her bathrobe on the bed and stepped back to the dressing table to dab on some of her favourite homemade White Musk and Ginger perfume. She reached into the delicate gown and carefully slipped it over her "new do." She picked through her crystals and gems until she found her rose quartz pendant with matching bracelet and earrings. A dainty pair of cream sandals with a slight heel completed the ensemble. Ten minutes later, Tessy descended to the kitchen looking like an angelic figurine with only one thing missing—the wings.

"Wow! Tessy, you look so beautiful!" Sarah gasped.

"Absolutely radiant is more like it," Cherokee added.

"Oh, ye girls! Stop it, now. And besides, it was the two of you that got me looking this way."

"We just enhanced what was already there," Cherokee smiled.

"And we were more than happy to do it," finished Sarah. "But we better get out of here before Grandpa catches us in the act. Have a wonderful time, Tessy, and don't worry, you'll be JUST FINE."

"Have a great time, Tessy. You look fantastic; enjoy every second," Cherokee gushed.

"Oh, thank ye so much again, girls. I don't know what I'd do without ye. You two are such a blessing." Tessy gave each of the girls a hug and a kiss, taking extreme care not to smudge anything. Amazingly, feeling very much like a fairy princess, she then calmly sat down at the kitchen table and remained quite still, waiting for this new chapter of her life to unfold.

The girls exited via the back trail through the trees behind Tessy's property so as not to get caught; however, given their present state of excitement, subtle was not exactly in their demeanour. They giggled and romantically chattered about the date all the way to Sarah's backyard. Pulling themselves together enough to hide their undercover operation, they entered the house in time to see Penny fussing over her father.

"Dad, hold still while I brush this lint off your jacket. You're worse than a little boy for fidgeting. There, that's better. You look so handsome." Penny stepped back to survey her father.

"Are you sure I shouldn't wear a tie? I don't want to seem too casual. I'd like her to think I can look respectable."

"Dad, you look great; and no, you do not want to wear a tie. Nobody wears a tie anymore unless they're going to a formal wedding or a funeral. Now, you better get going or you're going to arrive late."

"Good lord. Look at the time. Well, I guess this is it — no backing out now. Wish me luck."

Penny reached up and gave her father a peck on the cheek. "You'll be just fine, Dad. Have a wonderful time. Oh, Dad. Don't forget the flowers — they're in the fridge. I'll go get them."

"After seeing her flower gardens, I can't imagine why I am even bothering. The ones we got can't hold a candle to hers," Marshall called after her.

"Trust me, Dad, a girl always appreciates flowers, no matter who they're from or what the occasion."

"Okay. 'Bye. Wish me luck!" Marshall repeated as he dashed out the front door.

"Grandpa cleans up real good! Tessy is going to be very impressed," Sarah giggled.

"Oh, so you do know, do you?" Penny smiled as she wrapped one arm around Sarah's shoulder and the other around Cherokee's. "And by the way, just where have you girls been for the last couple of hours?" Penny really didn't have to ask, as she was fairly sure what the girls had been up to.

"Oh, just helping out a friend in need. Call us when you want help with supper." Sarah called as she and Cherokee headed up the stairs doing their best to continue on with their charade.

Marshall rehearsed his opening line all the way to Tessy's house. Driving up her long, winding lane, he could feel the quickening of his heartbeat and he smiled with anticipation. Leaping out of the vehicle like a college student on his first date, he gathered up the flowers in one hand and smoothed his lapel with the other and headed for the front entrance. Giving the beautifully structured doors a confident, firm knock, he stood back a couple of steps waiting for what seemed a lengthy while.

Tessy heard the knock and froze for a moment. She brought herself back to reality, straightened her dress and hurried to the foyer. Glancing out the lace-curtained front doors, she graciously opened them with a welcoming smile and an apology for her tardiness. Marshall stood silent staring at her with his mouth slightly open wanting something to come out but was momentarily stupefied. He finally collected himself enough to hand her the flowers and to comment on how utterly stunning she looked.

"Well, thank ye kindly. You're looking rather dapper yourself." She blushed. "Welcome to Ashling Manor. And thank ye so much for the lovely flowers. Please come in while I put them in some water. Make yourself comfortable. You can go on into the parlour or ye can follow me into the kitchen, if you wish." Tessy continued as she headed down the hall into the kitchen.

"Oh, if you don't mind, I'll just come with you. Always more comfortable in the kitchen," said Marshall as he followed Tessy.

"Oh, not at all. You're a kitchen man, are ye, then?" asked Tessy.

"Well, I don't mean to boast but I make my way around a kitchen fairly well, if I do say so myself," Marshall bragged.

"That's a fine thing to boast about. There's nothing wrong with a good man in the kitchen," Tessy chuckled as she set the flowers in a cut crystal vase and placed them on the kitchen table.

"My, these are lovely flowers. Where on earth did ye find lilacs at this time of year? Mine are all spent by now."

"The flower shop in town said they just got these in but I don't know where they're from. I am so impressed with the shops and restaurants here. You are really very lucky to have such an amazing retail community available in this area."

"Aye, on that you are right," Tessy agreed.

"Speaking of which, I made reservations out at the Inner Peace Bistro for 7:30, if that's okay?"

"Oh, lovely, lovely. I haven't been there for some time, and it is such a wonderful spot. Oh, but look at the time, we should be on our way, should we not? It's a wee drive out there." Tessy swept some fallen leaves off the counter and into the sink then wiped her hands off on a towel.

"After you." Marshall stood aside and motioned with a slight bow, allowing Tessy to pass by him, heading out to the foyer. Her scent was intoxicating! He was amazed at how easy it was to be with her and still be himself tonight. So much for rehearsed lines!

Once on the veranda, he waited for Tessy at the top of the stairs while she locked the door then offered his arm so he could assist her down the steps. He walked her around to the passenger door and chivalrously opened it then waited for her to get settled in before closing it. Again, feeling like a much younger man than he was, he literally ran around to the other side of the car and jumped in. He glanced over at his companion and said, "We're off!" with a smile that would put even a Cheshire cat to shame. All the way to the restaurant, to their mutual relief, they comfortably chatted non-stop.

The chalet was situated on a grassy slope overlooking the far side of Ladyslipper Lake, with beautifully manicured grounds and huge pine trees bordering the property. The setting and the evening could not have been more perfect. The sun was still warm, casting long, narrow shadows while a whispering breeze gently played with Tessy's loose curls. They took their time wandering up the path to the main entrance, enjoying the gardens along the scenic view. Once inside, they were greeted by Cherokee's Aunt Dawn who was standing at the reservation desk.

"Tessy. How good to see you. Welcome, come in." She stepped around the desk to give Tessy a hug.

"Thank ye, Dawn. It's wonderful to see you, too, to be sure. I'd like ye to meet Penny Tucker's father, Marshall Tayse." Tessy turned toward Marshall then stepped aside so they could shake hands.

"Nice to meet you. Oh, yes, Dr. Tayse, we have your reservation. I didn't realize you would be dining with Tessy tonight. If the two of you will follow me to the upper level, we will get you seated. I have chosen a quiet table by the windows overlooking the lake. Since it's so warm we have opened the windows but if you find it too cool please let me know." She pulled their chairs out for them and placed leather-bound menus at their place settings. "May I bring you some refreshments from the lounge or do you need a moment?" she inquired.

"If you don't mind, we would like to take a minute to look over your wine list." Marshall volunteered.

"Not at all, please take your time. I'll send your waitress, Jacquie, over in a few minutes to see how you are making out. Enjoy your evening." Dawn smiled and backed away.

"Wow! This is some place. I am already impressed and I haven't even tasted the food yet." Marshall said as he glanced at the majestic surroundings.

"Oh, you'll not be disappointed," Tessy answered. "I've not had a bad meal here yet nor am I ever about to, I am quite sure."

"Well, in that case, let's not hesitate. What would your wine preference be or would you maybe prefer a cocktail first?" Marshall offered.

"Oh, no, no. Wine would be just fine, thank ye. I have no real preference, so you please go on ahead and order for the pair of us. I'm sure ye have fine judgment on such things."

Marshall laughed and, perusing the wine menu, said, "Okay then . . . Let's see, I think maybe . . . oh, good, they do have it . . . all right, I think we're ready." Marshall glanced up in time to see a beautiful young aboriginal girl approaching their table.

"Good evening, folks. I'm Jacquie and I will be your server for this evening. Do you have any questions regarding any of the wines on our list?"

"No, thank you. I think we have decided on a bottle of your number 16." Marshall closed the wine menu and laid it back down on the table.

"Good choice," Jacquie agreed as she wrote it down on her pad. "I'll be back in a minute with your wine, then." She returned promptly, opened the wine with great flair, and poured a small amount in Marshall's glass for him to sample.

"Perfect. Thank you." Marshall raised his glass to her.

Jacquie poured them each a generous glass, proceeded to announce the evening's specials, then left them alone to enjoy their wine and each other's company.

"Well, here's to the beginning of a wonderful evening and an even better friendship." Marshall held up his glass, and Tessy reached over and tapped it with hers.

"*Slainte . . .* Aye, a fine evening seems to be in store, to be sure." Tessy smiled, took a sip of wine, and picked up her menu to hide her pink cheeks.

And a fine evening it was. They talked and laughed and even shared their heartaches. They witnessed the sun turn from a golden yellow to crimson to amethyst, while enjoying the lonely call of a loon out on the water. There was a brief lull in the conversation, and it was then that Tessy noticed the restaurant was lit only with candles and almost empty. She looked at her watch. "Oh, my stars. Look at the time! Where did the hours go?"

Marshall then checked his watch. "Wow! I've been having such a wonderful time, I had no idea it was this late. Well, I suppose we should go and let these good people finish up for the night. I'll just take care of the bill and we'll be off."

"Aye, and while you are doing that, I'll be off to the ladies' room and meet ye at the front desk." As Tessy rose, Marshall rushed over to pull out her chair and to assist her with her wrap. Tessy glanced up at him and felt her cheeks flushing once again, not sure, at this point, whether it was the gesture or the wine that turned their colour. When Tessy returned, she found Marshall at the front desk chatting with Dawn. As Tessy approached, they both turned toward her.

"Tessy, thank you so much for joining us tonight." Dawn smiled and reached for another hug.

"Oh, it was our pleasure, for sure; the meal was delicious as usual. I'm so sorry we stayed to such a wicked hour. I hope we haven't detained your staff over their limit," Tessy apologized.

"Oh, no, no. Marshall was just saying the same. Not at all. We loved having you. Please come back and see us real soon," Dawn assured them.

"Well, we're off, then. Ready, Tess? After you, my lady. Thanks again, good night." Marshall held the big log door open as Tessy passed through.

"Good night," Dawn called after them.

Outside, the frogs and crickets serenaded Tessy and Marshall. The path to the parking lot was softly lit with solar lamps, which allowed them to easily view the vast night sky. It exploded with millions of twinkling stars and a waning moon that hung on a slight angle. The air was still and warm with a scent of sweet grass and fresh lake water. There were benches along the path, and without much persuasion, they sat down on the one that best overlooked the lake. The reflection from the night sky in the gently rippled water was incredible. As they sat in silence for the first time the entire evening, Marshall impulsively picked up Tessy's hand in his. Startled, she drew it away then she put her head down and returned her hand into his, then looked up at him. They spent a minute gazing at one another, smiling, then without a word, got up and, hand in hand, continued to the car in silence.

The drive home was quiet, yet still comfortable. It seemed they had said everything that needed to be said for that evening. Both were tired, relaxed, and probably a little mentally exhausted from the day's anticipation of their "date." Marshall pulled into the long lane, and when the headlights lit the row of willows, it was like entering an enchanted tunnel. Marshall suddenly had the thought: Enchantment was the way this place — and Tessy, for that matter — made him feel. He glanced over at her, and there it was: that aura. He could actually see it. He blinked his eyes a couple of times to see if it would disappear, but it didn't. She was glowing. *This is silly*, he thought. *I am a doctor, for heaven's sake; people don't just light up. There has got to be a logical explanation. I'm just tired and the lights reflecting on the trees are making it seem like she's glowing. That's it.*

Tessy could sense his uneasiness. "Marshall, is there something wrong? What is it?"

"Oh, nothing. I think I'm just a little tired, that's all," Marshall assured her. He pulled the car into the circle drive at the front entrance and shut off the engine. They sat for a second, then Tessy looked over at him and said, "I had a lovely time tonight, Marshall Tayse. Thank ye so much for a delightful evening. I haven't laughed so much in a very long while." She chuckled.

"The pleasure was definitely all mine," Marshall graciously answered. "But I certainly hope it doesn't end here. I would love to see you again — if you'd allow it?"

"Oh, my . . . well, yes . . . of course, I'd enjoy your company again, to be sure." Tessy blushed. "Well, it's late — I should be getting in now. Thank ye again, Marshall."

Marshall leaped out of the driver's seat and rushed around to open Tessy's door. Tessy took his arm as they slowly made their way up the steps. Once at the front door, Marshall took Tessy's keys and opened the door; then, returning them back to her, he pulled her hands in his and brought one up and kissed it. "Good night, my fair lady of Ladyslipper." He then gallantly bowed, turned, and descended the stairs. He waited there until he was sure she was safely inside and heard the door latch and lock.

He was about to get into the car, but, for some strange reason, he decided to check around back just to make sure everything was locked up tight. It was very dark in the backyard, and his memory was not serving him well as to where everything was situated. He was approaching the back step and, not knowing exactly where the edge was, he stumbled . . . and then there was a loud banging, echoing crash! He had happened to trip over the galvanized watering can Tessy had left at the back door.

All of a sudden, the back light flicked on, the door flew open, and two very large dogs came thundering over top of Marshall. As Marshall lay motionless on the ground with the dogs standing over him and barking to beat the band, he looked up on the steps and there was Tessy. Her first expression was of shock, then concern, which soon turned to amusement when she saw who it was and that he didn't appear to be injured.

"Duke, Darby, it's okay . . . good dogs . . . come now." And with that, the dogs came over and sat close to Tessy. "Is there something I could be helping ye with, Dr. Tayse?" Tessy quipped.

"Uh, no, thanks. I just wanted to make sure the doors were all locked and that you were okay." Marshall volunteered as he picked himself up off the ground and proceeded to brush himself off.

Tessy started to laugh heartily and came down the steps. "Are ye all right? You know you can really hurt yourself skulking around in the middle of the night in dark places. Would ye like to come in and sit for a spell until ye get your sea legs back?"

"No . . . thanks . . . I think I'd better go before I do anything else really stupid. Hopefully, so far, the only thing I've damaged is my pride." Marshall shook his head.

"No, that was a very thoughtful thing you were trying to do, and I thank ye kindly. Not stupid at all. Aye, I agree, maybe a wee bit hard on your pride, but most times I've found it's not a bad thing to bruise one's pride on the odd occasion."

"Very kind of you to say so, Tessy. Well, good night, then, and I promise I will actually leave the premises."

With that, Marshall limped his way around the house and climbed into his car to lick his wounds and, if at all possible, restore his deflated ego.

Bruschetta

6 medium red or yellow tomatoes
2 cloves minced garlic
1/2 cup (125 ml) thinly sliced green onions
1/4 cup (50 ml) chopped fresh basil
1/8 cup (25 ml) chopped fresh parsley
1/2 tsp (2 ml) coarse ground pepper
Optional: 1 cup (250 ml) grated Parmesan cheese (if baking)

Mix ingredients in medium bowl and chill before use. Transfer to Mason jar if transporting. Spoon 2 Tbsp (30 ml) of the mixture onto a fresh baguette and enjoy! Optional: Sprinkle with Parmesan cheese before baking on toasted baguette.

Soothing Herbal Bath Salts

1 cup (250 ml) Epsom salts
1/2 cup (125 ml) sea salt
1/4 cup (50 ml) sodium borate
2 Tbsp (30 ml) dried, crushed, rose petals
1 Tbsp (15 ml) ground lavender flowers
1 Tbsp (15 ml) ground chamomile flowers
1 Tbsp (15 ml) ground lemon balm leaf

Grind the dried herbs in a coffee grinder dedicated to this purpose. Combine all ingredients and add 10 drops of your preferred essential oil — e.g., lavender, rose, neroli — and mix well. Add 4 Tbsp (60 ml) to your bath and relish the experience!

12

A Fresh New Day with Not One Mishap . . . Yet

Tessy lay in bed the next morning unable to stop herself from giggling uncontrollably over Marshall's midnight misfortune. She really did feel bad for him . . . sweet man but . . . oh, my gosh, he looked so funny lying on the ground seeming so befuddled! And away off she went again, giggling so hard she had to bury her face in her covers to keep the tears from rolling down her cheeks. "Okay, stop it now," Tessy scolded herself as she got out of bed shaking off her hilarity fit. "There. Enough." She huffed out. *My, wouldn't it be grand to laugh like that every morning before one's foot hits the floor. However, not over such an embarrassing antic, to be sure*, were her thoughts as she made her bed. She put on her housecoat and headed downstairs to let the dogs out with an oversized grin on her rueful face. After such a late night, she was feeling extremely exuberant.

Down the street at the Tuckers', there was also a face buried under the covers, but for entirely different reasons. Marshall held the covers over his head and kept repeating, "Why? Why? Why me? No. No, not again. Everything was going along beautifully and then . . . why? Why? Stupid, clumsy fool. I had to go and screw up a perfectly good evening. She probably thinks I'm a complete idiot. She'll never want to see me again, and I can't say I blame her." He flung the covers back and slowly crawled out of bed, experiencing a twinge of stiffness resulting from his tumble. He hobbled over to his ensuite and turned on the shower to as steaming hot as he could get it. He climbed in and let the hot water loosen up his sore, aching muscles, while drowning his sorrows at the same time. He did let out a few mournful groans, not so much from the physical pain, but more from the injustice of it all. He realized he was possibly being a bit melodramatic, but right at the moment, he didn't particularly care and enjoyed wallowing in his despair.

Marshall got dressed and made his way to the kitchen, disguising his limp as best he could.

"Good morning . . . you old fox." Jim was the first to make an account of the time in which Marshall got in the previous night.

"Yes, who would have thought a first date could have gone on to all hours of the night," Penny continued.

"Very funny, you two. That'll be enough of that from either one of you." Marshall playfully scowled.

"Dad, what's the matter? Are you limping? What happened? She flip you like a pancake?" Penny teased, but with some concern.

"No, no, no. I'm fine . . . flipped me like a pancake, really! I just had a little tumble last night, that's all. I don't want to talk about it." Marshall waved his hand in the air.

"What do you mean you 'had a little tumble'? I saw your jacket had grass all over it and couldn't imagine where it came from. What happened?" Penny was now insistent on getting the whole story.

"I need a cup of coffee," Marshall groaned as he noticeably limped over to the counter. He picked out the largest cup he could find and filled it to the brim with the rich, black, strong brew and gently eased himself down into a chair at the table.

"Spill the beans. Now! The kids are all still sleeping. It's just us three. Come on. You can't keep us in this kind of suspense," begged Penny.

"All right . . . but you have to promise not to laugh.

"We had a wonderful evening. The restaurant was fantastic, and we talked and laughed non-stop. Everything was perfect until we got to her house—"

"I knew it—you did get fresh with her," Penny interrupted.

"NO! Will you stop that and let me finish?" Marshall said, throwing Penny a wide-eyed glare. "Anyway, as I was saying. When we reached her house, I walked her to the door, and once she was safely in, I decided to go around back and make sure everything was locked up. Well, it was extremely dark, and to make a long story short, I tripped on the back step and knocked over a watering can, which made a thundering crash. She came to the back door, flicked on the lights and let out her barking, monster dogs to run all over me. Scared the hell out of me!" Marshall turned slightly pale at the memory.

Well, that was just too much for either Penny or Jim. The explosion of laughter could be heard down the block. Even Marshall, now visualizing the outlandish predicament, had to exude a hearty chuckle.

Penny, wiping the tears from her cheeks, finally collected herself enough to ask her father if he was really okay or if maybe they should take him for X-rays.

"No. I'm fine. It's just my ego that's a little bruised. But I can't see how I can ever face her again. Oh well, I'll be leaving in a week, anyway. Guess I'll just have to avoid her until then," Marshall concluded.

"Dad, stop that. You can't leave without seeing her again or at least phoning her. I'm sure Tessy feels it was a thoughtful gesture," Penny sympathized.

"Well, that's exactly what she said, but I'm sure she shut the door and had a good laugh, too," groaned Marshall.

"Even if she did, so what? You said the two of you had a great time and had lots to talk about. I'm sure that is the most memorable part of the evening — not your tumble. Although, I must admit that was a pretty unforgettable tactic. She probably closed the door and gave you an eight-point-five. You know what they say . . . always leave them laughing," and then Penny started laughing all over again.

"Oh, put a sock in it!" Marshall smirked and crossed his arms.

By this time, the kids were all up and wondering what was going on downstairs. One by one, they sleepily invaded the kitchen. Little Emma was first. "Mommy, why are you laughing so much?" She crawled up on her mother's lap and cuddled into her shoulder.

"Sorry, honey. Did we wake you?" Penny kissed her forehead.

Emma just nodded while continuing to cuddle.

Next came Sarah. "'Morning. What's up with the noise down here? Sounds like you guys are having a party. How was your date with Tessy, Grandpa? OOOPS! Sorry!"

Matt was right behind her. "Date? What date? Oh, Grandpa . . . yuk! You didn't kiss her, did ya? Oh, yuk . . . gross!"

Poor Marshall had nothing left to say but, "This *just* keeps getting better and better."

"Okay, kids. That's enough. Everyone leave your grandfather alone and stop badgering him," Penny commanded as she leaned up to the counter.

"Yes. Your mother has already done a fine job of that," Jim teased.

Penny giggled as she set some dirty dishes in the sink. "Now, who's in favour of a nice, big Sunday morning breakfast?"

All day Sunday passed, and it was now Monday evening and Tessy still had had no word from Marshall. She was quite sure it was because of the backyard mishap, but they really had had a very lovely evening and surely he could put that fact in the forefront and gather himself enough to call. She was sitting at the kitchen table sipping her favourite tea, pondering, when she looked over at the sleeping Merlin and Cordelia and suddenly had a revelation.

"Well, sometimes a woman has to take affairs into her own hands. If a person allows his pride to rule his heart, 'tis the duty of a friend to show him the error of his ways." She grinned, got up, walked over to her writing desk, and pulled out a delicately scented sheet of writing paper. She removed her new pen from its decorative box and thought aloud . . . "Aye, let's see . . . Aye." Then she penned:

> Dearest Marshall,
> The fair lady of Ladyslipper requests your presence
> to join her for an afternoon picnic and walkabout.
> Location: Ladyslipper Lake Park
> Date: This Wednesday Next
> Time: 1:00 p.m.
> I bid you shall come as I look forward to our visit.
> Yours very truly,
> Tessy McGuigan

She read it over, smiled, and placed it in a matching envelope. She addressed it, "Attention: Doctor Marshall Tayse, care of the Tuckers," along with their house number, and put a stamp on it. Tessy gave the envelope a gentle pat. "There, ready for Roger to take in the morning."

She had decided that she wasn't even going to go to the seniors' complex in the morning until she made sure it was in Roger's hands.

Tessy was on her lawn tractor cutting the grass at the front when Roger arrived the next morning. When she noticed him, she put it high gear and drove toward him, waving her hands in the air and calling out. Roger stood waving back, wondering what all the fuss was about.

As Tessy got closer, she geared down and finally rolled up to him and cut the engine. "Aye, Roger, good day!" Tessy puffed, and pulled the letter out of the top pocket of her overalls. "Here, I have a wee note I'd like ye to deliver for me as soon as you are able, in fact, the sooner the better, if you don't mind."

Roger took the envelope, looked at the address, and, with a slight twinkle in his eye, replied, "Shouldn't be a problem, Tess. Be glad to take care of it for you right away. Is there anything else you need me to take?"

"No. No. Thank ye, Roger. I appreciate your promptness." Tessy, now feeling a little embarrassed at her overzealousness, smiled and sheepishly added, "Fine day. Doesn't look like there's going to be a cloud in the sky today."

"Yep. Supposed to be clear and sunny all week. Well, I'd better be off so I can finish up my route early. Connie has a 'Honey-do-list' for me this week as long as her arm." Roger chuckled and headed off down the lane. "Have a great day, Tessy."

"Aye, Roger, and you. And thank ye again!" Tessy called after him.

It was close to noon, and Marshall had kept himself busy playing bocce ball with Emma and catch with Matt for as long as Matt was around that morning. He and Emma were on their fifth match when Penny called them in for lunch.

"Emma, please go and wash up," Penny requested. Then she turned to her father with an impish grin.

"What?" Marshall looked at her suspiciously.

"This just came for you." She teasingly held up the envelope and sniffed it then waved it in the air toward him.

"What is it?" Marshall questioned.

Penny handed it to him, "I'm thinking you might want to read it in private," she suggested.

Marshall flushed slightly, took the envelope, and stepped out onto the deck. He sat down at the deck table and gingerly opened it, seemingly afraid to reveal its contents. As he read it, he chuckled heartily, shaking his head. "What a gal! One of a kind for sure!" He smiled.

Penny came out to join him. "Anything you care to share?" she asked.

"Not really." Marshall grinned as he gathered up the note and envelope off the table and walked past her into the kitchen.

"Oh, come on." Penny ran after him. "You've got to be kidding. Come on. Dad? Come on. *Please.*"

"Maybe tomorrow. I'm going up to my room now. I'll be down for lunch in a few minutes," he said as he nonchalantly continued on through the kitchen.

"I'm not feeding you until you come clean," Penny called after him.

Marshall chuckled all the way upstairs.

Once in the privacy of his room, Marshall read the note again and again. Now feeling even worse for not having had the courage or manners to give this precious lady a considerate call, he wondered how on earth he would make it up to her. What could he do or buy? What do you present to a woman like Tessy? A woman who has every blooming flower available right outside her door. A woman whose tastes are simple, yet exquisite. A woman who would appreciate any little token with grace. A woman like . . . Tessy McGuigan . . . There *is* no woman like Tessy McGuigan. Marshall remained in his room a little longer than he had planned. A knock at the door startled him back to reality.

"Dad, are you all right? I was just kidding about not feeding you," Penny sounded concerned.

Marshall opened the door. "I'm sorry, honey . . . I know you were kidding. I just got lost in my thoughts for a bit." He went and sat down on the edge of his bed again. "Penny, I've been such a stubborn old fool. I'm just not used to this dating stuff. I should have called Tessy on Sunday morning and told her what a great time I'd had instead of being so pig-headed."

"Oh, Dad, don't be so hard on yourself. I know Tessy. She'll turn this all into a silver-lined experience for everyone. Besides, most women appreciate a man making a fool of himself in front of her." Penny smiled rubbing her dad lovingly across the shoulders.

"Well, if that's the case, Tessy should be crazy about me! She's invited me to meet her tomorrow afternoon for a picnic, and I will show her then how sorry I am and somehow will find a way to make it up to her," Marshall concluded.

Wednesday was sunny and bright. Tessy packed a delectable lunch; enough to feed a small army yet would delight even the fussiest palate. She tied the picnic basket into the wire cage on her trike and pedalled out to the lake at around twelve thirty. She coasted along the well-worn path, enjoying the sights and smells along the way until she reached the park entrance. She stopped and looked for the perfect spot to lay the blanket and spread out her carefully prepared banquet. The afternoon would be warm, so she decided on a lovely spot under a gigantic willow tree. She was busily reaching into the basket when she felt a shadow block out the warmth of the sun. She looked up to see Marshall standing over her with that boyishly broad smile.

"Good day, my fair lady of Ladyslipper." He reached out his hand to help her up and, pulling her close, gave her a warm hug. "Before you say anything," he continued, "I would like to profusely apologize for my rude behaviour by not calling you and telling you what a wonderful time I had the other evening and how wonderful I think you are and how incredibly lucky I feel to be here with you."

Marshall freed her from his hug and gently kissed her then stood back with a look of such genuine sincerity and adoration that Tessy was momentarily stunned. Not knowing quite what to say to his honest outpouring, she too, stepped back and just smiled. She gathered herself and calmly shared some of her inner wisdom: "I read somewhere that if you have made a mistake or have fearful thoughts, give it to Heaven and ask that all ill effects be undone for everyone concerned." Then, deciding to lighten the mood, she added with a wink, "And as well, I find a good dose of humility does keep one's ego in check!"

Marshall laughed. "You truly are more than a wise woman and you haven't yet ceased to amaze me. Penny said you would put a silver lining on this situation and make it disappear, and you have. Thank you for being so gracious and understanding. I will do as you say and I have given it to Heaven. Now, let's enjoy our day together!"

"Aye, an enjoyable one it shall be," Tessy agreed. "Are you hungry now, or should we walk up an appetite first?"

"I had quite a late breakfast this morning so I would love to go for a walk along the lake first, if that's okay with you — if you're not too hungry?"

"Oh, I nibbled a bit while making this wee feast so I could last an hour or so, to be sure," Tessy chuckled.

"I parked the car in the shade, so we can just place the picnic basket in the trunk for now. Will everything be okay?" asked Marshall as he picked up the basket and blanket.

"Oh, it should be just fine. I put in a few ice packs to keep things cool, and there is a container of ice cubes for our iced tea. Not sure how they will fare, but everything else should be fine as frog's fur."

"Great," Marshall smiled, and they headed for the parking lot.

After locking the picnic in the trunk of the car, they started down the path toward the lake. It was sandy, yet well packed, and wide enough for them to comfortably stroll side by side. As they ambled along the sandy berm, Tessy contently tucked her arm in Marshall's and they prattled on about the past and the future. They continued on for a while then relaxed on a bench for a few minutes before turning back to enjoy their picnic lunch.

Marshall retrieved the basket and blanket, and they soon had the meal spread out before them under the "big ol' willow tree," as Marshall put it. Tessy plunked the few remaining un-melted ice cubes into two large tumblers and poured them each a generous glass of iced tea. They clinked glasses. "*Slainte*! Is that right?" Marshall checked and proceeded to gulp down the much-anticipated cold liquid. "Boy! Does that hit the spot," Marshall exhaled.

"Aye, we were both a bit parched, and I'm sure you are as hungry as a bear by now. Here, help yourself to some fixings. I'm hoping I packed something you'll find to your liking."

"Are you kidding? Look at what you have here!" Marshall announced with great gusto as he looked over the incredible delectables laid out before him. There was a fresh baguette, homemade bruschetta, havarti cheese, cut-up vegetables with dip, cold grilled chicken, and smoked salmon; and for dessert, there was fresh fruit with a yogurt-whipped cream dip, as well as mincemeat tarts and gingerbread cookies left over from Sunday's party. Marshall displayed the healthy appetite of a teenager and helped himself to a good serving of everything.

Soon, very full and quite content, yet still nibbling on some grapes, Marshall leaned his back up against the roughly textured trunk of the willow. He fixed his gaze upon Tessy as she tidied up the unfinished bits and pieces, placing everything but the fruit back into the basket. Tessy looked up and caught him. "What is it you're staring at, sir?"

"Oh. Sorry. It's just that since I've met you I can't seem to stop wondering about you. I find you so absolutely intriguing . . . I have never met anyone of your calibre before."

"Ohh . . . go on with ye, now. I'm just a simple lass," Tessy blushed.

"Ohhh, no. You are definitely not a simple anything. That was immediately evident the first day I met you at your Christmas party. Did you know I spent that entire day trying to get you to notice me? And all I seemed to do was trip over myself!"

"Aye. Now that I think back, ye were about as subtle as a train wreck!" Tessy chuckled.

Marshall laughed. "Yes. You are probably very right. Oh, Tessy you keep me laughing." Marshall then became sober and asked, "If you don't mind my asking, how is it that you came to live in Canada?"

"I don't mind at all. When my twin brother, Keenan, and I were sixteen, we immigrated to Canada from Ireland after our parents had been killed in a horrific car accident. My mother survived for a few days, so we were able to say our farewells to her, but she eventually succumbed to her injuries. We were left in the care of Mum's sister, our godmother, Aunt Shannon, and her family in Winnipeg, Manitoba. We objected terribly at first, but the arrangements were set in stone. As big a change as it was, we were loved and eventually settled into our new surroundings."

"I'm so sorry. That must have been so hard on you both. Where is Keenan now?"

"Oh, that wandering minstrel! He chose to go straight back to Ireland immediately after we graduated from high school — to help out our uncle in the family business." Tessy smiled with love and pride for her brother.

"Do you see him often?" Marshall questioned.

"Not often enough. He's been back to Canada a few times, and Dermot and I made many trips to our beloved homeland throughout the years. I sure do miss him, though. We have a very special bond, he and I, being twins and all."

"I'm sure, and just so you know, I am truly going to miss you. In fact, I really would consider postponing my trip back home but I have patients scheduled for Monday morning."

"Well now, ye need to be going and caring for your patients. Your talent is a gift from God and you are the only one that can help those people right at the moment. Lord knows the world is short of good doctors and you being one of them are in demand."

"Oh, Tessy. Thank you. You have such a way of putting things into perspective. I appreciate your ability to pull me back to reality. But I am still going to miss you!"

"Aye. Companionship is a lovely thing, and I, too, shall miss our time . . . Oh, look . . . there's the children, bless their hearts. Hello, hello . . ." Tessy waved and called.

Sarah, Emma, and Becky came running over. "Hey, you two," Sarah smiled.

"Grandpa!" Emma ran into her grandfather's embrace. "Hi, Tessy," she mumbled, her head buried.

Tessy, too, was receiving her hugs from Becky.

"Hello, my dears! Have ye had lunch? Are ye hungry? I have a few smidgens left here that you are welcome to."

"Oh, no thanks, Tessy. We just finished lunch not too long ago and the girls want to go swimming," Sarah answered. "But thanks, anyway. We just came over to say hi."

"Well, here, be sure to take some gingerbread cookies for after your swim, then." Tessy said as she reached into the picnic basket. "Are Matthew and his friends apt to be at the beach as well? No matter. I'll give ye enough to share." Whereupon, Tessy crammed as many cookies as she could fit into a self-sealing baggie.

"Thanks, Tessy, these will really be great after our swim," Sarah said as she tucked them into her beach bag. "Come on, girls, we should get going. See you later, Grandpa. 'Bye, Tessy, and thanks again." And with that, the girls ran down to the beach.

Tessy stood and watched them in their excitement until they were out of sight.

"You really love those kids, don't you?" Marshall mused.

"Aye. Yes, of course. All children are a blessing. Unfortunately, Dermot and I were never blessed with children of our own, but as the years wore on, that pain lessened, and we relished our students and spent many a joyous holiday spoiling our nieces and nephews. Seeing the world through their eyes keeps a soul young, and I have no intention of letting my inner child or my soul grow old."

Again, Marshall heartily laughed and said, "I have no doubt, my fair lady, that that shall ever happen. Speaking of which, are you up to walking the full gamut round the lake?"

"Aye, and a fair bit quicker than you, I'm sure," teased Tessy.

"Ohhh, the challenge is on, then, my lady," Marshall accepted, as he energetically leaped up as best he could with his wounds and grabbed the basket and blanket to deposit them in the car. "I'll be back in two shakes. Don't start without me—or maybe I should let you have a head start?" He chortled over his shoulder.

"I'm thinking that won't be necessary, you cheeky devil. Just remember, you haven't tripped over yourself yet today, but it's still early," Tessy called after him.

Still laughing, Marshall grabbed Tessy's hand on his way past, and off they merrily trotted. "And I have no intention of looking that foolish in front of you ever again," announced Marshall with eyes twinkling as he kissed Tessy's hand and held on a bit tighter.

Gentle Insect Repellent

2 cups (500 ml) witch hazel
1 tsp (5 ml) vegetable glycerin
20 drops citronella essential oil
16 drops eucalyptus essential oil
16 drops lavender essential oil
5 drops peppermint

Combine all ingredients in one 16-ounce or two 8-ounce spray bottles and shake vigorously to blend. The oils will separate, so shake well immediately before each use.

Heavenly Dream Pillow

1 small, soft hand towel or any soft material of approximately
    same size as a small towel
Quilt batting
1/2 cup (125 ml) of dried herbs of choice
2 rubber bands
2 12-inch (30.5-cm) pieces of ribbon
2 small artificial silk flowers
Glue gun (optional)

Lay out hand towel and cut quilt batting to fit inside towel with at least a 3-inch (7.5 cm) margin on three sides. The end that you will be rolling up first should have the batting pulled right to the edge. Pick your herbs of choice—my favourites are lavender, hops, and chamomile or rose petals—mix together in a glass or plastic bowl and stir with a wooden spoon. Sprinkle the herbs on the batting and begin to roll the end that is lined up. When you have finished rolling it like a jelly roll, pinch the end and secure it with a rubber band. Repeat with the other end. If you like, you can spread glue along the open edge to further secure it. Tie the ribbons on each of the ends over the rubber bands and adorn with small silk flowers using a dab of glue. Tuck into bed with you, breathe deeply, and enjoy your heavenly dreams! Give the pillow a squeeze every so often to release the scent.

13

Bittersweet Feelings and New Beginnings

Tessy was glad she had prepared the groundwork for her last class a couple of days earlier. Yesterday's picnic was wonderful but it had pretty much eaten up most of the day. She merrily hummed while packing her herbs and oils into their baskets. The phone rang and she knowingly smiled as she picked up the receiver. "Good mornin' to ye," she chirped.

"And a good morning to you, my fair lady," Marshall returned. "What are you busying yourself with this morning?"

"Well, now, Doctor Tayse, after gallivantin' around the countryside yesterday, I best be busying myself. I'm preparing for my class this afternoon."

"Well, could you spare some time this morning to meet an old soul for a coffee and one of those sinfully delicious cinnamon rolls at Sheree's Sidewalk Café?"

"Ahh, you've succumbed to one of Sheree's rolls, have ye? A dangerous thing, to be sure. You make it hard for a lady to say no to such temptation."

"Then, that would be a . . . yes?" asked Marshall hopefully.

"Aye, I think I could squeeze you into my tight schedule. What time were ye thinking of being there?"

"How about thirty minutes?"

"My, you sure expect a girl to be up and ready, now, don't ye?"

"Well, when that girl is already as radiant as the sun, she doesn't have much to do."

"Go on with ye, now, and stop with your silliness. You cheeky man. I can be there in about forty minutes and now I'm going to say goodbye before you go on with any more of your nonsense!"

Marshall laughed. "See you in about forty minutes. And Tessy — thanks. I'm really looking forward to seeing you."

Marshall arrived early and was sitting out on the deck having a cup of coffee. When he looked up, he noticed a woman staring at him. He slightly nodded and smiled and she got up and walked toward him. When she approached his table, she said, "You are Penny Tucker's father, are you not?"

"Why, yes, I am Marshall Tayse. How did you know?"

"I am Mrs. Chamberlain and I make it my business to know what goes on in this town."

Marshall's expression drastically sobered "Oh. Yes, my daughter has mentioned you."

"Well, I've noticed she has not taken heed of my advice and is still allowing her children, your grandchildren, to associate with that — that witch, Tessy McGuigan."

Marshall wasn't even sure how to respond to this overbearing, opinionated, rude woman standing in from of him! He finally gathered his wits and, with gritted teeth, said, "Mrs. Chamberlain, I would suggest you keep your nose out of my family's affairs, your opinions to yourself, and remove yourself from my presence before I do or say something that would compromise my being a gentleman."

Mrs. Chamberlain drew herself up, raised her eyebrows, and glared at Marshall. "I have warned you," she huffed. "Just remember that!" and she turned and stomped away.

Tessy was quite relieved that she had already showered and her hair was almost dry. She ran upstairs and rummaged through her closet until she found her favourite denim skirt, matched it up with a salmon-coloured Tee, added a chakra amulet, earrings, and a wide sterling silver bracelet with stone insets. She whisked up her hair, lightly brushed her cheeks with some blush, and ran some coloured gloss over her lips. "There, Doctor Tayse, I'm afraid that's as good as it's going to get this morning," she announced aloud as she raced past the mirror.

Forty-two minutes later, Tessy pulled up on her trike. Marshall had managed to calm down. He was still sitting on the deck finishing his coffee and admiring the view that had just arrived. He rushed into the café and up to the counter to purchase two more coffees and a couple of cinnamon buns. Tessy joined him at the counter, and they headed back out to the deck.

"Good morning. You look lovely," Marshall sighed.

"Thank ye . . . And a good morning to you. You slept well?" Tessy inquired, wanting to move on.

"No. As a matter of fact, as the week moves on, I seem to be getting less and less sleep. Pretty soon, going to bed will just be a complete waste of time," Marshall complained.

"Oh, dear. Well, I have a mixture of herbs at home that will surely help with your problem. And here," as she dug into her emergency pouch, "put this howlite gemstone under your pillow. It will help with your insomnia; and I also believe I have a wee sachet of lavender in here somewhere . . . Yes. Here it is," Tess continued as she proceeded to look through her bag. "I truly wish you had said something a little earlier — I could have prepared the herbs and brought them with me this morning."

"Well, Ms. McGuigan, thank you, but *you* seem to be at the root of my problem," Marshall smiled.

"ME! What on earth have I to do with your not sleeping?"

"In a few short days, I am leaving to go back to a very large, lonely house in Winnipeg, and someone I have grown very fond of, in a very brief period of time, will be here in Ladyslipper — not to mention my family. Everything has changed, and certainly not for the worse, but I'm feeling torn and out of sorts. It's just not me, and I don't like feeling this way. Oh. Look at me wallowing in self-pity . . . Sorry. I'll be perfectly fine. It'll just take me a few days to readjust. However, I might stop by and pick up those herbs you were suggesting."

"Marshall . . ." Tessy reached over and placed her hand on his, "I, too, will be missing my new friend. But it certainly doesn't mean the friendship is over. The only thing that will be changing is the geography."

"There's so many things we haven't done yet. I haven't even had a chance to take you dancing," Marshall frowned.

"Now, that's a little harder to find in Ladyslipper — at least with music I'd care to dance to." She laughed, "And it's been so long I'm not sure your toes would be up to it. I do have a tendency to dance around the kitchen the odd day, but my cats and my faeries know to stay out of the way. One of my favourite sayings is: 'Dance like nobody's watching' — and *that* is one thing where I *do* practise what I preach!"

Marshall picked up Tessy's hand and kissed it. "Well, Winnipeg has lots of dance floors and I would love to see you cut loose on any one of them."

"Oh, now, listen to you. Don't be planning on me gallivantin' off to far places at the drop of a hat. We have just recently met, you know, and I'm not the kind of girl to be rushing into anything," scolded Tessy.

"Now, don't go getting that Irish temper all flared up. I'm just suggesting, at some point in time, that I'd love for you to come and visit. You could even bring the kids if that would make you feel more comfortable. As I said, I have a large house, and there's plenty of room for everyone."

"Well, I do still have my relatives in Winnipeg, and it has been a while since I've been to visit—so I suppose a trip, in the near future, might not be entirely out of the question . . ." Tessy mused.

"That would be wonderful!" Marshall exclaimed, a little more enthusiastically than he wished.

Tessy just laughed and touched his hand.

The next hour flew by with light conversation and easy laughter. Tessy looked at her watch and was amazed at how, once again, the time had so quickly disappeared. Marshall walked her out to her bike and stood towering over her. She looked so childlike with her large green eyes all bright, cheeks pink, and with that ever-present glow of wonderment. He picked up her hand and kissed it. "Join me here for dinner tonight? I could pick you up at six-thirty."

"Oh! My. I—I'm—I'm not sure," Tessy stammered.

"Please. We have such a short time left, and I'd like to spend as much of it with you as possible," Marshall begged.

"Well, all right, then, but I was just about to ask you over to my house for dinner tomorrow night. Kind of a farewell I was planning," blushed Tessy.

"That would be wonderful, too. I graciously accept, my lady. Thank you." Marshall beamed.

Marshall stood and watched Tessy until she was out of sight. He knew he was in trouble. He cared for her far more than he wished. Tessy was an independent, complicated, yet surprisingly simple woman. Not like any other. Not even his dear, departed Evelyne, as much as he had and always would adore her. Tessy is special, almost not of this world; he couldn't explain it if he tried. He reached in his pocket and pulled out the gemstone she had given him. "Howlite, I believe she called it." He tossed it in the air, caught it, and with a boyish smile shoved it back in his pocket. With an extra spring in his step, he turned and took off, whistling "On the Street Where You Live," as he strolled down Parkside Lane.

For Tessy's last class, she had planned on making the girls something decadent like chewy peanut butter-chocolate macaroons but wasn't sure she had left herself enough time. She got home and immediately set to work. She was just placing the cookie sheet in the fridge to let them cool when she heard a noise at the back door. Wiping her hands on her apron, she wandered over to the door and looked out. Not seeing anyone, she opened it and looked down to find a red rose lying on the step. Not being a variety found in Tessy's yard, she stepped out on the landing to see if she could spot someone. The dogs had been in the yard the whole time and they hadn't made a peep. She picked it up and brought it into the kitchen. She immediately looked over at the holly sprigs still sitting on the windowsill. Smiling and shaking her head, she placed the rose in with the holly and mused aloud, "Dermot, my darlin', you, too, are 'bout as subtle as a train wreck!" She took one more look at it before she turned and ran upstairs to get ready.

Tessy arrived at the Community Centre right on time to find most of the girls already there and more than eager to get started. She popped Desiderata into the CD player, and while the girls got organized, everyone sang with passion and flair. After it was over and the girls were settled in their spots, Tessy announced: "The herbal creations we will be working on for our last class are: Soothing Herbal Bath Salts; a Gentle Insect Repellent that ye may also use just as a refreshing body mist for those swelterin' summer days; and a Heavenly Dream Pillow for a peaceful night's rest. Now, we've not a minute to spare, so if ye could all join me in the kitchen area, please, we'll get started on our bath salts."

The girls tenaciously worked all afternoon, with each project proving to be even more enjoyable than the last. They were just finishing up their dream pillows when Tessy brought out the macaroon bars and the blender to make Berry Banana Boost Smoothies for all. After every macaroon had been devoured and the blender was empty, the girls took turns saying their goodbyes to Tessy and each other. Sarah, Cherokee, and a couple of the others stayed to help Tessy clean up and cart bins. As there were three weeks' worth of plastic bins and supplies to transport, Tessy had driven her car to the Centre. Sarah and Cherokee insisted they come along with Tessy to help her carry everything into the house. Grateful for the help, Tessy insisted on paying the girls five dollars each, to which the girls loudly protested, and Tessy paid little attention. They finally gave in, giving Tessy a warm hug with many thanks on their way out the door.

Tessy looked at the clock. "My stars, it's already four thirty. Marshall will be along in just two short hours, and I want to relax in a nice tub for a wee while." Tessy left all the bins where they lay and ran upstairs.

Now, in the main bathroom sits a beautiful, huge, claw-foot tub, and when Tessy just needs to feel pampered and refreshed, she climbs in and soaks. She often told Dermot that when one wants to get clean one can stand in the shower; however, when one needs a lavish experience, ye find your way to a claw-foot tub. When the tub was filled to almost where Tessy liked, it she dribbled in some of her homemade Serenity Bath Oil Blend, lit two beeswax candles, and stepped in to enjoy her steamy, heavenly experience.

At 6:30 sharp, Marshall tapped at her front door. Tessy flung it open with the exuberance of a teenager, wrap in hand and ready to go. The two "kids at heart" skipped down the steps hand in hand and were off. At the café, Sheree had reserved them a table outside at the far end of the deck. Their table was cheerfully draped in a red-and-white-checkered tablecloth with a lit votive and a long-stemmed red rose. As they were ushered to their table, Tessy noticed all the other tables had carnations in an array of vibrant colours. After they were seated and alone, she purposely asked, "Marshall, did you have anything to do with this red rose being on our table?"

"No, but I certainly wish I had, now that you've asked," he answered, a little embarrassed.

"Oh, my . . . I'm so sorry. I didn't ask to make you uncomfortable in any way — it's just that a funny thing happened this afternoon, and I needed to be sure. That's all. I'm so sorry."

"Anything you care to share?" Marshall questioned.

"I will be more than happy to share it with you, at some point in time, but just not quite yet, if ye don't mind. I need to get a handle on it meself first and set some things straight; but that's enough of all that for tonight. We're here for a fine evening and that's just what we shall have," smiled Tessy.

It was an exceptionally warm evening, and on Thursdays, in Ladyslipper, the stores remain open until 9:00 p.m.; so downtown was a hub of activity. Being out on the deck, Tessy and Marshall witnessed people's comings and goings; chatted to folks who passed by; shared amusing stories; and all in all, spent one of their most relaxed, enjoyable times together. They had finished their meal and were enjoying a cup of coffee while sharing a slice of Sheree's prized piña colada cheesecake when they noticed Jim closing up the pharmacy and motioned him over.

"Well, hey, you two. That sure looks good. Beautiful evening, aye?" he said as he leaned over the railing looking up at the evening sky.

"Couldn't be more beautiful," Marshall agreed, gazing at Tessy.

Tessy, being close enough to Marshall, gave him a sharp nudge and a smirk. "Aye 'tis a night for magick and mischief, to be sure."

"I'm all for that!" Marshall heartily volunteered.

"What am I going to do with you, Marshall Tayse?" Tessy said, shaking her head.

"You two sound like trouble. I think I'm getting out of here while the getting's good," Jim laughed. "Why don't you two stop by the house for a nightcap after you're done here? I know Penny would love to have a visit with you, Tessy. It looks like you'll be a few minutes, yet, which will give me time to get home and changed."

"What do you think, Tess?" Marshall shrugged.

"Well, that would be lovely — if you are sure Penny won't mind."

"Tell you what. Marshall, do you have your cell phone on you?" asked Jim.

"Yep, right here." Marshall reached over to the next chair and patted his jacket pocket.

"Good. Now, if it is a problem, which I know it won't be, I will call and let you know. If you haven't heard from me in — say — twenty minutes, it's a go. See you two in a while," and Jim was off with a wave and a smile.

An hour later, Tessy, Marshall, Penny, and Jim were relaxing on the Tuckers' back deck.

"Certainly 'tis an evening to be enjoyed outside," sighed Tessy. "And with such good company," she added, looking around the deck and raising her glass.

They all raised their glasses and took a drink.

"Tessy, it's so nice to finally spend some time with you. Usually the children are around demanding your full attention. We really do appreciate all the time you spend with the children. I hope they are not wearing you out. They just adore you, and you've made such a positive impact on our move here. Thank you so much."

"Oh, now . . . it's been my pleasure. The children are such a blessing.

You've done a fine job. They are amazing, fun-loving, good children. You should be very proud, as I know ye are."

"Well, thank you. They certainly keep life busy and interesting. Never seems to be a dull moment around here."

Jim spoke up. "Tessy, if you don't mind, there's something I've been meaning to talk to you about. I'd like to make you a business proposition."

"My. Me? A business proposition, ye say? Well, you could knock me down with a feather, ye could." Tessy was shocked and wide-eyed.

Jim chuckled. "Yes. You see, I've been fascinated with herbal remedies for years, but my former partner and I did not see eye to eye on the subject. He was truly a synthetic pharmaceutical fan and was not about to get into what he referred to as "voodoo medicine." But I think the two can work very well together and I would like to offer my customers that choice; and I feel you are the answer. I can't think of anyone else I'd rather have set up a natural healing department in my store than you. What do you think?"

"Aye, Jim. Herbs have made a great comeback, but there are still many misconceptions behind the mystery of herbs. As you know, there were many wise women, medicine men, Wiccans, and shamans put to death for just being natural healers. They were the first herbalists and naturopaths trying to heal people and they died unnecessarily, mostly out of fear and ignorance. 'Tis said that for every illness, God created a plant to cure it; and these gifted healers took that knowledge and tried to help Him do his work. Many of these remedies have survived the test of time, some over 5,000 years, and I truly believe they'll be around another 5,000 if we can, somehow, save Mother Earth. Oh . . . Sorry . . . listen to me go on and on. As you can see, it is my passion and you have struck a nerve, ye have."

"I totally agree with you. So . . . is that a yes, or will you at least think about it?" Jim asked.

"Aye. I think it a fine notion. There's plenty of room for modern medicine and herbalists to work together and learn from one another. But I must be letting ye know, some folks in Ladyslipper do call me the town witch, so they do. I feel ye might be taking a wee risk."

"Oh, I think I can handle whatever they might throw at me."

"Aye, I'd be careful with the term 'throw,' unless you're quick at ducking! Ye never know what it is they've up their sleeve."

They all had a good laugh then clinked their glasses in celebration.

"Well. Welcome aboard, Tessy McGuigan. If it's okay with you, we'll get together next week to go over the details and get some kind of an agreement written up."

The rest of the evening went by with no more talk of business or herbs, just light conversation and happy circumstances. It was getting late, and Tessy announced she must be on her way. After her farewells, Marshall took her hand and led her off the deck and around to the front. They were about to get into the car when Marshall suggested, "Tessy, if you're not too tired, how would you like to walk home? It's such a beautiful evening."

"Oh . . . aye, I suppose you're a bit weary and don't feel like driving all the way over there. I'll just be on me way, then. Good night to ye, Marshall." And she started down the driveway.

"What are you doing? Did you think for a moment I meant you were to walk home *alone?*" Marshall was absolutely appalled and grabbed Tessy's arm which immediately halted her.

Stopped in her tracks, she turned and said, "Well, I just thought ye must be tired and ready to go in."

"No, no. Oh, Tessy, I'm so sorry I made you even think that for a second. You are so precious. I would never let you out of my sight until I knew you were safely tucked into your home. Now, before you go on about being fine and independent, I realize all that, but I would like to think of myself as more of a gentleman than to let you trail off by yourself."

"Aye, Marshall Tayse. A fine gentleman, you are. All right, then, let's be on our way, and I thank ye." She took Marshall's arm and they were off.

When they reached Tessy's front porch, they sat down on the swing to rest and to watch the vast night sky lit in twinkling wonderment.

"Marshall, I've had a wonderful night. Even got myself a new job!" She laughed.

Marshall laughed and looked down at her, "Yes, you did." He picked her hand up and kissed it.

"And what are your views on the subject, Dr. Tayse?"

"Well, personally, I have been prescribing naturopathic medicine for years now with amazing results so you have my vote and greatest respect and I couldn't be more proud of you."

"You are truly a gem, Marshall Tayse, and I'm the luckiest lady in the cosmos."

Marshall beamed, "I always have a marvellous time when I'm near you — be it in this galaxy or the next."

"Oh, go on with ye, now," blushed Tessy, bumping up against him.

"Well, my lady, as much as I don't want to, I best go and let you get some rest. I will call you tomorrow to see if there's anything you need before I come over." He leaned over and gave her a gentle kiss. "Rest well, my lady."

As he got up, Tessy stood. "So I'll be expecting you tomorrow around six, then?"

"That sounds perfect. Six it is," Marshall all but sighed.

Tessy stopped and turned. "Now, not that I want to bring up past wounds, but please be careful on that uneven pathway in the dark. I don't want ye stumbling and hurting yourself."

"I'll be just fine, thank you. And just so you know, I will not be skulking around your backyard this evening." Marshall laughed as he descended the steps then waited for Tessy to go in and lock her door. As he walked down the path, he mused out loud. "Besides, how can a man stumble and fall when his feet aren't even touching the ground?"

Berry Banana Boost Smoothie

1 cup (250 ml) fresh or frozen raspberries
1 cup (250 ml) fresh or frozen strawberries
1 cup (250 ml) fresh or frozen blueberries
1 medium banana
1 cup (250 ml) cranberry juice

Put all ingredients in a blender and blend until smooth.

Herbed Soda Bread

4 1/2 cups (1.125 L) all-purpose flour
1/4 tsp (1 ml) sea salt
1 tsp (5 ml) baking soda
1 Tbsp (15 ml) sugar
1 cup (250 ml) buttermilk
1/4 cup (50 ml) melted butter
1 Tbsp (15 ml) dried rosemary
1 Tbsp (15 ml) snipped parsley
1/2 tsp (2 ml) marjoram

Preheat oven to 350°F (180°C). Combine flour, salt, baking soda, and sugar in a large bowl. Mix, make a well in the centre, and add buttermilk. Stir together until it makes a pliable dough. Lightly dust work area with flour, turn the dough out, and gently knead. Shape into a round loaf and place on a greased, floured baking tray. Melt the butter and stir in the herbs. Cut a cross into the top surface of the dough and brush with melted herb mix. Bake for 30–40 minutes or until brown. You can continue to brush the loaf with the butter mixture while it bakes.

14

Fond Farewells and Heavy Hearts

Tessy was planning on preparing some traditional Irish dishes for Marshall to sample: Herbed Soda Bread, Lamb Shank with Mint Chutney, pearl onions, and baby potatoes; but when the weatherman predicted another scorcher, she instead merrily fussed over a menu consisting of a much lighter fare. To start: a crisp spinach and strawberry salad with a poppy seed-raspberry vinaigrette dressing, grilled fillet of cod with Mango Salsa on a bed of brown and wild rice steamed in rich red wine; and the first of her green beans picked fresh from her garden topped with sliced almonds. For dessert, the fluffiest Light Lemon-Lime Mousse that would not only delight the palate but was sure to melt the heart. "Aye," she thought out loud, "should be enough to hold his stomach yet not heavy enough to weight him to his chair."

While preparations were coming along nicely at the McGuigan household, the day was not quite so cheery at the Tuckers'.

Penny had just finished the last of her dad's laundry and was carrying it into his bedroom when she found Marshall sitting on the edge of the bed lost in deep thought.

"Dad? What's the matter? Are you all right?" She reached over and laid her hand on his shoulder.

"Oh, Penny. Yes, I'm fine, dear, thanks. And thanks for doing up my laundry. You really didn't need to bother. Dotty will be expecting me to arrive home with a trunk-load of laundry for her to fuss over. As a matter of fact, when I called to see how she and Bert were making out and to let them know approximately what time to expect me home, she mentioned she'd be doing a large wash on Monday and wanted to know if I needed anything in particular for work. She'll probably end up re-washing everything I bring home anyway. That woman does love to fuss."

"Dad, you are so lucky to have Dotty and Bert. They are more like family than employees, and I am so thankful that they are with you so we don't worry about you so much."

"Yes, I suppose I am very lucky. They do take wonderful care of me, and it sure would be lonely rambling around that big old house all by myself; but there are times when that is exactly what I feel I am doing."

"Oh, Dad, I know. It's always hard for me, too, when you leave. I miss you so much—we all do. I was thinking, why don't Sarah and Cherokee come to visit you around Thanksgiving? It's early this year, and even though I don't have the girls' schedule yet, I'm pretty sure they will have a few days off."

"That would be wonderful. Do you think they'll actually want to come and visit their old grandpa?"

"Well, I'm pretty sure it wouldn't take much to convince them—especially the way you love to spoil them. I'll work on it and see what I can do."

Feeling much better, Marshall got up, hugged his daughter, and headed downstairs to challenge the kids to a game of bocce ball. They had been keeping track for the past couple of weeks and the kids were up on him; this was his chance to even up the score.

The rest of the afternoon pleasantly flew by, with Tessy primping and preparing, and Marshall lavishing his attention on his grandchildren in his last competitive effort to win.

As usual, Marshall was precisely on time. At 6:00, he tapped at Tessy's front door.

"My, ye are a man of your word, for sure, Dr. Tayse. Six sharp 'tis. Please come in, come in. Oh, what have ye there? Wine, is it?"

"Well, I wasn't sure what we were having so I brought a bottle of white and a red."

"Before long, I'll be able to open my own wine market . . . Very kind of ye to think of it. Thank you very much. I've still a thing or two left to do in the kitchen. You are more than welcome to sit out back on the patio and wait or you can join me in the kitchen."

"You know me, the man who loves a good kitchen. After you." Marshall bowed and swooped his arm in the direction of the kitchen.

"Well, since we've ample wine, ye could pop open whichever one tickles your fancy, and we'll have a wee splash while I'm finishing here."

"Sure smells amazing." Marshall took in a long breath.

"Well, not much brewing yet. It's just a little rice I have simmering, so far. As a matter of fact, I was planning on ye maybe rolling up your sleeves, wrapping yourself in an apron, and grilling the fish for me. Do ye think you're up for it?"

"I'm your man. I love to barbecue. Just point me in the right direction when the time is near."

"Aye, that would be grand, then, thank ye. A toast to kind friends, good food, and modern technology. *Slainte.*"

"*Slainte.*" They raised their glasses, tapped them, and drank. "However, I hope to be much more than just a friend; and as for modern technology, all I need is a computer and a phone so I can stay in touch with my Irish lass."

"Aye, we will stay in touch, I promise." Tessy stepped around the island, stood close to Marshall, placed her hand on his arm and affectionately looked up into his twinkling eyes.

"That's a promise I intend on holding you to, my lady." He took Tessy's wineglass and set it down on the counter along with his own, pulled her close, then bent and gently kissed her.

When the rice pot started to whistle and bang, Tessy jumped back. She rushed over to the stove. "I guess the temperature's a wee bit too high," she said as she fussed over the pot, not quite sure what to do next.

Marshall picked up both wineglasses, walked over to her, leaned close, and laughed while handing her hers. "Tessy, my love, you are a mystery. One minute you are this amazingly confident woman and the next you turn into an incredibly childlike angel. I never know what to expect."

"Well, to be perfectly honest, you've got me not quite knowing what I'm about to do next myself. Marshall, this is so unexpected. It's been a long time since anyone has got my blood up and my head spinning. I'm all sure with my suggestions and potions when it comes to everyone else but when it's my own heart I'm dealing with . . . now, that's a different matter. You've got me as flighty as a butterfly."

"I love butterflies. They're colourful, mysterious, graceful, and, most notably . . . beautiful. All the qualities I admire about you along with your wisdom and humour."

"Thank ye kindly for saying so. You're a wonderful man, Marshall Tayse — the only one who would even come close to my Dermot — and that's what's got me in this tailspin. I truly believe that he has got some hand in this. I know it sounds outrageous, but ye might as well know

now that I am a spiritual person. I believe the term they use these days is 'New Age,' however, that could not be further from the truth. What I am comes from an ancient culture of faith — long before Christianity was born — and with it comes some unusual gifts and practices. I don't mean to be scaring ye off, but you need to know what you are getting into."

"Tessy, I am not a Puritan nor do I care to be; nor am I shocked. I know how special you are. I knew it the minute I saw you standing in your festal garden. You were glowing, and I have since seen you glow many times. I also know how lucky — no, blessed — I am standing here with you, in your kitchen, or anywhere with you. Blessed that I have befriended you, enjoyed you, kissed you, and hopefully am establishing a meaningful relationship with you. I find your lifestyle exciting and challenging. I am a doctor. I have lived my life pondering over medical books and proving calculated theories; but in reality, I am only perfecting what ancient practitioners, herbalists, and yes, Wise Women such as yourself, accomplished centuries before. And in understanding that, I have witnessed my share of miracles and I do believe in that power beyond. I may not completely comprehend what your life entails but I want to learn. Just like I want you to learn about my life and be a part of it.

"Things may be happening a little fast between us, but let's face it, no offence, neither one of us is getting any younger. I don't mind admitting that you make me feel like a college freshman again and as frisky as a pup, so if it is your Dermot who's got his hand in all this, then I would surely like to be the first to shake it. In fact . . . Thank you and *Slainte*, Dermot!" With that, Marshall held his wineglass high, wrapped his free arm around Tessy, then gulped down his last swallow.

"Oh, Marshall! I had no idea you'd be so liberated and understanding. I was wondering how ye felt about my rantings and ravings the other night when Jim mentioned our business venture. I feel like the world has been lifted off my shoulders, and my heart is fluttering like a thousand butterflies. Now, fill up our wineglasses while I tell you about the extraordinary occurrences that I am sure Dermot has been providing for us." And while they collectively manoeuvred around the kitchen preparing their meal, Tessy described, in great detail, all the strange manifestations that had transpired over the past couple of weeks.

Both the meal and the evening turned out even better than Tessy could have hoped, and they were now sitting out by a crackling birch-wood fire and enjoying a snifter of Tessy's homemade blackberry cognac. Duke and Darby were lying at their feet, having long since forgiven Marshall for his late-night invasion; although it was well understood by all that should he ever step over the line, there would be dire consequences.

"Tessy, you are making it harder and harder for me to leave. Life just could not get any better than this." Marshall raised his cut crystal glass and swirled around the rich, dark liquid that glistened against the dancing flames. They were sitting in a wooden, two-seater lounge holding hands on the little connecting table.

Tessy gently squeezed his hand. "Marshall, we both know that if this is meant to be, there will be a way for us to sustain a meaningful relationship even with the distance between us."

The mood of the evening suddenly turned sombre and did not change. The warm, romantic glow along with the crackling and popping of the fire's last burning embers only made it all the more difficult for them to break away from the moment. Eventually, without speaking, they rose together and, walking arm in arm, made their way to Marshall's vehicle. They held tight to each other, with Tessy keeping her head leaning into his chest and her arms around his waist. Marshall's arms protectively gathered her close, and he felt he could hold her there forever. Neither one could have said how long they stood clinging to one another. Tessy finally raised her head and, with tears in her eyes and an obviously forced smile on her lips, piped, "Well, now, Dr. Tayse, you'd better be off and runnin'. You've a big last day with your family and some packing to do, to be sure, so ye best be gettin' your forty winks while ye can."

Marshall smiled down at her, melting her with those dazzlingly blue eyes. "Tessy, my love, you do have a way about you that makes the world a much better place. Yes, I suppose it is time for me to be off but I will call you tomorrow."

"Aye, that will be grand. I'll be looking forward to hearing from you."

Marshall leaned down and kissed her gently but firmly, and Tessy was not in any hurry to pull away this evening. She was surprised at how wonderfully warm and tingly she felt . . . could this really be happening? Marshall broke away first then reached down for a couple of extra little pecks and enfolded her in his arms, lifting her off the ground.

"Now, put me down, you cheeky man, and be off with ye!" Tessy all but giggled and playfully slapped him on the shoulder.

Marshall placed her on the ground and gave her another peck. "Good night, my fair lady of Ladyslipper. Sleep well."

Tessy waved as Marshall slowly drove down the lane. Then she returned to the backyard, walked over to the firepit, and moved the grate over the glowing embers. The dogs had gotten up and made their rounds one last time, ready to go in for the night. Tessy looked up at the huge sky scattered with millions of dancing stars. "I'm not sure what's about to happen, Goddess of Grace, but I'm putting my trust in you, knowing you've never steered me wrong. And ye, Dermot, my love, thank ye for loving me and helping me to move on. Ye always seemed to know what was best, even if it didn't always sit quite right with me . . . you and your quiet persuasion. Good night to ye both and may the angels guide me closer to finding the answers in my dreams. I'll be putting mugwort under my pillow tonight, to be sure."

Tessy got up the next morning and got right to work with a cup of coffee in hand. She planned on keeping very busy today, not giving any attention to that knot in the pit of her stomach. The herbs she had been drying in her screened herb cabinet were ready to be put into their various storage containers. She needed to replenish her more popular tinctures and oils to be ready for any new requests; and also to supply samples for Jim's approval before she ordered more supplies. Yes, it was going to be a busy day, and she was very thankful for the distraction. As she puttered around her back kitchen, conjuring up all sorts of mystical aromas, Merlin and Cordelia lay in their basket on the curved windowsill, occasionally jumping down to wind themselves in and around Tessy's legs, encouraging the odd petting and cooing she would lavish on them.

The phone rang, and Tessy froze. She knew who it was. She took a deep breath, wiped her hands on her crisp apron and reached for the receiver, "Good morning to ye," she merrily chirped, which even she knew had a little too much enthusiasm mustered into it. But whether Marshall noticed or not, he did not let on. "And a good morning to you, Tessy. How are you? Did you sleep well?"

"Aye. Like a wee one who ran about at the fair all day," Tessy lied.

"Good — me, too," Marshall answered, matching the fib. "Say, Penny wanted me to call and invite you to dinner here tonight with the family."

"Oh, now, I don't know about that. It's the last night with your loved ones, and I feel like I'd be intruding."

"Not at all. We'd love it if you'd join us . . . especially me. Please come, Tessy. Just be with me one more night."

"Oh, Marshall, to be perfectly honest, I don't know if I could sit with you one more night and then say goodbye. I'm not wanting to be a blutherin' bag-o-bones in front of your family."

"Tessy, they know how close we've become and couldn't be happier. Please come, my love."

"Aye, then, wild horses won't haul me from it. What time shall I be there and with what in hand to help out?"

"Fantastic! I'll pick you up early . . . say around five. Jim will be home shortly after that, and we can relax out on the deck before supper. I'm sure you don't need to bring anything but I know you — so here, I'll let you talk to Penny."

Lamb Shank with Fresh Mint Chutney

6 Lamb shanks
3/4 cup (175 ml) olive oil
3 cloves garlic, crushed
1 1/2 cup (375 ml) tomatoes, chopped
1 large onion
2 carrots, finely chopped
8 sprigs of fresh parsley
3 sprigs fresh rosemary
2 bay leaves
10 peppercorns
1 pint (500 ml) Irish stout or chicken stock
2 Tbsp (30 ml) honey

Preheat oven to 350°F (180°C). Heat oil in a large, ovenproof skillet. Brown the shanks and set aside. In the same pot, add garlic, onions, and carrots and cook for approximately 8 minutes. Add stout, tomatoes, peppercorns, bay leaf, parsley, and rosemary and season to taste with salt and pepper. Return lamb shanks to the dish and bring to a boil. Drizzle honey over the mixture, cover, and place in oven for 2 hours or until meat is tender. Serves 6.

Fresh Mint Chutney

2 cups (500 ml) lightly packed fresh mint leaves
1 medium onion
1 large garlic clove, chopped
1/2 cup (125 ml) fresh parsley, chopped
1/3 cup (75 ml) lime or lemon juice
1 Tbsp (15 ml) sugar
1 tsp (5 ml) sea salt
1 tsp (5 ml) canola oil

Combine ingredients in blender and pulse until it is well mixed. Scrape sides of the blender often to ensure even blending. For best results, prepare shortly before serving.

15

Not Goodbye . . . Just . . . See You in My Dreams

At 5:15, Marshall opened the front door and gently ushered Tessy into his daughter's home. Penny, wiping her hands on a dishtowel, came out to the foyer to greet them, giving Tessy a welcoming hug.

"Tessy, we're so glad you could join us. Please come in. Make yourself right at home."

Tessy followed her into the kitchen and placed a basket of appetizers containing a Spicy Herbed Cheese Ball, herb crackers, pesto for the adults, and the kids' favourite—a layered taco dip accompanied by a huge bag of chips.

"Oh, Tessy, these look wonderful. Thank you so much. I'll get some serving dishes out and we can put them on the patio table. Jim should be along any minute."

Marshall stood back, smiling. Here he was, in the presence of his two favourite girls, watching them fuss about preparing what was sure to be an enjoyable evening of great cuisine and even better company. Leaving here was not something he was looking forward to. He immediately shook those thoughts to the back of his mind. He was not going to let anything distract him from staying in the present and living every single moment of this evening.

"Dad, I made a pitcher of sangria—would you mind pouring us each a glass?"

"I'm on it. You lovely ladies go out on the deck and sit down, and I will be more than happy to serve you. If you don't mind, I'll just wait and have a beer with Jim." At just that moment, Jim came around the corner into the kitchen.

"Well, greetings, everyone. Tessy, how nice to see you. Glad you could make it. Did I hear someone mention a beer?"

"That, my boy, would be me. Here." Marshall backed out of the fridge with two beers grasped in one hand and the pitcher of sangria in the other. "Timing is everything," he winked as he handed Jim the beer.

Jim assisted Marshall in delivering drinks to the girls, teasing Penny by making her kiss him before he released her glass to her.

Jim held up his bottle in a suggested toast. "Cheers! I had a great day. How was everyone else's?"

Favourable replies, and all glasses were joined in response.

Sarah and Emma came running out onto the deck. "Hi!" they echoed as they took turns leaning down to give Tessy a hug. Emma climbed up in her daddy's lap and gave him a big hug and a kiss, scrambled down, then up on her grandpa's lap and remained. With everyone laughing and talking, at first no one noticed Matt coming up the stairs with blood running down his leg and elbow. Penny leaped up, once she saw him. "My Lord! What happened to you?" She was holding and examining him at the same time.

"Aah, Mom, it's nothing. I just fell heading down the new bike path we've been chopping out of the hills around the lake. I'm okay, honest."

By now everyone was up and looking over the bumps and bruises on the reluctant patient.

"Penny, darling. Do ye have any of that Tender Mend Antiseptic Salve left that I brought over for you and some witch hazel?"

"Yes, I'll run and get them."

"Aye, and a cloth and a pan of clean warm water, please, dear."

"Aah, Mom," Matt loudly groaned.

"Sit, sit—and never mind aahing your mum. Sarah, dear, could ye please fetch my pouch out of my bag and we'll get some lavender oil on this. Let's take a good look, now. Aye, it's deep, but not deep enough for stitches. Would ye agree, Dr. Tayse?"

Marshall leaned in to take a good look. "Yeah, it doesn't look too bad, but we need to clean the wound before I can really say for sure."

Penny and Sarah rushed back with all the necessary gadgets and ingredients, and before long, Tessy and Marshall had the disgruntled patient patched up as good as new.

"You two make quite the team. Possibly a new reality show in the making—The Good Doctor and The Wise Woman," Jim quipped.

"Very funny!" they echoed.

Soon everything was back to normal, and Matt was busy loading up a paper plate with a handful of chips followed by a hefty scoop of taco dip.

Supper was informal and comfortable, with everyone sitting around the patio table and enjoying the evening. The children cleared the table and filled the dishwasher before heading off to their specific zones. Sarah in the den on the computer designing the latest fashions with the new program Grandpa had just bought her, Matt in the family room watching the game and plucking on the new guitar Grandpa had just bought him, and Emma in her room playing with her new "Barbie Learning Laptop" that Grandpa had just bought her.

"Dad, you know you shouldn't be spoiling the children. You already buy them outlandishly expensive gifts for their birthdays and Christmas, and these gifts are for no particular reason at all," Penny scolded.

"Well, of course they're for a good reason. In fact, a number of good reasons."

"And what would they be?"

"Well, um . . . haa . . . for . . . passing their grades and for ummmm . . . a housewarming and . . . Oh, to heck with it—'cause they're great kids and I'm their grandpa and I don't get to see them and spoil them very often."

Penny just laughed. "Okay, Dad. Good enough." She got up, hugged her dad, and gave him an affectionate kiss on the cheek. "I love you . . . even if you *are* impossible."

Tessy had been just sitting back and enjoying the engaging playfulness between father and daughter when Marshall pulled her into the conversation.

"Tessy, I need help, here. This woman is suggesting I am impossible . . . please tell her this could not possibly be true. Someone as charming and debonair as myself . . . imagine that."

Tessy raised her eyebrows, lowered her chin, and smirked in Marshall's direction. "Aye, charming and debonair ye might be, but right at the moment I see more of the blarney in ye than anything else, and if ye carry on with this kind of gibberish, ye won't have a leg to stand on, at least not with this bunch."

Laughter filled the air.

The evening was wearing on; the children had challenged the adults to a game of bocce ball then they had one last game with Grandpa before joining together at the firepit. Emma was snuggled in tight on Grandpa's lap until Tessy brought out her basket filled with all the ingredients for making Campfire Fun Banana Boats. Then it was pretty much—catch you later, Grandpa!

With appetites satisfied and tongues tired, it was apparent the evening was coming to a close. Tessy thought it best to make her pardons and say good night. She was feeling tired after having not slept well the past few nights, and her heart was feeling heavy.

"Well, I best be on my way. You will all be getting up with the robins in the morning saying your goodbyes to this scalawag. Thank ye for a most enjoyable time." She smiled affectionately at Marshall.

Marshall stood and extended his hand to Tessy. "Come, my lady, your chariot awaits."

Tessy said her farewells, and she and Marshall strolled out to the car. He opened the door for her, and she got in without saying a word. Marshall, wanting to make the evening last as long as possible, asked her if she would like to go for a drive around the lake. Tessy kindly declined.

As they drove up Tessy's canopied lane, the silence was almost deafening. This was the first time since they had been together that there was any tension in the air. When the car came to a stop, they both began speaking at the same time, with Tessy apologizing and Marshall inquiring if he had done something wrong. Marshall stopped and let Tessy continue.

"Marshall, I'm so sorry. I'm just not myself this evening. I can't pretend that your leaving is not going to hurt me some and I don't know what I'm to do."

"Oh, Tess." Marshall reached over, picked up her hand and brought it to his lips. "I feel exactly the same way. When I came to visit my daughter, I certainly did not expect something like this to happen but I truly thank the Lord it did. We will just have to work it out somehow."

"Aye, as I've said before, if it is meant to be, it shall be. But it's sure plain to see I'm much better at fixing other people's woes than my own!"

Marshall laughed and went to hug her when he was abruptly reminded his seat belt was still buckled tightly, which, thankfully, lightened the mood, and they both had a good chuckle.

They sat on Tessy's swing on the front porch exchanging addresses and vows to stay in touch daily. They could hardly believe an hour had passed when the wind came up setting Tess's chimes in motion and blowing in the clouds that now crossed over the crescent moon. "Looks like you'll be driving in that shower they were predicting for the first part of your journey. I have a wee package here for your trip. A few things that would make me feel better knowing you have them with ye." She disappeared into the house and came back with a suede pouch. She sat down beside Marshall and opened it with care and reaching in, exhibiting great respect, she first pulled out a small bottle. "This is my Stay Alert Scent. Whenever ye feel yourself getting a bit weary and you are not needing to stop yet, just twist the top off this and take a good whiff. Here, smell." Tessy raised the bottle to just under Marshall's nose.

"Hey, that's not bad. I won't mind doing that at all. But Tessy, this really isn't necessary — I'll be fine."

The next item she extracted from the sack was a small indigo cloth pouch tied with a white ribbon. Tessy went on, ignoring Marshall's protest. "Now, the next thing I have for you is this wee 'Travel Protection' pouch to keep in your glove compartment. And last," she said as she pulled out three polished gems, "here is a yellow jasper, good for physical travel; jade, which is multi-purpose, as it protects and attracts good luck and friendships; and smoky quartz, used as an antidote to stress, lifts depression, brings emotional calmness, and manifests dreams."

"Well, what more could a guy need?" Marshall teased; then, realizing the significance this held for Tessy, he solemnly looked into her eyes. "Thank you, Tess. If my travelling with this type of protection gives you some comfort, I am more than honoured to take and use them as you wish."

"I thank ye, Marshall — yes, it does give me great comfort knowing you've got the extra protection from the bounties of Mother Earth with ye. I know not everyone believes as I do, and that is definitely something you'll need to reckon with; possibly while you're driving all those miles would be a good time."

Marshall laughed "Yes, that trip always gives me plenty of time to ponder; only this trip will be much more enjoyable, having you to think about."

Tessy stood and walked over to the railing with her back to Marshall. "Thank ye — and with that being said, I think it's high time you were on your way so ye can get some rest for your long journey tomorrow."

Marshall rose from his seat as well. "As usual, you are right. But I don't want to leave yet — and you're not going to send me off in this weather, are you?"

"A little water hasn't hurt a soul that I've heard of. Now, take your parcel and be off with ye, Dr. Tayse." Not wanting to show her true emotional state, Tessy was trying to be as casual and flippant as possible, but the tears in her eyes and the crack in her voice were betraying her.

Marshall took two long strides to where Tessy was standing and wrapped his arms around her without turning her. He nestled his lips into the nape of her neck, closed his eyes and inhaled her intoxicating scent one last time. "I am going to go. This isn't getting any easier for either one of us, and there is nothing that can change that right at the moment. I do promise you, this is far from over, and I am a man of my word." He whirled Tessy around and planted an affectionate kiss firmly on her lips that sent her spinning. Holding her by the shoulders to steady her, he looked her straight in the eyes and said, "This, my fair lady of Ladyslipper, is not goodbye but just 'see you in my dreams.'" With that, he gave her another kiss, stepped off the veranda into the rain, and, before he jumped into the car, he turned to take one long last look at her.

Mango Salsa

1 ripe mango
5–6 green onions, chopped
1 red pepper, diced
4 Tbsp (60 ml) extra-virgin olive oil
Sea salt and coarse ground pepper to taste
Juice of 1 lime

Peel, slice, then dice mango and mix with remaining ingredients in a bowl with lime juice and seasoning. Place in fridge to cool. Can be made a day in advance and left in fridge. When fish is cooked, spoon a generous amount of salsa on top.

Serenity Bath Oil Blend

1 tsp (5 ml) sweet almond oil
2 drops lavender essential oil
2 drops geranium essential oil
2 drops chamomile essential oil

Mix the above; run a warm bath then add the mixture just before you climb in. Inhale, relax, and enjoy!

16

And Life Does Go On

Tessy kept herself busy the next few days drying herbs, making potions, and preparing samples. She continued on with her life as she always had and with as much joy as she could muster. Her morning grounding and meditation practices, however, were a little more in-depth than usual and always entailed extra prayers for a certain someone. She was scheduled for a meeting with Jim mid-morning down at the pharmacy and was busy packing samples into a bin when the phone rang. "Good mornin' to ye," she answered.

"And a very good morning to you, too." It was Marshall.

"Aye, I thought you'd forgotten all about me, I did. How are ye doing, my dear doctor?"

"Not worth a darn without my girls but having to carry on anyway. I called Penny when I got home on Sunday, and she said she would give you a call."

"Aye, she did and told me you had made it safe and sound, so ye did. 'Twas good to hear. Said ye had no troubles, but a long drive."

"Yes, that it was. One forgets just how flat our beautiful prairies can be. I miss you."

"Now don't be startin' any of that, Marshall Tayse. I'm a wee long in the jaw meself, but it will be a bit yet before we meet up again. Penny was mentioning that the girls may be visiting you around Thanksgiving, and I was thinking they might need someone to drive them there."

"Really! That would be more than fantastic! Oh, yes — I'm sure they would much rather that than ride the bus. I'm thinking they really *need* someone, such as yourself, to drive them here for Thanksgiving."

Tess chuckled. "Well, then, I guess we'll have to see what we can do."

"Oh Tess, you have just made me the happiest man on the block. Hell, the entire country."

"Well, I'm glad I can still put a smile on yer face, all the way from here."

"Shoot, gotta go. My next patient is here. Tessy, thank you. This is going to be a Thanksgiving to be truly thankful for. I will talk to you soon, my fair lady of Ladyslipper."

"Good day, Marshall. You're in my thoughts and prayers, and I'm sending you as much healing energy as I can muster."

"Thanks, Tess . . . 'bye."

Tessy smiled as she hung up the phone. She hadn't wanted to spring the surprise visit on him so soon, but he sounded so lonesome. She finished packing up her samples and headed upstairs to get ready. An hour later, she was in Jim's office with an array of jars and bottles neatly displayed across his desk. She had designed her own labels and presented her products in professional, complementary containers.

"Very nice, Tessy. You have done a wonderful job. They look amazing."

"Thank ye, Jim. But it's what's in them that really matters. Please take all of these home with ye and try them all out on yourselves. Let me know what's working and what's not."

"Tess, I already know what you are capable of and I would really like to get these into the store as soon as possible. You have them all labelled with the ingredients and people in this town already know and respect you, so we'll let them decide. I'm not worried in the least."

"That's so nice of ye to say, Jim, but aren't ye taking a big risk? Making up a batch here and there for the folks that call for them is one thing, but displaying them in a store for the whole world is another. "

"What's life without a few risks? But if it makes you feel better, I will take these home and distribute them among the family, and we can hold off for another week; but I know it's not going to make one bit of difference."

"Thank ye. If nothing else, it will get my confidence up over the hump and give me time to get some more made to have on hand."

"Tessy, this is what you were created to do."

"Aye, it is my passion, for sure, but I never thought I'd be going global."

Jim just laughed.

Two weeks later, Tessy found herself busier than she had ever been in her life.

"What in the Mother's green earth did I get myself into?" She was talking to Merlin as he swooshed in and around her legs with his bushy tail held high in the air while she stood over a double boiler of beeswax and oils. Not only had sales been going extremely well, but she and Jim had decided to bring in a few bulk herbs and essential oils, due to many requests and a great deal of interest. She poured the melted liquid into a blender and turned on the timer; then, while she waited for it to cool to the proper temperature, she sat down at the table and continued on with her list of herbs and oils to order. "Busier than a leprechaun at a beer-tasting derby, I am. Now, let's see, we'll be needing the culinary herbs that folks are used to, then some medicinal herbs for people to conjure up their own remedies. Aye, those and those . . . and now the oils . . ."

There was a knock at the front door. Tessy slowly rose, still glancing down at the list, then removed her glasses and made her way down the hall. Through the lace curtains she could see it was Becky's mom, Susan. She pulled open the sturdy wooden door.

"Well, hello there, Susan. Come in, come in, my dear."

"Hi, Tessy. I'm just on my way home from work and thought I'd drop by to let you know the date of the faculty meeting you were asking about. It will be on September 14th, starting at 4:30 p.m. sharp. I did let the principal know that you had a proposal you wanted to share with us, and he was more than happy to have you present it."

"Grand, dear. Thank ye for helping me out with that. How is your new position working out? Are ye enjoying it?"

"Oh, Tessy, it's wonderful. I love it and it's great being so close to Becky all day."

"Aye, and how is wee Becky making out with your working all day?"

"Oh, she's just fine. It was so nice of Penny to watch her during the day while I'm at work for these couple of weeks before school starts. I don't know what I would have done if she hadn't offered. What a blessing."

"Aye, it's a blessing for sure; but I'm guessing that having Becky there to keep Emma company is a big help."

"Probably. Speaking of which, I have to run and pick Becky up now. See you soon."

"Thank ye again for your help, Susan. If I don't see ye before, will I be seeing you on the 14th, then?"

"Yes, I'm pretty sure they'll want me to take the minutes, so it's more than likely."

"Grand. See ye then, dear. Bye-bye, now."

Tessy closed the heavy door and leaned up against it for a moment. Then she heard the timer buzzing in the kitchen.

"Drat—forgot all about my mixture. I hope I don't have to start all over again!"

The next week flew by, with the kids getting ready to go back to school. There were books to buy, the latest fashionable trends to try on, last bonfires on the beach, and summer visitors to say farewell to.

Sarah's friend Jenny Bettray came for a week's visit mid-August, and the three girls, Sarah, Jenny, and Cherokee got along famously and did all the things young teenage girls love to do: shop, hang out, spend hours applying nail polish and makeup, listen to the latest CDs, and, of course, go to the beach and watch the boys play volleyball. Tessy saw very little of the girls during their time together. But she did have an opportunity to get acquainted with Jenny one afternoon and enjoyed listening to the girls talk and giggle non-stop. Apparently, Jenny had fallen for one of the "tallest, hottest beach volleyball players in the world," who just happened to live in Ladyslipper, so they would likely be having more visits from her in the near future. All and all, Tessy enjoyed every minute of being included in their "girls' club" for the afternoon.

How fast the summer slipped away. Tessy was sitting at the kitchen table thinking over the amazing turn of events in the past couple of months. A summer of friendships, new beginnings, romance, and enlightening. Who would have thought all that could possibly happen in such a short period of time. Life changing.

She felt a strong stirring within her to go into the library. She walked down the hallway and stood at the library door. It was closed, as it usually was these days; she opened it. The room was dim . . . not depressing, but more melancholy. She hadn't been feeling Dermot's spirit lately and she missed him. Had he left her now that she was having feelings for Marshall? She went over to the grand mahogany desk and ran her fingers over the smooth surface. She sat down in the large matching chair and swivelled one way then the next. She looked down, and there, on the European handwoven carpet, was a pure white feather. When she leaned down to pick it up, she caught a slight whiff of Old Spice cologne. She smiled and softly brushed the feather over her face. A tear rolled down her cheek and she knew Dermot was not far away.

"Thank ye, Dermot, darling. I'm sorry, I should have known better than to think ye would desert me. Ye were my first love, my only love for all those years; there was never another who would ever have turned me head. Yet, now — Marshall. Why is it you have picked him for me to fancy, and what is it you have in store for us?"

She sat in silence for a while, wishing, hoping for Dermot, an angel, God, whoever to give her an answer. With nothing clearly being shown, she got up and laid the feather on the desk top. As she walked out and closed the door behind her, she decided to place more mugwort under her pillow tonight, along with a lapis lazuli and an ulexite gemstone; if that didn't enlighten and enhance her dreams, nothing would.

Light Lemon-Lime Mousse

2 tsp (10 ml) lemon zest, grated
1/2 tsp (2 ml) lime zest, grated
1/4 cup (50 ml) fresh lemon juice
2 Tbsp (30 ml) fresh lime juice
3 egg yolks
1/2 cup (125 ml) sugar
2 Tbsp (30 ml) cornstarch
5–6 fresh lemon geranium leaves, lightly crushed
2/3 cup (150 ml) milk
1 1/2 cups (375 ml) heavy cream, whipped

Place stainless steel mixing bowl in freezer to chill. Infuse crushed lemon geranium leaves in milk over low heat for 20 minutes, let cool, then strain. Grate the zests from the fresh lemon and lime and juice the lemon and the lime. Combine the citrus zests, juices, egg yolks, sugar, and cornstarch in a medium saucepan and whisk in the cooled lemon geranium drink. Cook over medium heat, stirring constantly, until the custard has thickened and comes to a boil. Remove from heat and transfer the custard to the chilled stainless steel bowl. Set the bowl into the freezer to quick-cool, stirring occasionally to distribute the cold. Do not leave in the freezer for too long, as it needs to remain soft. When it has cooled, scrape into another bowl. Whip the heavy cream until stiff peaks form and fold it into the lemon-lime custard. Spoon mousse into parfait glasses and refrigerate until ready to serve. Serves 4.

17

Tessy Presents Her Crusade

Every Sunday without fail, Marshall phoned Tessy at exactly 7:00 p.m. Tessy looked at her watch; it was 8:26 p.m. What on earth could be keeping him? Any other day of the week he decides to call doesn't matter, as it varies; but Sunday night, never. She paced the floor wondering if she should call him to find out what was going on. Then the phone rang.

"Marshall, finally! I've been a mite worried, dear." There was a short silence on the other end, and then a woman's faint voice said, "Pardon me?"

"Oh, I'm terribly sorry. I thought you were someone else. Can I help you?"

"Is this Tessy McGuigan?"

"Aye, that's who I am."

"Oh, hello, Ms. McGuigan. This is Dotty — my husband and I attend to Dr. Tayse, and he's asked me to call you."

"Has something happened? Is he all right?"

"Oh, yes, he's just fine. I'm sorry. I didn't mean to frighten you. He is at the hospital this evening checking on a little girl he had to admit this week; he has been quite concerned about her. I believe he thought he'd be back home by now, but he got held up on the ward seeing another patient."

"Bless his heart, that sweet man, and thank ye kindly for letting me know. I'm sorry I was so abrupt with you. As I mentioned, I've been a wee mite worried, as he is such a reliable soul and he is very rarely late with anything."

"That's our Dr. Tayse. He is a man of his word. It's nice to know you see that in him. He is a wonderful man."

"Aye, that he is!"

"I understand we might be having the pleasure of seeing you soon. We are looking forward to meeting the lady who has captured our fine doctor's heart."

"Oh, now, I'm not sure about that, but aye, I am thinking of making a journey out your way and bringing Sarah and her friend Cherokee with me."

"Well, we'll certainly be looking forward to your visit. So, I guess we'll see you then. Dr. Tayse said to tell you he will call when he gets in if it's not too late. I'll say goodbye for now. It was very nice chatting with you."

"Aye, and you. Thank ye again. See ye in October. Bye-bye."

Tessy placed the receiver into its cradle and immediately began to scold herself. "You silly bird, ye. Getting all bothered and then finding out the man was just being his wonderful self. Well, I won't be acting that foolish again. It was a good lesson well learned." One of Tessy's best attributes was that she always tried to turn every experience into a lesson learned, whether it was her faux pas or someone else's!

Between keeping up with orders at the store and finishing up the proposal she was going to present to the faculty, Tessy had very little time for herself. She was thankful she had been jotting down notes and organizing her papers periodically over the summer. All she had left to do now was photocopy her sheets for distribution to the attendees. Before she knew it, it was September 14, and she was on her way down to the school to make her pitch.

She reached the parking lot just as the after-school mayhem was in full swing . . . parents picking up their kids, horns honking, kids running this way and that, traffic guards holding up their signs. *Aye, things haven't changed much,* she mused. From the time she left home she repeated her special little parking invocation: "Loving Mother full of grace, show to me my parking space!" She managed to inch into a parking spot not far from the main walkway. "Thank ye kindly," she whispered as she carefully opened her car door, gathered up her binder and briefcase, and started down the walk, dodging as many teenagers as she could.

She caught sight of Sarah and Cherokee coming her way. "Well, now, how are my girls today? Did ye have a fine day at school?"

"Hi, Tessy. We had a great day. What are you doing here?" inquired Sarah.

Before Tessy could answer, Cherokee piped, "I know—you're here to talk to the teachers about your environmental program, right?"

"Oh, right," said Sarah. "I remember you telling us all about that this summer. Can't wait to hear what they have to say about it. You had some awesome ideas."

"Aye, girls, that's why I'm here. Sorry, but if ye don't mind, I best be going so I'm not late. I have a few items to hand out before we get started. Wish me luck."

"You'll be fine, Tessy. You were born with the luck of the Irish. Let us know how it went," Cherokee added along with a hug.

"Thank ye, dear, I'll be sure to."

Tessy manoeuvred her way down the familiar hallways to the boardroom and immediately opened her binder and pulled the sheets out of her briefcase. Half an hour later, the meeting was called to order. After the reading of the minutes from the last meeting in June, new business was called. This was it — Tessy was up. She began by introducing herself, which for the most part was not necessary, then she distributed her sheets around the large oval table.

"Thank ye for agreeing to hear me out this afternoon. What I am about to propose is something I feel is extremely important — no, vital — to every living soul on the face of the earth but I'll just stay focused on our wee piece of the world first. I'm hoping every one of you will take a shine to it and climb on board. If ye could take a peek at the first page you have in front of you, we'll get started, as I'm sure a few of ye would like to get home to your loved ones sometime tonight."

Over the sound of shuffling papers, Tessy continued. "As ye can see, I've named it 'The Gorgeous Garbage Drive, or the GGD' and I've included some ideas for almost every class. Please follow along:

"To start, every Home Room would be expected to have their own recycling program to include paper, plastics, glass, garbage, and even composting.

"Business Ed: will do the actual running of the business part.

"Home Economics: could have a bake sale, sew up some cloth bags, make homemade environmental cleaning and beauty products to sell . . . I've a number of recipes I'd be tickled to lend for this.

"Social Studies: could start up an Environmental Economics program and write letters to our MLAs expressing concerns regarding local pollution, herbicides, etc.

"History class: could write an essay on the causes and effects of pollution through the ages.

"Art Department: could creatively paint waste bins and sell them to commercial businesses, one for pop cans and one for garbage. The art classes could make sculptures from smaller recycled items and have an auction to sell them. Also have each student make their own living journal from old magazines and catalogues.

"The Trades program: could make larger pieces of art by welding old bikes, bedsprings, lawn chairs, mowers, wheelbarrows, whatever; and they, too, could be sold at auction. As well, perhaps they could construct attractive wood receptacles to contain the waste bins.

"Drama department: could put on a play or musical regarding the environment. Possibly called something like *Environmentally Sound . . .* just throwing that out there.

"I would also like to see a Saturday or two set aside for volunteers to go from home to home collecting bottles and other recyclables, along with the annual Fire Department Rally collecting old batteries, cans of paint, household chemicals, etc. But that'll be a matter I'll be talking to the Town Council about. I'll also be talking to them about having businesses donate things like garbage bags, garbage cans, and gloves; and even putting weekly articles and announcements in the local newspapers regarding the progress the students and town have been making."

With that, Tessy took in a long breath and finally concluded, "So, there, in a wee nutshell, is what I've been plannin' and hopin' you'll take a likin' to. And if ye have any further ideas to add, that would be grand. Are there any questions?"

The principal, Mr. Hambley, spoke first. "Well, Tessy, I'm impressed. I can see you have put a great deal of thought into this program of yours, and to speak honestly, I think it is a wonderful idea and truly one worth looking into. As you know, we won't be able to give you an answer tonight but we will definitely talk it over and let you know as soon as possible. The only glitch I can see right at the moment is that our class schedules have already been made up for the year, so this would mean some rescheduling would have to be done first. But it's certainly not unfeasible. Does anyone have any questions for Tessy?"

Tessy answered with ease and confidence the few questions fired at her. She was then excused and she made her way down the deserted hallways and back to her car.

When Tessy reached her lane, she realized how tired she was. *I guess I was a little more anxious about the presentation than I thought,* she mused. Duke and Darby were bouncing around the car as she pulled in.

"You two are like a couple of hares in heat. Get down now and behave. I'll be getting ye a treat in a minute." She gathered up her binder and briefcase and was getting her key out at the door when she heard the phone ringing. "Aye, just a minute, I'm coming." She answered the phone just in time to hear it click. "Drat. Oh, I guess if it's important I'll hear back from whoever it was." She fixed herself a bite to eat and was just taking her tea into the other room when the phone rang as she passed it.

She answered on the first ring. "Good evening."

"Only because I'm talking to you, my lady," Marshall replied soft and very assured.

"Oh, Marshall, what a welcome voice, ye are. How's my favourite doctor, then?"

"Good. Better now that I've finally reached you."

"Oh, it was you that called a wee bit ago?"

"Yes. I couldn't wait to hear how your presentation went. Did it go well?"

"Aye, seemed to be well received, it did. They'll be talking it over and letting me know as soon as they can. I'm just a wee worried that if they don't get an answer to me within the next week or so, I'll have to wait another month to talk to the Town Council."

"Why do you have to wait? Can't you see them now?"

"I could, but I know if I have the whole school backing me, the Council will have a hard time saying no."

"Why would you think they'll say no?"

"Well, I'm not a popular person with some of the high and mighty who sit on the board. A couple of them think I'm nothing but a quirky witch. I must admit, though, since I've been working at the pharmacy that notion seems to be diminishing a mite."

"Well, if it's that Mrs. Chamberlain, she can just eat crow or worse, as far as I'm concerned. Don't let those types of people worry you in the least."

"Oh, I don't. I've been subjected to that way of thinking all my life. In Ireland, it's different. There are many of us who carry the gift — it's just a way of life in the homeland. I'll admit there are times I miss it so much that I think of packing up and moving back. I especially did after Dermot passed. Was very close, I was."

"You've never told me or mentioned that is how you feel. Ireland is a very long way from Winnipeg. You do realize that, right?"

Tessy laughed. "Aye, I do realize it's a mile or two to Dublin."

"Good. Tessy, when you come out to see me, I want to continue with this conversation at length."

"Aye, we have many things we need to discuss. I've heard from my brother and I may be taking a trip home sooner than later."

"What? When did this come about?"

"I've had a couple of odd letters from him in the last few months, and then yesterday, I got a call from him. The letters were hinting at me coming to visit, but it was nothing too serious. He does harass me from time to time to come over, but the phone call was a bit more pressing. He's got something he needs to talk to me about in person. So ye see, I've only just found out meself."

"What are you going to do?"

"Well, I've made no plans as of yet. There seem to be so many things happening all at once that I'm having a hard time focusing on just one thing."

"This doesn't mean you'll be cancelling your trip here, does it?"

"No, but I am thinking it might be time for me to go home to Ireland for a wee visit."

"Well, don't worry about that now. We'll talk more when you get here."

"Aye, I suppose. It is a way off, so we still have time to make a plan. Anyway, me dear Marshall, if ye don't mind, I'm a wee weary and think I'll just have my chamomile tea and tuck myself in early."

"Not at all, Tess. Go and rest and we can talk about this later. Don't worry, we'll make this work."

"Thank ye, Marshall. You'll be in my prayers tonight, as well as in my dreams."

"As you will be in mine. Good night, my fair lady of Ladyslipper."

"Good night, my love."

Marshall hung up and then realized what Tessy had just said. She had never called him "love" before. By God, he was going to make sure everything, no matter what *everything* was, would work out for his beautiful Irish lass.

Spicy Herbed Cheese Ball

8 oz. (225 g) package cream cheese, warmed to room
    temperature
4 oz. (115 g) ricotta cheese
1 garlic clove, minced
1 Tbsp (15 ml) Worcestershire sauce
1/4 tsp (1 ml) cayenne
1/4 tsp (1 ml) lemon pepper
4 Tbsp (60 ml) finely chopped fresh chives
3 Tbsp (45 ml) finely chopped fresh basil
3 Tbsp (45 ml) finely chopped fresh parsley
1 tsp (5 ml) crushed pink peppercorns

Combine all of the fresh herbs and the peppercorns in a shallow dish
and set aside. In a medium bowl, mix the cream cheese, ricotta, garlic,
Worcestershire sauce, cayenne, and lemon pepper and beat until smooth.
Add in 4 tablespoons (60 ml) of the herb mixture and mix well. Form
into a ball and roll in the remaining herb mixture. Wrap in plastic and
chill for 4 to 24 hours.

Pesto

1 cup (250 ml) fresh basil leaves
1 cup (250 ml) fresh parsley leaves
1/2 cup (125 ml) extra-virgin olive oil
2/3 cup (150 ml) Parmesan cheese
1/3 cup (75 ml) pine nuts
3 large cloves garlic
Sea salt and coarse pepper to taste

In a food processor or blender, combine basil, parsley, cheese, pine nuts
and garlic cloves and blend until well mixed. Slowly add olive oil until
desired consistency is reached; add salt and pepper to taste.

18

Victory for a Wise Woman

As it turned out, Tessy did not have to wait long for an answer from the school board. The motion was unanimous for the Gorgeous Garbage Drive. Classes were already setting up to get under way as soon as possible. Now, all Tessy had to do was make her pitch to the Town Council, letting them know about the school's involvement. Tessy received a copy of each class's calendar of events regarding the drive and prepared herself to launch the presentation to the council at their next meeting.

Town Council met the last Monday evening of every month, and Tessy was waiting with briefcase in hand when the Town Office doors were unlocked and the session was called to order. She was surprised when the principal, Mr. Hambley, walked in and sat down beside her. She smiled, reached over to his hand, and gave it an appreciative pat. He winked, nodded, and returned the pat.

Tessy was finally called to present her proposal. She looked down, and there, sitting front and centre, was Mrs. Chamberlain. Tessy took a deep breath, surrounded herself with a protective shield of white light, and did a fine job of delivering her Gorgeous Garbage recommendations. She answered a number of questions once again with such ease it was quite evident that she was very well prepared. She was about to step down when Principal Hambley asked if he could say a few words.

"I have come here tonight to show not only my full backing of this project but also the entire school's. Ms. McGuigan has always displayed a true concern for this community and its residents, especially its children. This project will not only enhance the beauty of our community but will teach our children to respect the environment and give them an appreciation of what teamwork can accomplish. With your help, I feel this will be a truly positive venture for everyone; and who knows, maybe even a prototype that could prove beneficial for many other communities. Thank you. I hope you will all join me in recommending this worthwhile project. Good night."

Mrs. Chamberlain spoke up: "Mr. Hambley, I am extremely surprised that someone of your stature and position would back such a person."

"Mrs. Chamberlain, if you would look past your prejudiced opinions for just one moment and focus on what is for the good of this community, we would all benefit from it. Good night."

Tessy and Mr. Hambley decided not to remain for the entire public portion of the meeting and left. When they got out to the parking lot, Tessy turned to him. "Thank ye kindly for those strong words of encouragement. I'm sure they'll go a long way in encouraging a positive decision. You're a good man and an even better teacher."

"Oh, Tessy, it was my pleasure. I only hope it did some good. And don't let that old battleaxe bother you. She's just full of bad wind. Good night. We'll stay in touch."

"Aye, and thank ye again. Good night to ye, Mr. Hambley."

When Tessy arrived home, she felt like a great weight had been lifted. She set her briefcase down in the entry and headed toward the library. She opened the door. It was dark, the only light shining in from the hall. She walked over to the desk and switched on the study lamp; still there on the desk was the white feather. She picked it up and brushed it against her cheek. "Thank ye, Dermot, my love. I know ye were there beside me tonight. I felt your presence and I do appreciate it. We still make quite a team, you and I, don't we?" Tessy felt a slight breeze gently stir the soft curls that tickled her neck and she knew. She placed the feather in the top drawer, switched off the lamp, and walked out, closing the door behind her. "Good night, love," she whispered as it latched.

The next morning, she got the call from the Town Office about Gorgeous Garbage. After much discussion, it had been approved; however, it had not received quite a full, unanimous vote. She immediately called Mr. Hambley to thank him again and give him the great news. Then she called Marshall. The phone rang six times and she was about to hang up when a woman answered puffing into the receiver. "Yes! Hello! Dr. Tayse's residence."

"Hello, there. Is this Dotty?" Tessy asked.

"Yes, it is."

"Hello, Dotty, this is Tessy McGuigan. Sounds like I caught ye running the derby."

"Oh, Ms. McGuigan. How are you? Yes. We are doing some rearranging in one of the guest rooms."

"Sorry to catch ye at a bad time—and please, Dotty, call me Tess. I'm just fine, thank ye. I was wondering if Marshall . . . er . . . Dr. Tayse might be about?"

"Oh, I'm sorry—he's out on some errands right at the moment, but I don't expect he'll be long. He's so excited about you ladies coming to visit he's been picking up all sorts of goodies," Dotty chuckled.

"Has he now? What a man. He loves to spoil ye, that one, bless his heart."

"For sure he does. Would you like me to ask him to give you a call when he gets in?"

"Aye, that would be grand. Thank ye. I'll let ye get back to your chores. Don't be overdoing, it now. Looking forward to having a fine visit with you."

"Yes, Tess. Me, too. See you soon, and I'll let Dr. Tayse know you called. 'Bye."

"Bye-bye, now."

Tessy hung up the phone and busied herself with some orders for the pharmacy. In large part, she felt her main mission to the Gorgeous Garbage Drive was over. Of course, she would continue on with whatever she could do to help, but preparations were under way, and now all she had to do was make sure everyone kept up with their obligations. Down deep, she knew everything would turn out as it should but she felt such a relief to have all the "protocol" over with. Now she and the community would be setting the "ideas" into reality. She was so looking forward to finally seeing her vision come to fruition.

"Aye, actions do speak louder than words," she said, looking over at Merlin and Cordelia lazily lounging on their pillows. "However, I would think action requires that ye have at least one eye open!"

As Thanksgiving was fast approaching, the girls were coming over to Tessy's after school so they could plan their trip to Winnipeg. Tessy was in the kitchen preparing some snacks for the girls. It was sunny, but there was definitely a fall chill in the air. She decided some nice, warm treats from the oven would hit the spot. She was just taking the steaming Spiced Rhubarb Muffins out of the oven when she heard a knock, and the girls came giggling in the back door.

"Hi, Tessy!" the girls chimed.

"Boy, does that ever smell good," Sarah said as she took a long sniff.

"And man, am I starving!" added Cherokee.

"Well, then, it's a good thing these are out of the oven in time. Sit, sit. How was your day?"

"Just a normal day . . . nothing major to report," Cherokee answered as she got up and pulled out some plates and knives.

"What would ye like to drink? There's tea, hot chocolate, apple cider, milk . . . well, ye know what's here."

"Well, if my nose is correct and those are your famous rhubarb muffins, I will just have a glass of milk," Cherokee laughed.

"Aye, your nose has not failed ye."

"Milk's good for me, too," Sarah agreed.

Tessy retrieved two glasses and a large pitcher of milk and set them on the table then went and placed the kettle on the stove for her tea.

The girls were finishing up their second muffin each when the phone rang.

Tessy answered with her usual greeting.

"Hello, my lady," came the welcome reply.

"Marshall, how nice to hear your voice. I'm just sitting here with your lovely granddaughter and Cherokee."

Both the girls yelled, "HI, Grandpa!" in unison. Cherokee had adopted the honorary name over the summer.

"Your grandfather says hi back," Tessy relayed, then continued. "We were just sitting here making plans for our wee trip. So far we've decided to leave early Friday. The girls are taking Friday and Tuesday off school so we can spend the whole weekend with you. It should take us between six and seven hours to get there, so we should be on your doorstep mid- to late afternoon. Before supper, for sure, at any rate."

"That sounds fantastic, Tessy. I can't wait to see all my girls."

"Well, you'll be getting your wish fairly soon. We'll be on our way in less than a week. And we're getting pretty excited, as well. The young ones, here, are floating like dandelion fluff in the wind. The time will pass quick as a jig, and we'll be there before ye know it."

Tender Mend Antiseptic Salve

1 cup (250 ml) refined coconut oil
2 Tbsp (30 ml) grated beeswax
2 Tbsp (30 ml) calendula essential oil
20 drops eucalyptus radiata essential oil
10 drops lavender essential oil
10 drops sage essential oil
5 drops clove essential oil
5 drops thyme essential oil

In a double boiler or a glass bowl set over a saucepan of water over medium heat, combine the coconut oil, beeswax, and calendula oil and melt. Remove from heat, add the other essential oils, and pour into containers. Let set overnight or place in refrigerator to cool.

Campfire Fun Banana Boats

Banana
Semi-sweet dark chocolate chips
Unsweetened shredded coconut
Mini-marshmallows
Walnuts, almonds, or pecans (optional)

Slice a banana lengthwise down the middle and place on a sheet of tinfoil large enough to wrap around the banana. Sprinkle on chocolate chips, coconut, marshmallows, and nuts, if desired. Loosely wrap in foil and place on edge of firepit or on barbecue until banana is warmed and chocolate/marshmallow is melted (doesn't take long!). Can top with whipped cream or ice cream and garnish with sprinkles and a cherry. Indulge — enjoy! Single serving.

19

Come East, My Ladies . . . Come East

The morning was cool but clear when Tessy pulled into the Tuckers' driveway at 7:45 a.m. sharp on Friday. The girls flew to open the front door and were dragging their suitcases down the steps before Tessy could hop out of the car and pop open the hatch.

"Good morning, Tessy!" they chimed.

"And a good mornin' to you, too, dears!"

Penny and Jim followed behind to help get the girls loaded up.

"Good morning, Tess," Jim greeted as he reached her first.

"Good morning, Jim. Penny, 'mornin' to ye."

"'Morning. Well, it seems like it's going to be a nice day for travelling," Penny added.

"Aye, that it does. Are Matthew and Emma about? I would like to thank them again for looking out for me pets."

"Matt left early this morning for basketball practice, and I'm afraid Emma is not taking this well, so she's still sitting at the kitchen table with her arms crossed."

Jim started hoisting the girls' suitcases into the hatch while they stood huddled excitedly chattering. Little Emma came out of the house with a huge pout on.

"How come *I* don't get to go?" she huffed as she plunked herself down on the bottom step.

"Oh, honey, we've talked about this. When you get a little older, you'll be able to go on special trips, too." Penny sat down beside her youngest daughter, trying to console her.

"Emma, dear." Tess leaned over her. "I truly need someone I can trust to look after Duke and Darby and Merlin and Cordelia. They love you very much, and I know you will take such good care of them. Between you, Matthew, and my neighbour, Mr. Baker, I can go away and not worry about my animals. You remember Mr. Baker, don't you? He was the nice man who took ye on the hayride at the Christmas party."

"Yes!" Emma brightened. "Do you think maybe he will let me pet the horses again?"

"I'm sure, if it's okay with your mummy and daddy, he would love for ye to go over to his farm and see all his animals. He has cows and horses and chickens and ducks. I think he even has some bunny rabbits. Maybe Matthew would like to go with you and your mum and dad?"

"Oh, Mommy, can we?"

"Well, I'm not sure, honey. We'd have to check with Mr. Baker first."

"I have already spoken to Danny, and it was his suggestion that the wee ones are more than welcome to pop over if they would like. I was going to leave his number with you anyway, as he will be checking Ashling Manor for me while I'm gone. And I hope ye don't mind but I left your number with him so if he needs to get in touch, he can. You can give him a call and arrange a visit when it's a good time for all."

"Yeah! Oh, Mommy, can we go today? Can we, can we? Please?"

"We'll see, Emma. Maybe after school. Right now, we have to get your sister off first."

Fifteen minutes later, after plenty of hugs and more "final" instructions, Tessy, Sarah, and Cherokee were buckled in and backing out of the driveway, with the teenagers leaning halfway out the windows madly waving. Before they reached the outer town limits, the girls had already gone through their purses, ensuring that their wallets and other essentials were safely in place.

"I can't believe we are finally on our way!" Sarah reached up to the front seat and gently squeezed Cherokee's shoulder. "This is going to be so much fun. Tessy, thank you so much for doing this for us."

"Oh, my dears, this is not just for you. I am looking forward to seeing my relatives — and, of course, your grandfather. This is as much a wee getaway for me as for you."

"I know . . . look at us . . . almost like 'Thelma and Louise' — well, plus one," Cherokee added.

"I don't think either of your parents, nor your grandfather, nor I would appreciate this wee adventure being anything like 'Thelma and Louise's', thank ye very much! That is one movie I did see and as I remember it didn't turn out real well for those young ladies."

"Oh, yah. I guess you're right. Good point. Well, if you give me some time, I'll think of a better one. There's probably a Disney film that turned out perfect, just like this trip is going to be."

"Great idea, Cherokee!" Sarah all but squealed. "Let's play a movie guessing game. We'll call it 'Name That Famous Film.' I'll start."

The first two hundred kilometres fairly flew by. They were enjoying new made-up games, non-stop chatting, and eating the goodies that Tessy had packed. There hadn't even been a quiet enough moment to discuss or miss what music to listen to.

"Ye know, girls, when you're travelling along the highway and you're looking for a good spot to eat, ye can always tell by how many truckers are stopped outside the restaurant. So, keep your eyes open because in about an hour we will be in Brandon and we can stop for a wee bite to eat and rest up a bit—if you girls would like?"

"That would be great. I'm getting TB and would love to stretch," Sarah yawned.

Cherokee turned to look at her friend. "TB?"

"Tired Bum."

The front seat erupted with laughter.

When they reached Brandon, they were ready for a nice meal and a good stretch. They spotted a gas station restaurant franchise along the highway and decided it was a good pick. They counted nine semi-trailer trucks parked close by!

"If it's only a one-seater, I'm in first. I've had way more to drink than you two," Sarah piped as they drove into the parking lot. She was out of the car before Tessy even cut the ignition. The other two were not far behind.

After a relaxing meal, they strolled out to the parking lot for a walk and some deep breaths of fresh air before climbing back into the car and gassing up. It was agreed that Cherokee and Sarah would switch places, with Sarah now in the front for the duration of the trip.

Sarah popped open the glove compartment and started going through some of Tessy's CDs. "Who are these guys?" she asked.

"Oh, that would be my Bobby collection," Tessy laughed.

"What do you mean 'Bobby collection'? Isn't that what they call British policemen?"

"Well, aye, that is what they call police officers, but that has nothing to do with these Bobbys. Let's see . . . in there you should find Bobby Cartola, Bobby Vinton, Bobby Darin, Bobby Vee, and Bobby Rydell."

"Are you serious? Was everyone called 'Bobby' back then?"

"Oh, no! They weren't all Bobbys. I have some other wonderful CDs in there from that era like Paul Anka, Neil Sedaka, Johnny Mathis, the Four Seasons, Leslie Gore. Then after that, the British Invasion hit North America like great boulders from the heavens."

"British Invasion?" echoed the girls.

"Aye, bands like the Beatles, Herman's Hermits, Dave Clark 5, Rolling Stones. They came over the pond from England to perform here, and all the lasses went crazy."

"You've lived through all that?" exclaimed Sarah.

"Aye," Tessy laughed, "and more. You'll also find all my CDs from the '70s in there somewhere. Now, that was more *my* era, so it was. But I love them all. Ye can pop a couple in and have a listen, if ye like."

Sarah and Cherokee thought they might as well give it a try just to see what old-fashioned music was like.

"Now, give the words a real listening to. They were a romantic lot, those Bobbys."

The girls were so surprised at how much they actually enjoyed the ballads that they were going back again and again to the same songs, and all three sang along like it was karaoke.

"Wow! Some of those lyrics are so romantic. I would faint if a guy said those kinds of things to me. But I'm really surprised they talk about making love so much. Was that okay back then?" Sarah asked.

"Well, now, back then, making love was holding hands, making eyes at one another, and maybe a little smooching — but that was it. Certainly nothing like today's definition," Tessy explained.

"Well, that's good — otherwise, there sure would have been a lot of teen pregnancies."

"Now, don't get me wrong. There were some of those at that time, too, but it was quite a bit tougher, then, especially on the girls. Today's teens have so many choices . . . but until you reach a certain age, abstaining would be my wish for young teens. When you're young, ye get led astray with your hormones all dancing around and ye just don't always think wisely."

"How old do you think a girl should be, Tessy?"

"Oh my, that would be something ye should be talking over with your parents, not an old widow like myself."

"Tessy, you are not old," Cherokee exclaimed.

"And you're hot! Just ask Grandpa," Sarah added.

"Now, ye girls stop embarrassing me with your blarney."

The next hour passed pleasantly with more tunes, laughter, and all-around good female camaraderie. The girls were momentarily quiet and taking in the scenery when Cherokee thought out loud, "Wow, it sure is flat country out here."

"Aye, this is definitely one of the flatter landscapes of the prairies. Has its own beauty, though, doesn't it? When the fields of sunflowers are all in bloom, there's nothing lovelier . . . or a beautiful field of bright blue flax . . . and rich, fertile land with plenty of sunshine to go with it."

"Tessy, you have a way of making any place sound magical," Cherokee sighed.

"That's because every place *is* magical if you just open your heart to see it. Canada is so bountiful and every bit of it has its own beauty, right from the mountains to the prairies to the oceans. Wouldn't it be boring, now, if it all looked the same across this country."

"Someday I am going to travel across Canada. Wanna come with me, Sarah?" Cherokee chirped.

"You bet. Count me in. We'll have to give ourselves a name—but obviously not 'Thelma and Louise.'"

Before long, the scenery turned into a skyline of buildings, and the girls were now leaning against the windows taking in all the sights that rushed by.

"Are there no really tall buildings here?" asked Cherokee.

Sarah was the one to reply, "Silly, we're not even close to downtown, yet. Grandpa lives a long way from the really tall buildings."

"Aye, we won't be going to the core of the city today, but just wait until we do. We'll visit the infamous Portage and Main. You'll be seeing some good-sized buildings then."

"Why is it infamous?"

"Well, it's said that it is the windiest intersection of any city in Canada; but I think it is an amazing sight to see and a powerful experience. We'll go and stand there while we're here and then you can tell me how it makes you feel."

"Really, Tess, we haven't ever done that. I guess Grandpa just never thought of taking us there."

"Aye, I suppose if you live someplace for so many years, ye just take those things for granted. But trust me, it is a humbling experience to stand amongst those towering buildings and all the city's commotion and just take it all in. And oh, feel that breeze on your face."

"You mean gale-force winds, don't you, Tessy?" Sarah laughed.

"Aye."

They travelled down Portage Avenue for a few kilometres farther, and then Tessy started checking out the cross streets.

"Now, girls, I think we should be turning off soon, so if you could help me look for the Kenaston Boulevard turnoff, it would be much appreciated. It's been a long while since I've done any driving in this part of the city."

"There. There it is. I recognize it. Tessy, turn at the next exit." Sarah pointed.

Once off the main throughway, they soon found themselves driving down a beautifully treed street with luxurious homes.

"This is Wellington Crescent," Tessy all but whispered. "This is one of the oldest, wealthiest districts in Winnipeg. Aren't those homes a grand sight to see!"

"Yah, Grandpa just lives a couple streets down. We're almost there," Sarah chirped.

"REALLY!" Tessy and Cherokee exhaled in unison.

"Yep, and if you keep going that way," Sarah pointed again, "you end up in Assiniboine Park and the zoo."

They continued on until Sarah yelled, "There, right there. Stop. Turn, turn. Yeah, we're here!"

Tessy slowly drove up to the mansion, not believing what she was seeing, feeling the nausea forming in the pit of her stomach.

Cherokee said it all. "Holy crap! Are you kidding me? Sorry, Tessy."

"No worries, dear. 'Twas not far from my thinking, as well," Tessy vacantly answered, staring at the massive structure.

"*This* is your grandpa's house?" Cherokee gasped.

"Yah, come on, hurry!" Sarah answered as she jumped out of the car and ran up the steps. "Come on," she said again, turning and waving her arms. When she reached the top step, the door flew open, and her grandfather stepped out and embraced her. Tessy and Cherokee slowly emerged from the vehicle and mounted the steps, still mesmerized by the grandeur that stretched before them.

"Tessy, Cherokee — well, you made it! Please, come in! How was the trip?" Marshall asked as he gave them each a welcoming hug. "Please, this way." He ushered them through the front door.

Once they were in the foyer, a full-figured woman came rushing down a hallway toward them. "Sorry, Dr. Tayse, I was just seeing to things in the kitchen. Oh, Sarah, how wonderful to see you, my dear," she continued as she gathered Sarah up in a most earnest hug.

"Dotty, it's so good to see you, too. I'm so excited to be here."

Marshall carried on with introductions. "Dotty, this is Sarah's good friend, Cherokee Amiotte, and this . . . this is Tessy McGuigan. Ladies, this is my guardian angel, Dotty Mitchell."

"Finally, a chance to meet you both—it's a pleasure. Dr. Tayse has talked about little else since he got back from Ladyslipper. We have been so looking forward to your visit. And don't pay any attention to that one. Trust me, I am a far cry from any angel," Dotty laughed as she threw a sheepish glance at Marshall then continued, "My husband, Bert, should be along any minute to collect your bags and take them up to your rooms."

The girls followed Dotty up the stairs to their rooms, leaving Tessy and Marshall alone in the foyer. Marshall picked up her hand and kissed it.

"It is so good to see you," he whispered into her hand while gazing into her eyes.

"Aye, it's good to see you, too," Tessy replied, returning the gaze. "I do have to admit, though, I was not expecting such grand surroundings . . . leaves one a bit shaken, it does."

"Oh, Tessy, no. It's not that big. Well, maybe it's a bit large for just me to be rambling around in, but I'll give you a tour and you can see for yourself. Come with me." Marshall, still holding her hand, pulled her toward the hallway.

As promised, Bert delivered the luggage and was introduced to Cherokee. The girls unpacked and returned downstairs. They were in the kitchen helping Dotty with some vegetables when Marshall and Tessy returned through the patio doors from the backyard.

"Hey, there you are. We were wondering where you two got off to," Sarah remarked.

"Aye, your grandfather was just showing me about. My, what a lovely piece of Mother's earth. Takes your breath away, it does."

Bert was also in the kitchen visiting. "Hello, you must be Tessy. I'm Dotty's better half, Bert." He stretched out his hand and gave Tessy one of the brightest smiles she had ever seen. "Pleased to meet you."

"Well, a pleasure, to be sure, Bert." Tessy smiled back, firmly taking his hand.

Cherokee piped up, "You mean I missed the tour?"

"Grandpa, would you mind if I showed Cherokee around?" Sarah offered.

"Not at all. Go ahead — look around all you want. There's really not that much to see."

"Are you kidding? This place is fantastic. It's like a fairy-tale fortress!" Cherokee gushed.

Everyone laughed.

"Aye, I can see how she would think that," Tessy nodded.

"Now, Tessy. When Evelyne and I bought this place, we had five kids, which of course included the twins, and we wanted everyone to have their own room. And besides, it's all relative. The price back then was not anything like the market price today. It was really quite reasonable when we purchased it. Anyway, enough of this talk. Let's get you unpacked and settled so we can start our Thanksgiving."

Stay Alert Scent

10 drops of lemon essential oil
10 drops of geranium essential oil
10 drops of rosemary essential oil
5 drops of clove essential oil

Put drops directly into a small brown bottle and shake to blend. When you feel you need a "lift," just place under your nose and breathe in deeply.

Spiced Rhubarb Muffins

3/4 cup (175 ml) vegetable oil
1 1/2 cups (375 ml) packed brown sugar
3 eggs
1 tsp (5 ml) vanilla
2 cups (500 ml) flour
1 cup (250 ml) rolled oats
2 1/2 cups (625 ml) finely diced rhubarb
2 tsp (10 ml) baking powder
1 tsp (5 ml) baking soda
2 tsp (10 ml) cinnamon
1/2 tsp (2 ml) nutmeg
1/2 tsp (2 ml) allspice
1/4 tsp (1 ml) sea salt
1/2 cup (125 ml) walnuts or pecans (optional)

Beat together oil, brown sugar, eggs, vanilla, and nuts, if desired, in a large bowl. In another bowl, combine flour, oats, baking powder, baking soda, spices, and salt. Add dry ingredients to creamed mixture alternately with rhubarb. Spoon into greased muffin cups and bake at 350°F (180°C) for 25–30 minutes or until done. Yield = 24.

20

Winnipeg-on-a-Whirlwind

On Saturday morning, everyone was up and going at the crack of dawn. Dotty was in the kitchen preparing a hearty, full breakfast "with all the fixins'," as Tessy put it. While waiting for breakfast, Marshall gave them each a list of attractions and events that were going on at the time. They each went over their copy and ticked off what they thought they would most like to see. Sarah had been to most of the attractions on the list already but there were a number of them she loved to repeat every time she was in Winnipeg and she didn't want Cherokee to miss out on any of them. After some discussion, the major picks were decided on, and breakfast was served.

Dotty made sure their guests would be out the door well fed and able to tour a long while before having to stop for anything to eat.

"Where to first, Grandpa?" Sarah asked.

"Well, this morning, I thought we would drive around to the main highlights, kinda like a mini-hop-on-hop-off tour so you can see where some of your choices are and we can go from there. We only have a couple of days to fit in as much as we can, so I suggest we go ahead and do the ones you really want first."

"Sarah, you've done most of this stuff. Where do you suggest?" Cherokee asked.

Sarah grabbed her sheet and scanned the list. "Well, you said you wanted to see some skyscrapers, so let's start with a drive down to Portage and Main, take some fun pictures of us on the corner, then carry on to St. Boniface Cathedral, then . . . Grandpa, is there anything going on at the English Gardens this time of year? Tessy said she would like to see them if there is time and if they are still open."

"Yes, the Conservatory and the Gardens are open all year round, and, since the weather has been so beautiful thus far, the colours will be spectacular; but I was thinking we might want to leave that until Sunday or Monday morning. Reason being, the grounds at Lower Fort Garry are also open to the public at this time of the year, but all the buildings are closed up and the only way you can see them is to book a tour; so I went ahead and booked us one for this afternoon and I am really glad you all had that on your list! I checked with some of the hospital staff to see if they would be interested in getting their family members together and joining us. It will still be a limited tour compared to what is going on at the Fort in the summer months, but it should still be fun.

"So if we do Portage and Main, St. Boniface Cathedral, and then maybe head down to the Corydon district for some shopping and lunch, that should be perfect timing to get out to Lower Fort Garry for our tour. How does that sound?"

"I'd say you sound like a tour guide fit for royalty, ye do! But don't be talking to me about eating any time soon, I don't think I can swallow another bite."

"Oh, I'm pretty sure by the time we tramp around downtown, take in the cathedral, and fit in some shopping, you'll work up an appetite. And now, ladies, we best be on our way . . . your tour bus awaits you!" Marshall swooped his arm and bowed toward the front entry and they trundled down the hallway, out the foyer, and into the large SUV.

They toured, laughed, shopped, took dozens of photos, and just thoroughly enjoyed the day and each other's company. By the time they got back to the house, they were exhausted, but the girls still had enough steam to tell Dotty and Bert all about their adventures over drinks and a plate of homemade nachos.

That evening, Dotty and Bert were taking the girls out to a special eatery just outside of town famous for foot-long hotdogs and then dropping them off at a glow-in-the-dark miniature golf course. Meanwhile, Marshall had planned a very special evening with Tessy. Around four p.m., all she was told was that she should go up and put on her loveliest dress and meet Marshall in the living room when she was ready. Marshall heard Tessy descending the stairs about an hour later and he got up to meet her at the bottom. When he looked up and saw her he had to catch his breath. She looked radiant in a simple gown of warm chestnut carrying a hooded cloak woven in a tapestry of vibrant fall colours. The girls came around the corner from down the hall to say goodbye before they left and stopped dead in their tracks. "Wow!" they echoed.

"Ditto!" was all Marshall could come up with at the moment as he stood there with his mouth gaping.

Tessy blushed. "Well, thank you. It's appropriate for what ye have in mind, then?"

"Appropriate doesn't even come close, my love. You look absolutely breathtaking." He reached out his hand to assist her down the last few steps.

"Well, you look rather dapper yourself, Dr. Tayse."

"Thank you—but after seeing you, I'm thinking I should go upstairs and dust off my tux."

"Why you look just dashing in the fine threads you're in. The most handsome rogue I've ever seen, to be sure." She winked then laughed.

Just then the doorbell rang, and Marshall answered it. "We'll be right there, thank you." He said and closed the door.

Tessy looked puzzled as Marshall took her cloak and placed it around her shoulders.

"Our ride is here, my lady." He bowed, and, as he swung open the door, there waited the longest limousine Tessy had ever set eyes on.

"Marshall, what have ye gone and done now?" she gasped.

Once again, the girls said, "Wow!"

"Ditto!" Tessy echoed.

The driver held the door open for Tessy and Marshall to enter. Immediately, they noticed the ice bucket with champagne and glasses. Marshall did the honours of popping it and pouring them each a glass. "*Slainte*, my love. Tonight is going to be a night to remember, I promise." They tapped their glasses, took a sip, and he leaned over and gave her a kiss.

"Marshall Tayse, I have no idea what ye have in store for this evening but I can agree it will not be forgotten anytime soon, I'm sure."

They toured Wellington Crescent along the Assiniboine River and drove into the park, where the driver stopped to let them out so they could take a short stroll under the magnificent elm and maple trees. Soon, they were back in the limo and headed for their dining destination, which happened to be the luxurious Fort Garry Hotel. As they were pulling up to the main entrance of this most regal structure, Tessy couldn't have felt more like a fairy princess even if she had looked down and discovered she was wearing glass slippers. The driver opened their door, letting Marshall out first so he could help Tessy.

"I will have the limo waiting here for you promptly at 7:30 p.m., Dr. Tayse," the driver assured him.

"Thank you, Colin. That might be cutting it a little close, but we should be fine." Marshall gently slapped him on the back. "See you then."

"Good leapin' leprechauns, what on earth else do ye have up your sleeve, man?" Tessy shook her head at Marshall. "Is this not enough?"

"Not for you, my lady of Ladyslipper." Marshall smiled as he bent and kissed her on the nose.

"I plan to woo you tonight."

"I think you've already accomplished that."

Their reservation was confirmed, and they were quickly seated at an elegantly set table in the dining room. The music, the ambience, the wine, and the food were amazing—but none held a candle to the company. They drank and talked and ate and talked and talked some more. It seemed like they could have sat there all night, but when Marshall checked his watch, he was startled back to reality. "Oh, darling, we have to finish up and be on our way. The limo will be here any moment and we have someplace else to be."

"Well, I'm hoping a girl has a minute to freshen up first," Tessy quipped as she dabbed her mouth with her napkin and jumped up.

Marshall called the waiter over, and before they knew it, they were back in the limo. They hadn't gone far when they were already coming to a halt. Tessy peeked out the windows to see if she could tell where they were. Another lovely building, and *my, look at all the well-dressed people going in* she thought. Again, the driver opened their door.

"Didn't really seem worth the time and gas we wasted to get here," Tessy said as she gave Marshall a puzzled look. Colin tried to hide his smirk, while Marshall just laughed out loud.

"Welcome to the home of the Winnipeg Symphony Orchestra, my love," he announced.

"Marshall . . . really? Oh, I've always wanted to hear them but have just never had the opportunity. Oh, Marshall, how did ye know?"

"Just a good guess, I'm realizing. Shall we?" He placed his hand on the small of her back and gently led her into the lobby. "I believe our seats are this way."

For two hours, chills ran up and down Tessy's body while the orchestra played medley after medley. Sometimes she would close her eyes and just let herself be carried off to another realm. It was enchanting and exhilarating at the same time. Before she knew it, they were applauding the final bow, and it ended almost as suddenly as it began. Marshall took her arm in his, and they stepped outside to see a long chain of limousines waiting for their passengers. Colin waved at them down the line a bit, and they waited for him to make his way to them. Before he reached them, Tessy looked up at Marshall and sighed, "Marshall, this has been the most magical evening I have ever spent. Thank you so much."

"Well, my love, it's not over just yet." He smiled down at her as their limousine pulled up.

They toured the city and then drove along the river again to watch the lights reflected off the water. Tessy was cozy and comfortable against Marshall's shoulder and she was feeling somewhat intoxicated from the effects of the number of refreshments provided throughout the evening.

"Don't nod off just yet, my love." Marshall kissed her forehead.

"Marshall Tayse, you're going to put me in an early grave if ye have much else planned."

Marshall laughed. "Well, I only have you for a couple of days so I am going to make the best of it."

"Aye, but all in one night?"

Tessy looked out the window and noticed they were pulling up to Marshall's home, and a sense of regret yet relief crossed over her. Obviously, the evening was coming to a close, but she was getting very weary.

Colin opened their door for their final exit. "Good evening, Dr. Tayse. It was a pleasure driving you and your lovely companion this evening."

"Thank you, Colin. I'll be letting your employer know what a fine driver you are."

"Thank you, sir." Colin bowed as he shut the door behind them and waited for them to enter the house before pulling away.

"Now, my lady, one more surprise before you head off to bed. Close your eyes and take my arm, and no peeking."

He led her down the hall and into the dining room. "Okay. Open your eyes."

Tessy couldn't believe her eyes. The table and chairs had been moved off into the living room, there was a ballroom glitter globe hanging in the centre from the chandelier, the lights were low, and there were rose petals scattered around the edge of the room.

"What in the land of leaping leprechauns have ye done?"

"Well, when I was in Ladyslipper, I promised I would take you dancing but I couldn't find a place with romantic music playing while you were here — so I created one. Wait right here." Marshall stepped over to the stereo and hit PLAY then walked back to Tessy and held out his hand. "May I have this dance?"

"Oh, Marshall . . ." She placed her hand in his and they glided across the floor. She had scores of questions as to how and when, but they would wait for another time.

On Sunday morning, Tessy awoke with a flood of thoughts and feelings pouring over her from the night before. Had last night actually taken place? She smiled and sighed into her soft sateen weave sheets. She was starting to feel like a lovestruck teenager and she quite liked it. She lay in her cozy bed for a while longer, lingering in romantic, smoky thoughts of this amazing courtship. She was, at first, enjoying them then she began to scare herself with even the possibility of what might happen. She threw open the covers and placed her feet "firmly" on the floor. "There, no more of that," she told herself.

Downstairs, everyone was in the kitchen at various stages of a buffet-style breakfast.

"Well, good morning, sleepyhead." Marshall raised his coffee cup and shot one of his most adorable smiles at her.

A little embarrassed, Tessy bowed her head to hide her flushed cheeks and replied, "A good morning to ye all. I apologize for my tardy pace this morning. I hope I haven't made anyone run late."

Dotty came to her defence. "You just never mind — don't let the good doctor rattle you. You are not far behind any one of them. It seems that we are all running a bit late this morning. Coffee?"

"Aye, that would be grand. Thank ye."

It wasn't long before the kitchen was cleaned up, and they decided to get ready and head out for some fresh air before helping out with preparations for Thanksgiving dinner. Tessy's Aunt Shannon had been invited to join them for supper. It had been some time since Tessy had had a visit with her, and she was quite excited to see her once again. Her uncle had passed two years earlier, and that was the last time she had seen her aunt — or her brother Keenan, for that matter.

The English Gardens and the Conservatory at the Assiniboine Park were open at 9:00 a.m., so Marshall, Tessy, and the girls were there shortly after. It was a brisk sunny morning, and everyone was dressed accordingly. They decided to check out the Conservatory first so that it could warm up a bit outdoors before they wandered through the gardens. About an hour later, they were all back in the vehicle and heading for home. Dotty was working on the dressing for the turkey, and Bert was drying off the bird. Everyone immediately pitched in, and before long, the kitchen was filled with tantalizing aromas. After everything seemed to be well on its way and under control, they were off to the Manitoba Museum for a couple of hours.

When they got back, Tessy and the girls could not stop raving about it.

"Dotty, I was absolutely amazed. Have ye ever been?" Tessy marvelled.

"Why, yes, but it's been a few years now. It was called the Museum of Man and Nature back then. It is quite something, though, isn't it?"

"Quite something! Are you kidding? WOW!" Cherokee gasped. "I could spend an entire day there and still not see and do it all. The planetarium was awesome!"

"Yah, that's probably my favourite, and even though I've been there lots of times, I always have a great time when we go. And I still haven't done it all, either," Sarah agreed.

"Well, I'm really glad you all liked it. We've certainly crammed a lot into a couple of days," Marshall said as he shook his head.

"Yep, and we have one day left. What's on tomorrow?" Sarah continued.

"Don't you two ever get tuckered out?" Marshall laughed.

By the time Aunt Shannon arrived, the dining room was festively decorated, the house smelled delicious, and everyone was well dressed. After introductions, Aunt Shannon was ushered into the living room for a visit and a glass of wine. Appetizers were enjoyed over some shared "Tessy stories," which everyone found amusing except perhaps Tessy.

"Now, Auntie Shannon, stop with your tales. Nobody cares to hear about such goings-on."

"Says who?" Marshall laughed. "In fact, Shannon, I'll just fill up your wineglass while you carry on with your next story."

"You just never mind, Dr. Tayse, I'm sure I heard Dotty say it was time to be carving the turkey, so be gone with ye."

Again, Marshall laughed but did make his way out to the kitchen, along with the girls, leaving Tessy and Aunt Shannon alone to visit.

"Tessy, dear, 'tis so good to see ye — and so happy, as well. Your mam would be so proud to see what a fine woman you've become. Speaking of which, I have a wee parcel of your mam's in me bag that I was told to hang onto till my time was getting close; then I was to give it to ye. Would ye mind passing my bag to me, dear?"

"Well, I don't mind getting your bag for you, but you're not going anywhere anytime soon. I won't have ye talking like that, now."

"Tessy, dear, I may be your mam's younger sister, but that still puts me in my eighties. Growing old 'tis a privilege, and I have been blessed with that privilege, which I am truly thankful for; but when it's my time, I'll be thankful for that as well."

"Aye, but I'm not ready for you to say your goodbyes just yet." Tessy gently squeezed her hand before placing the bag in her lap.

"Now, ye have to promise me to not open this wee parcel until after I've taken my last breath and that only Keenan is with ye when ye do. No one else must know until after it's opened, and what's inside has been discussed between the two of ye. That was your mam's final wish, and I'll not be breaking it." Aunt Shannon stared deep into Tessy's eyes until she was sure her message was perfectly understood.

"Aye, Auntie, I promise," Tessy solemnly replied.

Their powerful moment was abruptly interrupted when the girls came giggling down the hall.

Sarah said, "Dotty says we're ready to move into the dining room, if you like?"

Tessy quickly stashed the package under her wrap. "Aye, I think we're ready to sample those wonderful smells that have been teasing us all afternoon. I just have to run upstairs for a moment and then I'll be right in."

Marshall put on some soft dinner music and got Aunt Shannon seated at the amazing banquet laid out before them. Tessy soon joined them, and a prayer of Thanksgiving was most earnestly offered. As the meal went on, everyone had a turn at sharing what he or she was thankful for, and why. Dotty was first, and as everyone took their turn to speak,

Tessy was just truly thankful for being in this space, at this very moment, with people she loved and enjoyed; while knowing that upstairs was a special gift left from her mother so many years ago.

The rest of the evening was spent with much laughter, more stories, and wonderful songs from the old country, with Aunt Shannon gracefully gliding her fingers over the piano keys. Before they knew it, it was ten p.m. and past her bedtime.

"Well, now, look at the hour. I must get home, as I will be doing this again tomorrow at my grandson's house, and an old lady such as myself can't be out this late too many nights in a row!"

"Shannon, Bert said he'd be glad to drive you home," Marshall said.

"Aye, that would be much appreciated. Thank ye kindly, Bert."

"No problem. I'll just go and pull the car around to the front and meet you there," Bert offered.

"Auntie Shannon, it was so nice to see ye. It's been too long—but I'll be in touch, I promise." Tessy gave her aunt a big hug and held on for a few moments, rocking her slightly.

"Now, now, dear. We'll see one another again either in this life or the next," Aunt Shannon said as her kind, knowing eyes shone up at her.

Marshall helped her on with her coat. "Well, Shannon, it was certainly a pleasure meeting you, and thank you for all the entertaining stories. Some of them will come in handy on occasion, I'm sure," he said as he shot Tessy a wink.

"Ye just never mind, Dr. Tayse," Tessy nudged him.

"Aye, and thank ye. It was grand of ye to have me . . . and my, what a wonderful meal, Dotty. Now, ye promise to call me with the recipe for that casserole?"

"You bet, Shannon. I've got your number in the kitchen." Dotty smiled.

"Girls, it was wonderful to meet ye. Enjoy your young lives, the years go by quickly," she said as she waved to them.

"Great to meet you, too, Aunt Shannon," the girls echoed.

"Thank ye all, now, good night, good night," she said as Marshall took her arm and helped her out the door and down the stairs.

Tessy dabbed her tears with a hankie as she watched her favourite aunt disappear down the drive.

Monday morning arrived with as much welcome sunshine as the

previous day.

"Wow, you have great weather here!" Cherokee said between bites of her waffle.

"Not always, but I will agree it has been pretty nice this fall," Dotty said as she pulled off the next waffle.

"Good mornin' to ye all. Did ye have a fine night, girls?"

"Yep," Sarah nodded.

"So, what is it ye have in store for your last day, then?"

"Grandpa told us about this awesome corn maze just outside of the city. He just went to call and check to see if it's open today."

"And yes, it is," Marshall announced as he came around the corner.

"Awesome! I can't wait! How much fun is this going to be?" Sarah squealed, grabbing Cherokee's hand.

"Good morning, Tessy. Are you up to it?" Marshall affectionately gazed at Tessy.

"Am I up to it . . . huh! Just let me get a cup of coffee into me and maybe one of those sinfully delicious-looking waffles, and watch out. I'll take ye all on," she laughed.

The corn maze was another big hit, and everyone came home tired and very fulfilled.

Marshall was sitting on the edge of Tessy's bed watching her pack. "Tessy, I can't believe your visit's over already. Tomorrow you'll be gone, and I'm going to miss you all so much."

"Aye, the time did go by quickly, but we've had such a wonderful time. I want to thank you so much for all you've done and all the places you've shown us."

"Yes. I don't think we could have fit one more thing into these past few days. It's been pretty action packed."

"Aye, ye could say we've done Winnipeg-on-a-whirlwind!"

Travel Protection Pouch

Equal parts of juniper, fennel, Irish moss, rosemary, mint, coarse
   rock salt
1 pine cone
1 clear quartz crystal
Indigo-coloured pouch
White ribbon

Either purchase or make an indigo-coloured pouch, fill with the
ingredients above, and tie with white ribbon. Place in glove compartment
of vehicle.

French Canadian Popcorn Balls

6 quarts (6 L) freshly popped popcorn, in large, lightly buttered
   bowl or a bowl sprayed with vegetable cooking oil
1 1/2 cups (375 ml) sugar
1/2 cup (125 ml) water
1/4 cup (50 ml) corn syrup
3/4 cup (175 ml) pure maple syrup (not imitation)
1/4 tsp (1 ml) cream of tartar
8 Tbsp (120 ml) butter
1/2 tsp (2 ml) baking soda
1 1/2 cups (375 ml) pecans and/or sunflower seeds (optional)

Heat sugar, water, corn syrup, maple syrup, butter, and cream of tartar
in a heavy saucepan over medium heat to a hard boil (260°F [126°C]
on candy thermometer, if used). Remove from heat and *carefully* stir in
baking soda then pecans and sunflower seeds. Pour over popcorn and
toss to coat. Once cooled enough, using buttered or sprayed hands,
quickly form into 3-inch balls. Set aside to cool, then individually wrap
in cellophane or plastic wrap. Yield: approximately 28 balls.

21

Ghosts, Goblins, and . . . Gorillas?

Driving up her lane and seeing Ashling Manor patiently waiting for her was a welcome sight. Tessy was tired after the long drive, not to mention packing a week's sightseeing into a couple of days. She missed her familiar surroundings as well as her own comfy bed. She parked outside the front door and immediately went to the backyard to let Duke and Darby out of the kennel. With such a reunion, she was lucky to remain on her feet as they jumped and wagged themselves into a frenzy. After sufficient pats, tummy rubs, and hugs, they followed Tessy out to the car while she retrieved her bags and packages. When she opened the door, the inviting aroma of drying herbs was her first sensation, and a smile came to her lips. The next was the coolness, so she dropped her bags in the entryway, walked over to the thermostat, and cranked it up a few notches.

"There, now, that ought to blast the chill out of the autumn air. I'll be having to put a hot brick in my sheets tonight." Duke and Darby weren't even listening—after not being in the house for days, they were too busy sniffing about to see what they had missed.

Tessy went upstairs to unpack and to make sure one wee package in particular was securely tucked away until that inevitable time in the distant future. A promise is a promise.

The weather had turned, and mid-October was proving to be a bit more blustery than most. Tessy was sitting at her kitchen table with a cup of freshly brewed tea and going over her list for Halloween. As she breathed in the heavenly scent of her Autumn Herb Tea, she glanced over at Merlin and Cordelia curled up on their pillows nestled in their large basket.

"If it stays like this, you two will not be seeing the likes of outdoors until May," she said, shaking her head while watching the leaves swirl outside the window. "And, oh, the wee ones on Halloween. I just hope the snow holds off until after then."

Halloween—or Samhain, as Tessy knows it—is a very important

holiday for her. It is the final harvest of the season when nature is receding into the quiet of winter. It is a time to know that all things are possible; to remember and honour our departed loved ones and their gifts; to believe in enchantment, tell stories, and have fun. All the children and their parents are welcomed into her home that evening to enjoy the decorations and refreshments. Every year, she would try to outdo herself with silhouette depictions of witches, goblins, haunted houses, cats, and bats all throughout the house. To greet you, the lane is fluttering with ghosts, while scarecrows on the lawn reach out their long arms to grab at you; and the walkway, steps, and veranda are lined with dozens of gourds and carved and uncarved pumpkins. Inside, you will find beautiful crystal bowls filled with treats as well as punch bowls of fragrant fall ciders that sit among the candelabras, pumpkins, spiders, and cobwebs that adorn the long dining room table. In the middle of the table, the entire scene is complete as the black cauldron with steaming dry ice resides in its honoured spot.

The only thing that changes ever so slightly from year to year is Tessy's witch's costume. She is always the storytelling witch. Every year, she tells a scary story to the children at special intervals. The first story is at 7:00 p.m. for the small children, and is usually not very long or very scary at all. Then, at 8:00 p.m. the story becomes a little more spooky for the next age group. However, at 9:00 p.m. there is a terrifying story for the teenagers. It comes with sound effects and props that always delightfully frighten them!

In the weeks before Halloween, Tessy had the children over after school to help put up the ghosts, build the scarecrows, and carve pumpkins.

"Man, this is way more fun even than decorating for Christmas in July," Sarah laughed as she straightened one of the scarecrows Matt had just pounded into the ground.

"Yah, this is kinda cool. I didn't help out that much for the Christmas thing, but this is great," Matt agreed.

"Looks awesome, you guys," Cherokee called out from the veranda where she was helping Emma and Becky clean out pumpkins, as well as all the leaves from their hair after they had finished jumping in the piles scattered around the yard.

"Well, that was the last scarecrow to go up. What's next?" Matt asked.

Sarah pointed to a stack of sheets and said, "I think the ghosts can go up, now. The stepladder is just inside the garage door, so if you and

Brendon want to do that, I will help Cherokee and Jason carve pumpkins with the kids."

Just then, Tessy called everyone into the house for some snacks and hot chocolate. "My, ye children have done such a wonderful job. As I've said numerous times before, many hands make light work."

"Yah, but this is more like fun than work," Matt added.

"Well, I'm glad ye think so. I've almost finished the dining room. When you're done your hot chocolate, you'll have to come take a look and let me know what ye think."

The kids walked down the hall and stood looking into the dining room, which had been transformed into an amazing haunted cavern.

"Wow! This is so cool!" was the general consensus.

The last week was spent primping costumes, last-minute decorating, and fledgling excitement.

Tessy got her wish. Her favourite day of the year, October 31, was crisp but sunny, with just enough of a breeze to set the ghosts in motion and send the leaves dancing and tumbling down the lane. She couldn't have awakened feeling any happier or more blessed. She peered out her bedroom window as the sun was coming up in a beautiful shade of lemony orange, reminding her of all the pumpkins lying in wait for their time to shine. She quickly dressed and ran down the stairs, being careful not to disturb the cobwebs delicately entwined around the banister. When she reached the kitchen, she saw Merlin sitting on the windowsill among some small gourds and pumpkins, with his tail slowly twitching.

"Aye, don't ye look perfect sitting there with your black coat gleaming in the sun. It's your favourite time of the year as well, isn't it? Black cats and Halloween are like bees and nectar."

She spent the day filling bowls with treats and candy, wrapping French Canadian Popcorn Balls and preparing her famous fall ciders, one for the adults and one for the children. She was almost giddy by the time the kids stopped by on their way home from school to see if there was anything they could help with before they went home to change into their costumes. After a short visit, she sent them home with some candies and a popcorn ball each, along with some extra Halloween safety tips for later on.

In past years, children started arriving as early as five p.m., so at four o'clock, Tessy fixed herself an early supper. As Samhain is a time to remember, honour, and communicate with your departed loved ones, she arranged a full place setting for Dermot and served up some of her hearty root vegetable soup with a whole-grain bun and a glass of cider for each of them. She lit a white candle in remembrance and ate her meal in silence while fondly remembering cherished moments with Dermot. After she was done, she cleared the table, snuffed out the candle, and headed upstairs to get ready. She wanted to be in costume when the children arrived. This year, she had made her witch costume a little less traditional. The main part of the dress was made with long, black velvet back and sides with a front lace-up bodice. Underneath was two-tone, with black satin print down the front and sage green satin side insets. The long puffed sleeves were black chiffon gathered at the wrists with a slit down the arm. The pointy witch's hat was made of matching sage green satin with black chiffon netting and long, black feathers strategically placed. She laced up her black granny boots to finish the enchanting ensemble and reached for her special witch's hearth broom. She gazed into her full-length mirror at her bewitching image and smiled. *Not a person in the world would be afraid of this witch,* she thought as she ran her hands over the luxurious materials. She turned and went downstairs to light all the candles and make sure everything was perfect for her guests.

An hour and a half later, the house was full of ghosts, goblins, power-rangers, fairy princesses, and yes, even witches. She was waiting for Emma and Becky to arrive so she could sit the smaller children in the front room to tell them their story, when a very large gorilla appeared. She hadn't noticed a gorilla in the group earlier, and you would think that a gorilla might stand out. He kept nudging up to Tessy and cocking his head one way then the other. Tessy did her best to avoid him as much as possible, but he kept on getting right in her way and didn't seem to want to move. She was really starting to get annoyed with him when the girls finally showed up.

"Well, now, look at my two wee faeries. Aren't ye beautiful? Look at those wings, all sparkly and pretty."

"We're pixy fairies and we have pixy dust and everything. But Mommy said we can't sprinkle it inside — only outside," Emma reported.

"Oh, isn't that lovely. Well, come and sit, and I'll tell ye a wee story before ye get on your way trick-or-treating."

She arranged all the wee ones on the floor of the front room and, just as she was about to begin her story, she noticed the gorilla standing at the door. She flashed him a blazing glare that would have put the fear of death in any wild animal, and, without a word, he turned and swaggered down the hallway. Tessy began her children's story. After she was done, the children all followed her back to the dining room where she gave them each a bag of goodies and a popcorn ball before they left to continue on with their trick-or-treating. She was standing just inside the doorway watching the children go on their way when she felt breathing on her neck. She turned around, and there he was, that irritating baboon. Never in all the years of her hosting this celebration had she run across anyone so obnoxiously rude and annoying. It hadn't seemed like he had come with anyone in particular and he'd already been around for at least an hour. Well, that was it.

"Mr. Gorilla, may I have a word with ye in the kitchen, please?" Tessy hissed as she grabbed one of his fuzzy paws.

The gorilla silently followed her into the kitchen, and she closed the door.

"Mr. Gorilla, whoever ye are, you are most welcome to join in the celebrations but must ye be at my elbow the whole time? Now, when we go back out to the other guests, I expect ye to keep your distance and out from under my feet. Is that perfectly understood? Because if it's not, I'll be showin' ye the door!"

Gorilla sadly looked at Tessy and cocked his head from side to side.

Tessy instantly felt a pang of guilt, as if looking into the eyes of a real gorilla whose feelings she had just crushed.

"Well, now, that may have been a little harsh; but ye have got to leave me a little breathing room, if little else."

Gorilla nodded his head and patted Tessy on the shoulder, and they left the kitchen friends. However, that did not last. It was not long before Gorilla soon became his irritating self, and Tessy dragged him back into the kitchen. She threw up her arms. "Uncle! I give up," she huffed. "What is it that ye want?"

Gorilla turned his back to her and took off his mask. "You," he said. When he turned around, Tessy almost lost her balance.

"Marshall Tayse! What in the devil are ye doing here? Oh, I should have known it was you up to no good out there." She didn't know whether to swat him or fall into his arms.

"I'm sorry, Tess," Marshall laughed. "I missed you so much and I just couldn't resist when I heard about your party. But man, I didn't realize how easy it was to get your Irish dander up."

"Ye just never mind about my dander. I can't believe you would do such a thing. Just like a bratty teenager, ye are. I was about ready to take ye by the ear and toss you out on your behind!"

"Come here, you." Marshall reached out his hairy arms and pulled the lovely witch into them, telling her, "You look absolutely gorgeous," before giving her a most affectionate kiss.

"I should be madder than hops at you but I just can't. You are such a brat." She slapped him on the shoulder then hugged his neck. "I'm so glad you're here. How . . . why—" was all she got out before he kissed her again.

"Enough of that, now. I've got guests to attend to. Put that silly mask back on and join me."

For the rest of the evening, Gorilla didn't seem near as annoying.

It was getting close to nine p.m., and everyone had left, leaving Tessy and Marshall alone for a few minutes. Marshall took off his mask. "Boy, it gets pretty hot under there," he said as he wiped his face with a napkin.

"Would ye like a damp cloth and a drink of cider?" Tessy asked as she headed for the kitchen.

"That would be great!" Marshall followed her.

"Does anyone know you're here, Marshall?"

"Only Penny and Jim know. The kids have no idea."

"Oh my, that could really work to our advantage," Tessy smiled.

"What do you mean?"

"I know how good ye are at annoying people but how good are you at scaring them?"

Sarah, Cherokee, the boys, and some of their friends showed up for their nine o'clock story after dropping the little ones off at home from trick-or-treating. When they arrived, the house was especially dark and quiet, with just some eerie, creepy music playing. Tessy was nowhere to be seen.

As they slowly crept down the hallway toward the front room, Tessy suddenly appeared almost as if floating out from behind the door. She did not smile or greet them with her usual enthusiasm; instead she motioned with her hand for them to step into the darkened room, not taking her eyes off them.

This behaviour, being so uncharacteristic of the Tessy they had all come to know and love, was really starting to freak them out.

Still not saying a word, she again motioned them to be seated. The only light in the room came from candles and the low burning embers in the fireplace. Even with the fire, there was a chill in the room. All of a sudden, there was a creaking sound, and a door slammed at the top of the stairs. The kids jumped and grabbed at one another. Tessy did not take her eyes off them but stared deeper into each one of them.

"Shall we begin?" she asked with everyone well aware it was not really a question. "I shall tell the story of 'The Hook' this evening," she began, looking around the room.

"There was a Lover's Lane where all the young people would go to show their passion and affection, share their dreams and aspirations, and make plans for their futures. However, one summer evening, experiencing a future was deemed almost impossible for one couple. You see, a few miles away was an insane asylum where the most dangerous, deranged criminals resided. The most notorious was a young man they had named 'The Hook.' He had lost his hand when he was a child in a horrible act and, when he got older, he replaced it with a hook. This horrible act had left this man angry, scarred, and mean, which prompted him to a life of crime and murder. With his sick, demented mind, he performed these murders by mercilessly clawing at his victims with his hook, mostly vulnerable street people and ladies of the night. He was finally caught, sentenced, and locked in the insane asylum for the rest of his life. At least that is what was supposed to have happened."

Another door slammed shut upstairs and the sound of heavy footsteps could be heard. The front room filled with teenagers' screams. Tessy didn't even blink and continued on. "Well, just a few short years into his sentence, he escaped and it was said he lived in the forest close to Lover's Lane. The teenagers believed it was just a story made up by their parents to keep them away and out of trouble so they ignored the warnings and continued to go there.

"It was summer, and the young people did what young people do, went swimming, played summer sports, and, of course, drove out to Lover's Lane.

"One particularly warm evening, Lover's Lane was very busy with young people doing what young people do. A nice couple by the name of Sandy and Joe were sitting in Joe's car when they thought they heard something at the back of the car. Joe, who was the high school star quarterback, was not afraid of anything so he decided he would get out and take a look. It was very dark, and Sandy begged him not to go, but she couldn't stop him. He got out and slowly moved around to the back of the vehicle, but it was too dark to see anything. Just as he was getting back into the car, he felt something hook around his ankle."

All of a sudden, two more doors slammed and the sound of running water was heard coming from the kitchen. The kids screamed and covered their faces while clinging to one another.

"He frantically started screaming and tried to shake his leg free. He shook and he shook. Sandy was screaming, 'Get in! Get in!' He could see his pant leg turning red with blood. Joe finally broke free and jumped into the car. He managed to quickly lock the doors and started fumbling to get the keys into the ignition. The car started, and they roared off as fast as they could. When they pulled into the police station and got out of the car, Joe turned around to close the door and there it was . . . the bloody hook dangling from the bumper.

"Two questions remain . . . did The Hook get anyone else that night . . . and . . . where is he today?"

Suddenly, Gorilla jumped into the middle of the room and roared. The screams were heard all over the neighbourhood.

After everyone finally calmed down, they all laughed and clapped their hands.

"Wow, Tessy! That was awesome. I've never been so scared in my life. In fact, that is the best one I've heard you tell so far," Cherokee said, still holding her chest.

"Well, that's the only one I've heard her tell and I'm not sure I want to hear any more, especially if they get any worse — er — better . . . whatever . . . than that. I'm not going to be able to sleep for nights." Sarah shuddered.

Tessy started to laugh. "Oh, my dears, I'm sorry if it was a mite too gruesome."

"And who was your cohort in all this?" Sarah asked as she stared at the gorilla.

"Oh, I'd like ye all to meet a very close friend of mine — Mr. Gorilla."

Gorilla bowed and waved his hands to the small crowd.

"I think we should all go into the dining room and get some refreshments. Ye definitely all deserve some treats after surviving that little performance. And I want to have a good look at everyone's costumes," Tessy said as she led them out of the front room.

After all the kids had some appetizers and a glass of punch in their hands, Tessy got them to stand so she could view their outfits. "Now, let's see. I know what some of you are . . . there is a bumblebee, very cute, dear; a vampire . . . love the teeth — not easy to eat with, I'm sure; Matt, you are a pirate."

"Actually, Tessy, I'm not just any pirate. I'm Jack Sparrow," Matt boasted, throwing out his chest.

"My, quite a handsome fellow, for sure." Tessy smiled. "And then we have a gypsy; a flapper girl; a Flower Power hippie; and you are Cleopatra, Cherokee?"

"Good guess, Tess."

"Lovely, all of you girls. Good job. Now the rest of you boys I don't quite get. Some kind of a robot; someone with way too much makeup and you, well, I just don't know about you."

Matt spoke up for the rest of the guys. "Well, Tess, the robot is Iron Man; the makeup guy is the Joker from *Batman*; and this goof," he laughed and messed up Jason's hair, "is Austin Powers. It's no wonder you were having a hard time with him."

"Well, now, ye all look wonderful and ye did a fine job with your costumes."

"Okay, now it's our turn. We want to see who Mr. Gorilla is," Sarah laughed.

Gorilla shook his head and started to get up to run away. The kids ran around the table to block him into the dining room. He was caught and he had nowhere to go. He was looking at Tessy for support. Tessy just laughed and said. "Oh, no, Mr. Gorilla, you're on your own. The only vine I see here is the one you're dangling from. Serves ye right — you're just getting a little of what you've been dishing out. Looks good on ye." Tessy stood smiling with her arms crossed waiting for the inevitable and waiting for the reaction that would go with it.

After a few minutes of tag around the table, Gorilla finally gave up and slowly removed his mask.

"Grandpa!" Sarah gasped then leaped into her grandfather's arms while Matt and Cherokee stood with mouths gaping.

"Who is he?" asked the bewildered vampire.

"It's Sarah and Matt's grandfather, silly," answered Cherokee.

"Oh," was all he said then shrugged his shoulders, pulled out his fangs, and reached for another popcorn ball.

By eleven thirty p.m., all traces of human pirates, princesses, ghosts, goblins, and even gorillas had vanished, and Tessy was left to celebrate her favourite holiday in fine solitary tradition.

Earlier in the week, Tessy had set up a remembrance altar, covered in a black velvet cloth, with photographs and keepsakes of ancestors, close family, and friends who had passed over. Along with the keepsakes, there was a silver candle, a gold candle, and an orange candle; a goblet; and a seashell bowl filled with sage, patchouli, purple heather, and myrrh to cleanse and purify. And off to one side was a crystal bowl filled with pomegranates — the legendary food of the otherworld or Summerland. There were also four different coloured candles in the room to call in the elements: a green one in the north to call the spirits of earth; a yellow one in the east to call spirits of air; a red one in the south to call spirits of fire; and a blue one in the west to call spirits of water.

She lit the herbs in the shell bowl to cleanse and cast a circle by lighting the four element candles. She lit the green one, Earth, asking for protection and comfort from the flesh of the Mother. Next was the yellow, Air, asking to carry the words of the dead and to take her words to them. Then red, Fire, for purification, trials, and joys of life. Last was blue, Water, to bring peace.

She then spoke clearly and loudly. "I celebrate tonight for I know that death is a passage, not a state of being." She lit the silver candle to invoke the Goddess and said, "Lady, I ask that you join me, and may your love shine upon us in bounty and in loss." Then she lit the gold candle. "Lord, I ask that you join me, and, though gone for a time, your light will return to us." Then she lit the orange candle. "The light is now short, yet our harvest is plenty, and we wait for the light to rekindle another day." She poured some cider into the goblet, held it up to the altar displayed with all the beautiful memories, and made a toast:

Thank you all for cherished memories and love.
I celebrate and honour you as you watch from above.
I feel your presence and know you are close.
Protecting me, guiding me as if part of your post.
I am thankful for your wisdom and knowledge,
For you have proved to be my higher college.
On this special Eve when the veil is thin and weak,
I trust you will come to me; I will listen for you to speak.
Please continue to teach and protect me.

So mote it be.

She drank her cider; thanked the Lord and Lady for their
presence, bounty, and protection; snuffed out the silver,
gold, and orange candles, then the blue, red, yellow,
and green, thanking each element as she did. She then
took one of the pomegranates, cut it in half, and headed
outside. She picked out a spot in the garden, dug a small
hole, and buried it for any spirits that might be passing by
that night.

Tessy checked all the rooms to make sure every candle had been
put out and then headed off to bed to listen for any messages her dear
departed ones might have for her.

Autumn Herb Tea

1 part nettle
1 part fennel seeds
1 part dried cranberries
1/4 part cloves

Combine and steep for approximately 20 minutes.

Lice Eliminator Treatment

1/4 cup (50 ml) coconut oil
20 drops tea tree essential oil
10 drops rosemary essential oil
15 drops lemon essential oil
15 drops lavender essential oil

Caution: This formula is intended for children over six years of age.
 Always do a patch test on children or yourself. Rub a small amount on back of neck and leave for 12 hours. If no rash or itching develops, proceed with treatment.

Put all essential oils into a small container (such as a small jar). Melt the coconut oil in a bowl set in a larger bowl of hot water. Once it has melted, pour into essential oils, mix well, and cap. Rub mixture into dry hair and scalp, making sure you pull it down the full length of hair. Cover the head with a plastic shower cap then wrap in towel. After 1–2 hours, unwrap the head and shampoo well. Rinse with apple cider vinegar. You may have to repeat shampoo and rinse.

22

Six Weeks and Counting

Marshall remained in Ladyslipper for the next few days, occupying a great deal of a certain Irish lass's time and attention. As the departure day drew nearer, it was becoming more and more difficult for them to be apart. After their magical time in Winnipeg, it was very plain to see that they were meant to be together on a more permanent basis. Penny and Jim were ecstatic about Tessy and Marshall but they were also concerned about the geographical distance between them.

"I really do not see a solution to their living arrangements," Penny confided to Jim. "I can't see Tessy moving to Winnipeg and I don't know if Dad would ever move out here. Although, if he did, he could be with Tessy and he would have us here, too. Oh, I don't know, what do you think, Jim?"

"Well, I'm going to tell you exactly what Tessy tells her customers outright when they ask her about something that she feels is none of her business: 'It's not my journey.' And I am going to leave it at that. It's . . . not . . . OUR . . . journey, honey!"

"Oh . . . why are men so bad at this?" Penny huffed.

Jim just laughed, leaned over, kissed her cheek, and picked up his newspaper.

Those few days came and went, and so did Marshall. Before long, life was back to normal, and he and Tessy carried on with their long-distance romance. It was sadly settled that the next time they would see one another would be when Marshall came out for Christmas. It was going to be a very long six-and-a-half weeks.

Tessy busied herself by spending more and more time at the pharmacy, as she was becoming quite comfortable after all the positive responses she had been receiving. She was in the back aisle stocking some new essential oils that had just arrived when she heard Jim greeting Mrs. Chamberlain. Tessy stopped what she was doing to listen, though she did feel a little guilty doing so.

"How can we help you today, Mrs. Chamberlain?" Jim continued.

"Good day, Mr. Tucker. I am here to pick up my prescription."

"Yes, of course. It's ready. If you'd like to step to the back counter with me, I'll just be a moment."

As Mrs. Chamberlain was waiting at the counter, she noticed some baskets filled with crystals and gemstones alongside a stand of copper and hematite bracelets.

"Mr. Tucker, I am amazed that you would have these rocks in your store. I suppose that witch you have working for you is responsible for these," she huffed.

"Well, Mrs. Chamberlain, Tessy has neither confirmed nor denied being Wiccan, and her religion should not be of anyone's concern. What I do know and care about, however, is that she is an excellent herbalist. And these are healing crystals."

"Healing crystals! What on earth would you need those for?"

"Well, people value them for their healing abilities through their natural energy and vibrations."

"Pah, what nonsense! What energy can a rock have?"

"I realize they may not be for everyone, Mrs. Chamberlain, but I like to give my customers a choice."

Jim remained quiet while he finished up with her purchase then looked down at her wrist. "Mrs. Chamberlain, what a beautiful watch you have. Quartz, isn't it?"

"Well, thank you, yes. My husband bought it for me for our anniversary. It was quite — " she stopped, realizing what Jim was getting at. Glaring at him, she picked up her parcel. "Good day, Mr. Tucker," she snorted as she walked out.

"Have a nice day, Mrs. Chamberlain," Jim called after her. Jim couldn't help but smile as he heard Tessy softly titter in the next aisle.

The more information Tessy provided her customers, the greater her sales rose. Jim was beyond pleased. He was extremely impressed. They were in the office discussing the possible expansion of the Natural Healing section of the store.

"Well, with the winter season upon us, there will definitely be a need for more Eczema Salve and dermatitis products. And the schools always seem to have an infestation of head lice this time of year, with the children switching hats and what not, so I'd better order lots of the ingredients for my Lice Eliminator Treatment." Tessy chuckled. "I was wondering, also — I've had a good many ladies come and ask me for the recipe for my Yuletide Potpourri as gifts; so if we could order a little extra of those ingredients I think they would sell just fine."

"Tessy, you are the expert in this department so whatever you think will sell, by all means, go ahead and order," Jim confirmed with confidence.

"Thank ye for your kind support, Jim." Tessy blushed.

"Don't thank *me*; you're the one making this such a success. When I suggested this little venture, I had no idea it would grow into this. I am the one to be thanking you."

"Go on with ye, now," Tessy waved her hand then continued writing out her order.

On her way home from work, Tessy stopped by the post office to mail off her Christmas cards and parcels destined for Ireland. She wanted to make sure they arrived in plenty of time. Christmas always made her think of her faraway family and how they would be getting ready for the holidays there. She especially thought of and missed Keenan at this time of the year, and on their matching birthday.

Being early November in Saskatchewan, it was cold and dark by the time Tessy was walking up the shovelled pathway to Ashling Manor, and she pulled her favourite cable-knit outer shawl up around her neck to keep warm from the wind. When she got closer, she could see Sarah and Cherokee huddled under the winter throw she leaves on the bench on the veranda.

"Great leaping leprechauns! What on Mother's earth are ye two doing out here?" Tessy panted as she scurried up to them. "Come in, come in. You'll be half frozen."

"Hi, Tess. No, we're fine. We haven't been here very long," Sarah said as she threw the wrap off them and stamped the snow off her boots.

"Yah, we just wanted to come and talk to you about something before we go home for supper," Cherokee added, also stomping the snow from her boots.

"Of course. Come, come." Tessy unlocked the door and they all entered the foyer. "I'll put on a nice pot of Yuletime Tea, and ye girls come in and warm up."

The girls kicked off their boots then stripped away layers of coats, vests, hats, and scarves and hung them on the large hooks in the entryway. By the time they reached the kitchen, Tessy already had the kettle on and was spooning the fragrant spices into the teapot.

"Now, tell me, what is it ye girls were wanting to ask me?" Tessy asked as Cherokee set the cups out on the counter.

"We're in the middle of career studies at school, and, well . . . last summer you said something that has stuck with me and it keeps gnawing at me," Cherokee answered slowly with great thought.

"Well, now, I have always found that if the Divine's whisper turns into a roar, it's not to be ignored."

Cherokee scrunched up her face. "I think I know what that means," she said.

Just then, the kettle started whistling, and Tessy poured the water. She asked, "What is it that's got you thinking so hard, dear?"

"You said something like . . . that I could become an herbalist or naturopath or something. Do you really think that it's possible and do you think there would be any kind of future in it?"

"Of course it's possible. You can do anything you put your mind to. And a future, aye, I think there is going to be a great demand for more and more natural healing of all kinds. Ye can also check into areas like homeopathy, reflexology, acupuncture, massage, reiki. There's many different fields to choose from. Just look at what has happened in the wee town of Ladyslipper in the short time it's been available here."

"Well, that's kinda what we were thinking," Cherokee added.

"Sarah, then you're thinking of a career in the field, as well?"

"Yep. I think it's pretty cool. I was thinking of going into nursing anyway, so this would just be a different way of helping people. And Dad just can't believe what's happening with it at the store."

"There's more and more notable educational institutions offering what you're looking for now. In my day, they were few and far between. I did take some wonderful correspondence courses and received a good number of my certificates that way."

"Really? Isn't that a harder way to learn?" Sarah asked.

"No, especially not if it's a passion and ye love what you're learning. It is a pleasure. 'Knowledge is a treasure but practice is the key to opening it.' That comes from a scholar and statesman by the name of Ibn Khaldoun Al Muquddima, who lived in the 1300s."

"That's really cool. They said a lot of neat things back then."

"Aye, they did. What do your parents have to say about your idea?"

"Well, we thought we'd come and talk to you first. We both really want to try this but we weren't sure if it was even possible. Now that we know it is, we can't think of a reason why our parents wouldn't be fine with it. Thanks, Tessy. We feel so much better." Cherokee got up and hugged Tessy.

"Glad I could be of help but I really didn't do much." Tessy reached out and squeezed each of the girls' hands.

Sarah looked at Cherokee and gushed, "Guess we better go talk to our parents and then start checking into colleges!" They both started bouncing up and down in their chairs and clapping their hands.

"Oh, one more thing," said Sarah. "Tomorrow is Fabulous '50's Days, and we are having something called a sock-hop dance in the gym and we were wondering if we could borrow your 'Bobby' CDs? We promise we'll take really good care of them."

Tessy started to chuckle. "Of course ye can, dears. I believe they are still in the car, so just grab them on your way out."

The girls finished their tea, bundled up, and set off for home to talk to their parents. Tessy was left to her thoughts. "Oh, to be young and starting out fresh," she said to her pets as they all lined up waiting to be fed.

"Look at ye now, you'd think you were all starving. Come on, then, let's get your dishes, ye poor wee skeletons."

The next morning, Tessy stayed home to make product and fill some of her regular orders. She was scooping and measuring her Sore Muscle Soak into individual pouches when the doorbell chimed. She wiped her hands on a tea towel and threw it over the back of the kitchen chair as she ran past it and down the hall. She glanced through the lacy curtains to see Roger standing with a parcel in his hands.

"Good day to ye, Roger. A grand sunny one it is."

"Hi, Tess. Yep, couldn't ask for a better one at this time of the year."

"What have ye there?" Tessy asked as she motioned him into the foyer.

"Looks like a little something special from Winnipeg," Roger gleamed. "I just need your signature here and I'll leave it with you."

"Aye, Winnipeg, is it? And ye just never mind with your gloatin', there," she said as she glanced up at Roger while signing the register.

"Yes, ma'am," Roger smirked. "Well, better get my rear in gear and carry on. Have a great day, Tess. See you tomorrow."

"Thank ye, Roger. You have a fine day, as well," Tessy absently answered as she stared at the box and closed the door.

"Now, what have ye gone and done, Dr. Tayse?" she said out loud.

She walked into the library and set the parcel down on the desk. She slowly opened the top drawer and removed scissors while still staring at the box. Almost afraid to open it, she gingerly cut the string that tightly held the brown wrapping. She turned the parcel over and methodically started pulling at the tape. The plain wrapping fell away to expose a lovely, textured burgundy box. She lifted the lid, and there was a beautiful china horse and a note pressed into the lid of the box. She pulled out the note and unfolded it. Right away, she recognized Marshall's handwriting. It was more of a riddle than a note:

> In the six weeks to come you will find
> Little tokens to show you are on my mind.
> Each one has a purpose you'll see
> To bring you even closer to me.
> Now this fine horse is no grey mare
> For she belongs in a grand affair.

Tessy turned the note over looking for more. She was not sure what she was looking for, but it didn't make any sense to her, and she was hoping Marshall had sent some other clues or something. She carefully lifted the horse from its moulded container and examined it. It was exquisite and expensive, made from fine bone china. But a horse, why a horse? The only horses they had even seen together was when Danny Baker brought his team over for the hayride. Surely that can't be it, can it?

Tessy placed the horse on one of the bookshelves in the library. It was the perfect spot, and it seemed to fit in so naturally.

"Well, Dermot, my love, looks like I'm gonna have my hands full with this cheeky rogue you've picked for me. Don't be slipping off anywhere too far, because I have a feeling I'll be calling on you from time to time with this rascal."

She put the note back in the box and left it on the desk. She gathered up the brown wrapping, folded it up, and took it with her into the kitchen and threw it in the recycle bin.

She spent the next few days churning the riddle over and over in her mind, still not coming up with anything. Finally, she couldn't stand it another moment and picked up the phone.

Dotty answered the phone. "Dr. Tayse's residence."

"Dotty, love. Hi, it's Tess."

"Tessy, hi. How are you? We sure miss you around here."

"Aye, I miss you all as well. I see you're having some nasty weather. How are ye faring?"

"Oh, we're hunkered in for a day or two yet. It's supposed to break by Saturday."

"Good, good. Is the fine doctor about?"

"Yes. He's just helping Bert hang a new fixture. Hold on for a moment, I'll get him for you. 'Bye, Tess, take care."

"Aye, you, too, Dotty, and say hi to Bert for me."

Tessy waited patiently for Marshall to take the phone.

"Tessy, how nice to hear from you. What a surprise."

"Funny ye should be talking to me about surprises, Dr. Tayse."

"Oooh . . . 'Dr. Tayse.' Sounds like I'm in trouble of some sort."

"Aye, of some sort. If I may be so bold, why is it that you're sending me a horse and nothing but a riddle to go with it?"

Marshall heartily laughed. "Oh, it arrived, then."

"Aye . . . And . . .?"

"You'll find out soon enough, my fair lady, and I can't give you any more than that."

"You can't—or you won't?"

"Be patient, my love, and all will be revealed . . . eventually."

"Eventually? What am I going to do with ye, Marshall Tayse?"

"Oh, I have a few suggestions."

"None of that, ye cheeky rascal. I'll deal with you when I see you next. Well, if I'm not going to get any more information out of you, I'll let ye get back to your chores."

"Thanks for calling, Tess. Sorry I couldn't be more help," Marshall teased.

"Aye, I'm sure. Don't be falling off any ladders," Tessy teased back.

"'Bye, Tessy. Love you."

"Aye, I'm still fond of you, too, regardless of all your trickery. 'Bye, ye scalawag."

Marshall just laughed.

Tessy put the mystery out of her mind as best she could and continued on with her daily routine. She dropped by the pharmacy to check and see if her latest order had arrived. She was heading to the back when she noticed two young girls standing by the makeup. Thinking nothing of it, she acknowledged them with a smile and proceeded on. She was in the storage room for about ten minutes and when she came back out, those same girls hadn't moved. She nonchalantly watched them for a few moments and saw one of them slip a lip gloss into her pocket. Tessy slowly made her way over to them. "How are you young ladies today?" she gaily asked.

"Fine," the girls chimed, nervously looking at one another.

"Good. Ye know, when I was a young lass over in Ireland a clever shopkeeper shared some wonderful wisdom with me: 'Karma sees everything yet forgets nothing.' I always remembered that wee quote and maybe it would be wise for you girls to do the same," and she walked away.

A few minutes later, Tessy hid her grin when she saw the girls doing the right thing at the checkout counter.

Eczema Salve

3/4 cup (175 ml) coconut oil
1/4 cup (50 ml) olive oil
1/4 cup (50 ml) beeswax
1/4 cup (50 ml) oats, finely ground to powder/flour consistency
8 drops calendula essential oil
8 drops lavender essential oil
8 drops rosemary essential oil
8 drops chamomile essential oil

In a double boiler or a glass bowl set over a saucepan of water over medium heat, combine the coconut oil, olive oil, and beeswax and melt. Stir in ground oats and remove from heat. Add the remaining ingredients and whisk. Pour into containers, let cool, and cap.

Yuletide Potpourri

2 cups (500 ml) rose hips
1 cup (250 ml) whole cloves
1 cup (250 ml) star anise
1 cup (250 ml) pine cones (each cone about an inch in length)
1 cup (250 ml) cinnamon sticks (2-inch lengths)
1 cup (250 ml) curly pods
1 cup (250 ml) juniper berries
1/2 cup (125 ml) whole allspice
2 drops bayberry fragrance oil

Combine all ingredients in a large zip-lock bag or airtight container and let blend for 1 week, remembering to gently shake daily. Open after 1 week and see if it needs more drops of bayberry or is lacking in any other scent. Add if necessary. Place in decorative bag or container and add small Christmas baubles or ornaments for gift giving.

23

Christmas Riddles and Sound Advice

Tessy had been out Christmas shopping and was unloading parcels out of the back seat of her car when Roger came whistling up the walk carrying another package.

"Hi, Tessy. Can I help you with some of your load, there?" Roger asked as he stood beside her car.

"Roger, hello there! Aye, that would be grand." She handed him two shopping bags while she gathered up the rest.

"I have a stack of Christmas cards here for you, Tessy, along with another parcel from Winnipeg. It's nice to see that Dr. Tayse knows how to treat a special lady."

"Now, go on with ye! I'll have ye know, he's actually just being a brat."

Tessy opened the door, and they put all the bags down while she signed the register. "And I can see that you're laughing behind those twinkling eyes. You men are all in cahoots." Tessy smirked at Roger.

"I have no idea what you mean, Ms. McGuigan."

"Aye, I'm sure. Now be off with ye. Thanks for helping me with my bags."

"No problem. See you tomorrow." Roger waved as he headed down the walk.

Tessy set the parcel down on the table in the entryway while she carted all her shopping bags into the kitchen. She put a few things away before she returned and retrieved it. Again, she took Marshall's gift into the library and placed it on the desk. The other box was still where she had left it. She took out the scissors and repeated the process as before. She pulled the wrapping off another pretty box and opened the lid. She started to laugh. In it was a bright pink piggy bank with a soft, blue cloth bow tied around its neck. In the lid was the riddle to go with it.

Here's the next surprise it's number two
a special little gift just for you.
It will keep you guessing and amused
with each one chase away your blues.
As you can see it's a piggy bank at play
So you can save for that rainy day.

This riddle made no more sense than the last; first a horse, and now a pig. Obviously, she was to start saving for something, but what? He really was a cute little guy, though, made of lovely ceramic and hand painted and with a very playful demeanour. Tessy decided this little fellow needed to sit on the corner shelf in the kitchen just above the sink where she could look at him and smile. She would also remember to put a little something in him every day. "What next?" she giggled. She was actually beginning to look forward to more of this odd puzzle but she was wondering if and when it would start making sense.

Christmas or Yule in December was quite different than Christmas in July. Christmas in July is always a little over the top, as it is forced and quite out of season. Tessy believes that Yule in December waves a magic wand over Ladyslipper. It approaches softly and arrives as it should with carollers, skating and toboggan parties, bell-ringing Santas, and plenty of goodwill. She was out on the veranda swagging a garland and placing large red bows while waiting for Sarah and Cherokee to arrive. They were coming over to wrap some of their Christmas presents and hide them at Tessy's. She was about half finished when they showed up.

"Hey, Tessy. That looks beautiful," Cherokee called out.

"Hi, me dears. Thank ye."

"Would you like some help finishing up?" offered Sarah.

"That would be grand. Then we can go in for some hot chocolate."

The girls carried on with the garland and bows while Tessy threw a black and red wool blanket over the willow chair by the front door, arranging some sprigs of cedar and holly with a few red berries, willow sticks, and bows into a basket beside it. Then she placed a very large, festive wreath to match on the front door. Before long, the veranda looked like a period Currier and Ives Christmas card scene.

"Wow, Tessy! This looks so beautiful," Sarah said as she stood back in amazement.

"Aye, it does look inviting. Thanks for your help, girls. Now, let's go in and get warmed up."

Just as they were about to head in, Roger came up the walk.

"Wow, Tess! Looks great. Nice job," Roger said as he stood back and admired the sight.

"Thank ye, Roger. We're about to go in and have a cup of hot chocolate — would ye have a minute to join us?"

"Oh, thanks, Tess. That sounds great, but I'm afraid at this time of the year I'm going full tilt. Maybe some other time. Got another package from Winnipeg for you. Pretty small this time, but you know what they say — nice things come in small packages!"

Tessy was a little flustered, as she hadn't mentioned anything to anyone about the mysterious riddled deliveries. She remained silent as she took the register and signed it.

"Well, better get going. See you tomorrow, Tess."

"See ya, Roger." The three ladies chimed.

"Another package from Winnipeg? What's up, Tessy? Is it from Grandpa?"

"Aye, come on in, and I'll bring you up to speed on this wee adventure."

"Adventure . . . ooooh . . . sounds intriguing. What's Grandpa up to now?"

"Aye, my question exactly."

"What? What?" Sarah asked.

"Well, come in, and we'll get the kettle going, and I'll tell ye."

Tessy explained about the parcels showing up every week, read them the riddles, and showed them the horse and the piggy bank; but they were no help whatsoever in suggesting any useful clues.

"Well, open this one and see if it helps us out at all," was Cherokee's suggestion.

"Guess it can't hurt. Here we go." Tessy picked up the bubble-wrapped envelope and shook it. Nothing. She turned it over and pulled it open. There was a tiny box; she lifted the lid, and, of all things, there was a pack of chewing gum . . .? They all laughed.

"What?" blurted Sarah, shaking her head in disbelief.

Tessy took out the riddle and read it to them.

This little gift may seem a little strange

you might even think I may be deranged
But don't give up and you will see
these all connect as handy as can be
This pack of gum don't use for glue
just close your eyes and really chew.

"What?" Sarah repeated a little louder. "No kidding, it's a little strange, Grandpa. Tessy, do you think he'll talk to me?"

"No. Not a chance in all of Ireland. I've gone down that wee path and it didn't take me anywhere."

"Man, your grandpa's pretty impressive. What a romantic," Cherokee snickered.

"Romantic, my foot! The man's an impossible brat. Keeping a girl in such a flap for weeks!"

"Ahhh, Tessy. I think it's so sweet," said Cherokee.

"Really, do ye, now? Well, I suppose the man does have a kind heart and a playful way of showing it. I guess there's nothing wrong with a bit of the inner child poking through." Tessy couldn't help but grin and blush just a little.

"Well, I guess we'll have to play it out and see what the end result will be. Now I really can't wait for Grandpa to get here for Christmas!" Sarah exclaimed.

"Aye, that makes two of us."

As the weeks went on, so, too, did the parcels. Just like clockwork they arrived, and, just as before, each one was as baffling as the next. Tessy was quite relieved to have a couple of allies in this adventure, but they, too, remained stumped. The next one was also a fairly light, small package. Tessy opened it with the girls hovering over her. A sleeping mask for over the eyes? And, as usual, the riddle was of no real help.

We're into week four not long to go
Though I do feel the time goes slow
Looking forward to seeing you soon
I see your face in every moon
It's okay to wear this mask and sleep
For I will be there to share your dreams so deep.

"Nope. Not a clue," was all Sarah could come up with.

"Me either. Sorry, Tess." Cherokee shrugged.

"Aye, what a frustrating man. And every time I talk to him on the phone he just gets as smug as a crafty fox. He's going to have to do some pretty fancy talking when he gets here to smooth this lass's feathers," Tessy huffed as she marched off to the kitchen.

"Looks like Grandpa's in pretty hot water. I sure hope I get a chance to give him a heads-up before Tessy gets ahold of him," Sarah playfully whispered to Cherokee.

"Well, he's going to have to learn sooner or later . . . she IS Irish," Cherokee giggled.

Tessy kept busy with regular orders plus making up containers filled with thoughtful homemade recipes, remedies, potpourris, and delicious goodies to be delivered and shared with her friends and neighbours. She always celebrated with a real tree and, as it was still early December, she hadn't gone to pick one out yet. She insisted that it come only from a renewable source so she always got hers from Danny Baker's Christmas tree farm. Danny and his wife, Betty, had a few acres set aside for a local Christmas tree farm where people were welcome to come and scout out their own Christmas tree. They could then either cut it down themselves, or, for a small fee, Danny would do it for them. Then, in January, Danny would drive around Ladyslipper picking up the trees, take them back to his farm, and chip them up for mulch to be sold in the spring. It had turned out to be quite a profitable little business. It was like selling the trees twice and not wasting a thing.

Tessy was delivering the Bakers' gift basket and decided she would pick out her tree today, even though she was not ready for it to be cut yet. Danny allowed "special" customers to come in and tag a tree with a SOLD ticket, and Tessy was one of those people.

"Good day, Danny boy," Tessy greeted as she met Danny in the driveway.

"Tessy, wonderful to see you. Come on in. Betty just called me in for a cup of tea. She'll be so glad to see you."

Tessy was warmly greeted with smiles and hugs as she presented her festive basket. Betty opened it up to find the Soothing Herbal Bath Salts and oil mix that she especially loved; and then there was a jar of Herb Jelly and the Spicy Herbed Cheese Ball that Danny could never get enough of. And, of course, there were the gingerbread cookies that Tessy included in all her baskets.

After they had had their tea and some fresh biscuits, Tessy and Danny headed out to pick a tree.

When they had found and tagged the perfect specimen, they headed back to Tessy's car. Betty stood on the step and called out to Tessy, "We're looking forward to your annual get-together. We'll see you then. Thanks again for the lovely basket!"

"You're more than welcome. Looking forward to seeing you, as well. 'Bye for now, Betty dear."

As Danny was holding the car door open for Tessy, she added, "Oh, that reminds me, are ye able to have the team harnessed up to the sleigh that evenin' for a while?"

"You bet. Wouldn't miss an opportunity to show off my girls and take people for a ride. They love it as much as I do!"

"Hopefully, it will be a fair night and with no biting winds."

"Well, even if it is a chilly night, we'll just wrap quilts around everyone and bundle up."

"Aye, thank ye kindly, Danny. See ye soon."

It was beginning to look like Christmas everywhere. The storefronts were all decorated inside and out. The windows were sprayed with artificial snow, and rolls of cotton batting were laid out covered with toys and unique gift ideas. Store hours had been extended in Ladyslipper, and it was becoming very busy, so Tessy spent the next couple of days working at the pharmacy. People were extraordinarily pleasant and seemed full of good cheer . . . well . . . with maybe the exception of Mrs. Chamberlain.

Tessy was up on a ladder in the front window hanging beautiful crystals of all shapes and sizes when Mrs. Chamberlain entered with her usual demanding presence.

"Oh. You," she huffed as she glanced up at Tessy.

"Good day, Mrs. Chamberlain. How can we help ye today?" Tessy cheerfully greeted her.

"Well, YOU can't help me with anything. Where's Mr. Tucker?"

Tessy slowly descended the ladder. "Well, I'm afraid Mr. Tucker stepped out for a few minutes, so it looks like I'm it. So . . . if ye'll tell me what it is you're looking for maybe I can help."

"I don't need any of your rituals or spells or hocus-pocus. So I'll just wait. Thank you very much."

"Whatever you wish, Mrs. Chamberlain," Tessy said as pleasantly as she could through gritted teeth. "Mrs. Chamberlain, have ye ever enjoyed a birthday cake?" Tessy innocently inquired.

"Of course I have. What has that got to do with anything?" she snorted.

"Well, believe it or not, that is a ritual. Think for a moment, someone makes you a special cake. Decorates it. Puts candles on it. Lights those candles. Then tells you to make a wish. Blow out the candles but don't tell anyone what that wish is or it won't come true. Is that not a ritual of some sort?"

"This is preposterous. Tell Mr. Tucker I'm at the back of the store when he gets in."

"Certainly, Mrs. Chamberlain." Tessy smirked as she climbed back up the ladder.

A couple of days later, Tessy was at home during the day, as she had offered to work the evening shift. She was standing in the foyer; Roger had just dropped off yet another parcel from Marshall. This one was in a large puff envelope. Tessy carried it to the kitchen table, carefully cut the end off, and dumped out the contents, which looked like a CD with the riddle wrapped around it and secured with a rubber band. She snapped off the rubber band, opened it, and read:

> Not sure if you've guessed where this is going
> I want to keep it a surprise, it's not for showing
> Not long now and I'll be on my way
> Then in the snow we will frolic and play
> I hope the songs on this CD you'll like
> You can listen to them whether you rest or hike.

She walked into the front room and inserted the CD into the player. She was hoping whatever was on it might reveal a further clue—but no. As she listened, it was just a wonderful selection of the tunes they had danced to in Winnipeg. She drifted back to that magical night and realized just how much Marshall meant to her and how much she longed for him. This was becoming increasingly unbearable. What was going to happen? How is this going to continue to work? She hit the stop button and sat down on the edge of the couch and put her head in her hands.

Close to tears, she sat in silence, rolling everything over and over in her head. Then she plainly heard a whisper. "It's going to be okay. Everything is going to work out, my pet. Believe and have faith."

Tessy sprang up. "Dermot. Dermot. Are ye there?" She knew it had to be him. Dermot was the only person in the world that ever called her "pet."

She stood there slowly and deeply breathing in and out, drinking in his presence and feeling herself filled with his unwavering strength.

"Oh, Dermot. You and your Christmas miracles. All right, I'll be patient and, as Sarah says, 'Wait it out.' Thank ye, Love, for staying close and calming my fears."

Simple Shepherd's Pie

3–4 cups (750 ml–1 L) cooked potatoes (mashed leftovers)
2 lbs (1 kg) ground beef
1 large onion, chopped
2 cups (500 ml) frozen mixed vegetables (or leftovers)
2 Tbsp (30 ml) butter
3/4 cup (175 ml) beef broth
1 Tbsp (15 ml) Worcestershire sauce
1 tsp (5 ml) thyme
1/2 tsp (2 ml) basil
1/2 tsp (2 ml) marjoram
Salt and pepper to taste

In a large frying pan, sauté onions in butter until tender. Add ground beef and cook thoroughly. Add frozen vegetables, beef broth, Worcestershire sauce, salt, pepper, and herbs. Cook for approximately 15 minutes.

Pour mixture into a casserole dish, cover with mashed potatoes, and bake at 375°F (180°C) for 45 minutes or until bubbling and brown. Broil for the last few minutes to brown, if necessary. Serves 6.

Yuletime Tea

1 tsp (5 ml) raspberry leaves
1 cinnamon stick
5 whole cloves
2 cardamom seeds, slightly crushed
1/4 tsp (1 ml) ground nutmeg

Place in cup, pour boiling water over and let steep for 15 minutes. Single serving.

24

Final Riddle ... Yet No Clue

Christmas was just a little more than a week away, but even more exciting was that Grandpa was arriving in just four days, and the evening he gets here is Tessy's Yuletide gathering. This event is for adults only, which makes it a much smaller and a more intimate affair than her Christmas in July. She does have a children's get-together a day or so earlier with hot chocolate, snacks, and, of course, gingerbread cookies. The kids did come to help out but didn't have near as many duties as in summer. Emma and Becky helped string popcorn and cranberries again and spent a morning decorating gingerbread men, tasting a great many to make sure they were delicious enough to share.

Sarah and Cherokee were on their way over one afternoon to help finish the tree and gather up their presents to take home. "I can't believe Christmas is here already. Grandpa will be arriving in just a few days."

"And then, hopefully, we can find out about those riddles and what the heck is going on," Cherokee added.

"Well, we won't be the only ones really happy to have that solved—although Tessy does seem to be in great spirits lately and taking everything in stride."

The girls were almost at Tessy's when they saw Roger coming toward them.

"Hey, Roger," Sarah called out as he approached.

"Hey, girls."

"Are you just coming from Tessy's?" asked Cherokee.

"Yep. Just finishing up my run," Roger chirped.

"Have a nice evening, Roger. See ya," Cherokee said as they passed.

"The last time I talked to Tessy she hadn't received the last gift and riddle yet. Maybe today?"

Sure enough, they got there just in time to witness Tessy ceremoniously opening the final clue. She removed the brown paper wrapping to find another lovely textured box. She opened it and discovered a breathtaking, ornate leather-bound journal with a beautiful pen nestled next to it.

Tessy read aloud:

> One week from now I'll be in your arms
> Enjoying your laughter and all your charms
> This Christmas will be one of joy
> I will use every trick and every ploy
> To watch you pen in this journal your dreams,
> Your thoughts and all of your Irish schemes.

"Wow, Tess! What a gorgeous journal," Cherokee softly murmured.

"Isn't it lovely, girls?" Tessy picked it up and stroked the soft cover. Then she picked up the flawlessly balanced pen and studied it. "My, your grandfather is definitely a man of impeccable taste."

"Well, he picked you, didn't he?" Sarah said, looking at her most earnestly.

Tessy lovingly smiled at her, placed an arm around her, and pulled her close. "I am truly a blessed woman. It certainly won't be a difficult task sharing my thoughts with such an alluring journal. It's calling to me this very moment." As she untethered the leather lace that fastened it, the journal fell open, and she touched the fine, linen pages of antique cream. She drifted into a mild trance. Weeks ago, she had envisioned herself surrounded by a soft glow, sitting at a desk and writing in this exact journal with this exact pen. She shouldn't have been surprised — she had had many other past premonitions come to fruition, but this one was so surreal.

"Tessy, are you all right?" Sarah softly touched her shoulder.

"Oh! Aye, dear, I am. Sorry, just off in the land of foggy dreams. Let's trot to the kitchen and pour us some Yule Nog to sip on while we finish the tree."

Tessy's tree sat cradled in the bay window of her front room. Her ceilings were ten feet high, which afforded her the room for a large tree. However, one of the problems she faced every year was reaching the top. She had always managed to get the star up there and add a few decorations to finish it off, but it usually looked a little sparse. This year, with their collaborative efforts, the three of them produced a magnificent specimen. It was late in the day when they finished, and the room was quite dim. Cherokee squeezed in behind the tree and plugged in the hundreds of tree lights.

"Wow!" Sarah was dazzled.

Cherokee reappeared, and the three of them stood in awe of that magical moment one experiences when gazing at a beautifully decorated tree, lights blazing.

"It's a splendid sight, to be sure. Thank you, girls, for helping me finish. I'm sure Santa will be leaving each of ye an extra wee gift under it."

"Well, you tell Santa, thanks but that's not necessary." Cherokee put her arm around Tessy.

The girls had more gifts to carry home than they realized, so Tessy helped stack them into boxes and then drove the girls home. When she got back, the Christmas tree was brightly glowing in the window and it did look lovely. She stood out on the veranda admiring it for a few moments, feeling its inviting warmth. "I am the happiest, most blessed woman on the face of this Mother's green earth. Thank ye, Lord."

Tessy was about to go into the house when she thought she heard someone calling out. She stood very still and strained to listen into the crisp winter air. There. There it was again.

"Help! Please, someone help me!"

It was coming from down the lane and just past her hedge. She grabbed a flashlight and ran down to where the cries were coming from. She was pointing the flashlight in all directions when she saw a dark figure slightly moving in the snow. She ran over to it. "Blessed be, Mrs. Chamberlain. Are you all right?"

"Of course I'm not all right," the woman hissed. "I've been lying here in the cold and snow for half an hour."

"What have ye done? What seems to be the problem?" asked the concerned Tessy, as she took her cable-knit shawl off and wrapped it around the shivering Mrs. Chamberlain.

"I slipped on some ice and twisted my ankle and I can't seem to put any weight on it," she groaned.

"I'll run up and get my sleigh and we can get you back to the house and see just how bad your injuries are. Wait here — I'll be right back," Tessy ordered.

"Like I'm going anywhere!" was Mrs. Chamberlain's curt response.

A couple of minutes later, Tessy had Mrs. Chamberlain loaded up on the sleigh and they headed up to the house. Luckily, Ashling Manor had a ramp just off to one side of the house, which enabled Tessy to pull the sleigh right up to the door. Tessy helped Mrs. Chamberlain up on her good foot and supported her as she hopped into the front foyer.

Once inside, Tessy had her sit on the bench while she bundled her up in a comforter. She asked if she could perform some reiki before trying to remove her boot.

"I've told you before—I want nothing to do with your spells."

"Mrs. Chamberlain, reiki is not any kind of spell. It will help with the pain."

"Oh, do what you have to. Just get this boot off my foot," Mrs. Chamberlain howled.

Tessy realized that once the boot was off the swelling would probably become worse; but if she didn't get it off now, they would have to cut it off later. After much whooping, wailing and grumbling, the boot was off, and Tessy was able to take a good look at the damage. She was still unable to determine whether it was a bad sprain or a break so decided a trip to Emergency for X-rays was necessary. She dabbed a little lavender essential oil on a hanky and handed it to Mrs. Chamberlain.

"What's that for? Mrs. Chamberlain demanded.

"It's for mild shock. Just put it under your nose and breathe deep. I'll go and get the car and bring it around. Stay here and don't move until I get back."

When they arrived at Emergency, Tessy parked the car and ran in to get a wheelchair. Once inside, Mrs. Chamberlain asked Tessy if she would call her husband and let him know where she was. Only after all the paperwork was done and Donald Chamberlain had arrived to comfort his wife, did Tessy think it was time for her to return home.

She was hanging her coat on the hook when the phone rang. She scurried down the hall in time to pick it up on the third ring.

"Hello, good evenin'," she puffed.

"Good evening, my sweet lady," Marshall sighed into the receiver.

"Marshall. How nice to hear your voice," Tessy sighed in return.

"You, too, my love. What have you been up to? You sound bushed."

"Well, do I have a wee story for you!" and Tessy proceeded to explain in detail the evening's gripping events.

"Wonders will never cease," was Marshall's reply.

Getting back to a more enjoyable topic, Tessy piped, "I received your last gift today. It is absolutely lovely. Thank ye so much. Although it didn't give me any more of a clue than the rest."

Marshall laughed. "Well, I'm glad you like it. Soon, my dear, soon."

"Aye, and it's a good thing, because I'm not sure how much more anticipation I can stand."

"That's why I am calling. I have decided to leave a day early."

"Oh, what a wonderful surprise, and I'm glad you've decided to share it with me. So ye won't be making an illusive entrance as at Halloween, then?"

"No. I've retired my gorilla suit for now. Don't want to scare Santa."

"With the kind of misbehaving you've been up to lately, do you think Santa will even be visiting you this year?"

"I'm crushed you would even ask such a thing."

"Aye, are ye, now? Well, there could be a lump or two of coal under the tree when you get here."

"There now, I feel warmer already."

"We'll be discussing this a wee bit further when you get here."

"Yes, we will. In fact, you can bet every penny you've got in that new piggy bank on it."

"Marshall, with all the blarney aside, I am so looking forward to having you here close by. I've been missing you terribly."

"I miss you, too, my love. I will be there as quickly as I can."

"Well, don't be coming too quickly; I want ye here in one piece. Please promise you'll drive extra careful on those icy roads."

"I promise. It's supposed to be sunny for the next few days, so they should be fine. I'll see you soon. I love you."

"Aye. And Marshall, I love you, too. Good night."

She immediately hung up the phone. That was the first time she had actually said it . . . I love you . . . out loud . . . to him . . . and she wasn't sure how to deal with it. How did she get so lucky, so blessed? Some people go through their whole lives without finding even one special person to love and be loved by, and here she was, blessed with two wonderful men in her life. Feeling grateful and completely humbled, Tessy headed for the library. She needed to feel close to Dermot and express her gratitude to the Divine. She lit some candles and quietly sat in prayer and meditation, even though she already knew everything would work out as it should. She wasn't sure how long she had been meditating but when she opened her eyes she felt an overwhelming sense of peace and happiness. She drew in a long breath, got up, blew out the candles, and left. As she closed the doors, she turned, smiled, and whispered, "Good night, Dermot."

Peppermint Hot Chocolate

4 cups (1 L) milk
2/3 cup (150 ml) cocoa
1/3 cup (75 ml) sugar
1/4 tsp (1 ml) peppermint extract
Whipped cream or miniature marshmallows (optional)
Candy canes (optional)

Heat 1 cup (250 ml) milk with the cocoa and sugar in a saucepan over medium heat and whisk until well mixed and just comes to a boil. Whisk in remaining milk and heat thoroughly. Remove from heat and stir in peppermint extract. Pour into decorative cups, top with whipped cream, and garnish with a candy cane stirring stick.

Olde English Wassail

1 tsp (5 ml) freshly grated ginger
4 cinnamon sticks
4 coarsely ground cardamom seeds
1/4 cup (50 ml) sugar
1/8 tsp (0.5 ml) coarsely ground pepper
4 cups (1 L) red wine
1/2 cup (125 ml) brandy
Oranges and lemons, thinly sliced

Combine all spices and sugar in a large saucepan and pour in the wine and brandy. Bring to a boil and simmer, tightly covered, for 7–10 minutes. Remove from heat and strain out the spices. Serve in large wine goblets and garnish with a fruit slice. Refrigerate leftover wassail.

25

A Frosty Start

Tessy stomped the snow from her boots as she entered the back kitchen and dug in her pocket for a hankie to dab her nose. It was a chilly morning, and she had been outside for some time shovelling the walks, filling bird feeders then gathering twigs, pine cones, and spruce bows to make her centrepiece for the dining room table. As she stripped off her hat, scarf, and mitts, she glanced up at the reflection in the mirror and noticed her rosy cheeks and she quickly rubbed them.

"Aye, I think a nice hot cup of tea will warm me down to my toes."

She put on the kettle and set the bows and twigs on the kitchen table alongside some holly she had purchased. She also had found a clean block of birch wood to use as the base, into which she had drilled some holes. Some of the holes were big enough for candles, and some smaller ones would hold the branches. She went to the hall closet and pulled out a plastic bin full of festive ribbons and baubles and other pretty things. She rummaged around in the closet until she found her glue gun, placed it in the bin, and returned to the kitchen. The kettle was already whistling before she could spoon the tea into her cup. She was just doing so when the doorbell rang. She opened the door to find a delivery person standing behind a beautiful Christmas arrangement, which he handed to her and wished her a very Merry Christmas. Tessy quickly reached into her pocket and pulled out a five-dollar bill. "Thank you. Here, please take this — it's not much but it's all I have on hand right at the moment. Merry Christmas." She closed the door and took the arrangement into the living room, untied the plastic, reached for the card, and in lovely handwriting it said, "Thank you for your kindness — Margaret Chamberlain."

"Well, as I live and breathe. Bless her heart!" Tessy was stunned.

As Tessy fussed and primped over her homemade centrepiece, she tried to keep down her level of excitement, knowing Marshall was on his way and would be in Ladyslipper some time that evening. She felt having said she loved him put a whole new spin on their relationship — which they would have to discuss and maybe even do something about. But what? Well, she would just have to trust the Divine, that's all there was to it . . . there was nothing else to do. Right? *Oh, stop second-guessing yourself, the good Lord has never let ye down yet and is not about to now. What was it Dermot said not long ago? "Believe and have faith." Aye.*

The day went by more quickly than Tessy had expected. She had just put a Simple Shepherd's Pie in the oven when the doorbell rang. Wiping her hands on her apron, she headed toward the foyer, opened the door, and there he stood, as tall and even more handsome than she remembered. "Marshall! What on earth are you doing here?"

"Now, what kind of a welcome is that?" Marshall smiled down at her gathering her up in his arms and kissing her before she could answer.

"I-I-I wasn't sure I'd be seeing you at all this evening. I thought you would just be stopping off at the kids' and I'd be seeing you tomorrow," Tessy stammered, still in shock and deep in Marshall's arms.

"I wasn't about to drive right past the house of the woman I love and not even stop in to say hi." Marshall leaned over and gave her another gentle kiss.

"Please, come in, come in. Have ye got time for a drink and a wee visit?" Tessy ushered him in, holding his hand.

"That sounds wonderful, but I will give the kids a call, if you don't mind, so they won't worry."

"No, not at all. Ye know where the phone is — help yourself. Would ye like tea, a beer, a glass of wine, something stronger? What can I get ye?"

"Well, definitely not tea. Do you have any red wine?"

"Aye, if ye remember correctly, I think you brought enough bottles over last summer for me to start my own winery. I'm pretty sure I'll be able to hunt down one for us!"

Before long, they were snuggled close, enjoying a fire, fine wine, and each other's company while basking in the light of the beautifully lit Christmas tree.

"Oh, Tessy, this is going to be the best Christmas I've had in a very long time — maybe ever."

"Aye. It's surely going to be a special time; but I know you had to have had other wonderful Christmases with Evelyne and when the kids were wee."

"Of course. But back then, I seemed to just get caught up in my day-to-day life as it continued on without thinking about how time was slipping away. Now, I cherish every minute, especially when I'm with you and I realize that it's not going to last forever . . . so let's enjoy it to the fullest while we can."

"Aye, I suppose that's all we can do." Tessy wasn't quite sure what to think about his last comment and she straightened up.

Just then, the timer went off on the oven, so Marshall didn't notice Tessy's sudden distanced attitude as she got up and headed for the kitchen.

"Boy, that smells terrific. What is it?" Marshall sniffed into the air as he followed her.

"Just a wee shepherd's pie. There's enough for two, if you would like to stay."

"That would be wonderful, but I'd better get going. Penny said she would hold supper for me, and I've already stayed a bit longer than I promised — but thanks anyway. Can I take a rain check?"

"Aye, that would be grand . . . always room for a friend at my table."

"A friend! I'm hoping I'm more than just a friend." Marshall seemed taken back.

"Aye, aye . . . I was hoping so, too," Tessy answered, a bit flustered.

"Tessy, what do you mean?"

"Marshall, it's nothing. You had better get going so you and the kids can eat and have a visit before the wee ones go to bed. We'll talk tomorrow."

"Okay. You promise we'll talk tomorrow?" Marshall gathered Tessy's hands in his and pulled her close.

"Aye, I can promise ye that."

"Oh, I hate to go — but I guess I'd better." They walked arm-in-arm down the hall to the foyer. Tessy helped Marshall on with his jacket, pressed down his lapel, and wrapped his scarf neatly around his neck.

"There, now, that ought to keep you toasty until ye get over there."

Marshall bent and kissed Tessy again and again. He could sense something was not right but he knew now was not the time to push her. If nothing else, he had learned to be cautious of her fiery Irish heritage — if not downright frightened of it!

She had lost her appetite so decided to fill up her wineglass and sit in front of the fire for a while. She didn't want to read too much into one comment but she couldn't remember exactly how he had put it: "for as long as it lasts" — was that what he'd said? Or was it, "let's enjoy it while it lasts"? Oh, I can't think of what it was and how he phrased it. However he put it, it didn't sound like he was in for the long haul. Well, 'tis good to know. We'll just have a nice time together, and then he'll be back off to Winnipeg, and I'll continue on here with my perfectly fine life. There . . . done with it.

She went back into the kitchen again and dished herself up some shepherd's pie and another ample glass of wine. She trotted off to the living room to eat, her supper balanced on her lap, and stared into the fire for a bit longer. After finishing one more glass of wine, she eventually got up and, feeling a little woozy and quite sorry for herself, she plunked the dishes in the sink and headed upstairs to bed. She went into the bathroom and splashed water on her face to see if that would make her feel any better, but even that didn't seem to help.

Entering her bedroom, she noticed something on her pillow. As she got closer, she could see that it was a sprig of holly. "Not again!" she said out loud. "Dermot, what are ye up to?" She thought maybe one of the cats could have been playing with it, which would explain how it ended up on her pillow; but both cats knew they were not to be near her pillows, so she dismissed that idea. She stopped to recall the meaning of holly. Being a bit clouded just then, it took her a minute. "Let's see . . . protection, luck, increase a man's ability to attract a woman, and Yule . . . Too late, Dermot. It didn't work." Tessy held the holly in her hand, threw open the quilt, and fell into bed; maybe not to a peaceful sleep but an extremely sound one, nonetheless.

Christmas Eve Casserole

4 cups (1L) medium shell pasta
1 large onion, chopped
3 cloves garlic, crushed
4 Tbsp (60 ml) butter
1 lb (455 g) fresh large scallops
1/2 lb (225 g) medium shrimp
2 cups (500 ml) fresh spinach, chopped
1 1/2 cups (375 ml) light cream or whole milk
1 cup (250 ml) shredded mozzarella cheese
1 cup (250 ml) grated Parmesan cheese
2 tsp (10 ml) fresh parsley, chopped
1/2 cup (125 ml) bread crumbs
1 Tbsp (15 ml) butter
Sea salt and coarsely ground pepper to taste

Cook pasta as directed on the package to just underdone; drain and set aside.

In a large frying pan, sauté onions and garlic in 2 Tbsp (30 ml) butter. When onions are soft, add 2 more Tbsp (30 ml) butter with scallops, shrimp, and salt and pepper. Cook until scallops are lightly browned and shrimp is pink. Add cream and mozzarella to cover and cook over low heat for 5 minutes, stirring occasionally. Stir in spinach and cook until just wilted.

In a large bowl, mix cooked shells, Parmesan, parsley, and salt and pepper. When pasta is well coated, add scallop/shrimp mixture, and spoon into a sprayed or oiled casserole dish. Bake at 350°F (180°C) uncovered for 25–30 minutes. In a small bowl, combine bread crumbs with melted butter; sprinkle over casserole and continue to bake for another 10 minutes or until bread crumbs turn a golden brown. Serves 6.

26

A Magical Moonlit Affair

Tessy awoke with a start. She reached for her head and poked herself with the holly that was still clenched in her hand. "Ouch!"

It wasn't necessarily the scratch she was complaining about.

Going over what she remembered from last night, she groaned . . . then she looked at the clock and groaned again . . . she had slept in. This morning of all mornings. She had so much to do with a house full of guests coming this evening, and Christmas just a few days away. She slowly got up and sat on the edge of the bed to steady her legs then she promptly began to lecture herself: "Ye silly woman. Letting something get to you enough to put yourself in this state. Like my Uncle Wil used to say, 'Always do sober what ye said you'd do drunk.' I guess I should have talked it over with Marshall before he left then maybe I wouldn't be feeling like such a dishrag this morning. You'd think I'd learn by now, being the grown woman that I am. And Dermot, I thank ye for keeping your fingers in the pie, but I'm not sure what it is, at this point, you're trying to get across to me. I will do my best to pay attention, but if ye could pick it up a notch, it would be greatly appreciated." And with that, she stood up and headed for the washroom.

At the sight of Tessy, the dogs started to circle, wagging in, out, and all around her. "You two settle down, and out ye get!" She opened the door, and the blast of cold air felt refreshing. She stood there for a few moments, taking in deep breaths of the crisp morning air. She closed the door and turned to see Merlin and Cordelia giving her nasty glares as they crouched on their beds from the cold. "It's not hurting ye two to have some fresh air so ye can stop with the looks. I'm not in the mood for your attitudes just yet this morning."

She poured herself a very large glass of grapefruit juice to replenish her sugar levels and sat down at the table. After the juice, two cups of coffee, and a bit of breakfast, Tessy was starting to feel human again. She was getting her Belleek china serving dishes out for the party when the phone rang.

"Good mornin'," she answered.

"And top' o' the morning to you, too, my sweet sunshine!"

"My, aren't we a bit of a firecracker this mornin'."

"Ouch!" Marshall winced.

"Oh, I'm sorry, dear. I had a few glasses of wine after ye left last night and I've been trying to get the cobwebs out of my head ever since. Don't pay any attention to my awful mood."

"Tessy, are you okay? This really isn't like you. I wish I could have stayed longer last night. I knew something wasn't right."

"Marshall, this isn't your fault. You spoke your mind last night, and I had to analyze it to death and I know better than that. Again, here I am, not knowing how to fix my own problems yet I can help almost anyone else."

"Honey, I'm coming over right now. We have to talk, and I won't take no for an answer."

"Marshall, ye have your family to visit with and I have a million things to do today. I'll see you tonight."

"I'll be there in ten minutes and I can help with anything you need done. I am coming and I will bang on the door until you let me in. You're not the only one with a stubborn streak, you know."

"I see that. Well, all right, then, I'll see in ye in a few minutes."

Exactly fourteen minutes later, Marshall was at Tessy's door. "Okay, let's go into the kitchen and sit so you can tell me what's going on." Marshall grabbed Tess's hand and pulled her into the kitchen. "Sit! Please."

Tessy sat down in the chair as directed. Then she looked at Marshall and jumped up. "Would you like a cup of coffee or tea or maybe some nice hot chocolate?"

Marshall placed his hands on her shoulders. "Sit!"

Again, Tessy sat as instructed and sheepishly looked at Marshall.

"Now. What on earth is going on? Spill the beans — right now."

"Oh, Marshall. Last night when we were talking ye mentioned something about we should enjoy 'this' while it lasts. I was hoping that 'this' would last forever, but that's not what it sounds like you want."

"You silly girl. Of course that's what I want. I meant that for as long as it lasts — as long as we both live. Neither of us is getting any younger so we have to grasp the moment and live it to the fullest now. That's what I was trying to say, but obviously not well. I am so sorry if you thought I was just being callous and aloof."

"Oh, Marshall! It is I who should be apologizing. I know you're not that kind of person and I should never let negative thoughts ever enter my mind. From now on, let's promise to always talk things out before any misunderstanding gets out of hand."

"Agreed." Marshall stretched out his hand and they shook on it. "I'll take that cup of coffee now, if you're still offering."

They spent the rest of the morning preparing for Tessy's party. The kids arrived to help out with shovelling the walks, setting the dining room table, placing throughout the house the beautiful Belleek platters and bowls piled with chocolates and goodies.

By three o'clock, everything seemed to be done and under control. They all sat down in the kitchen savouring a cup of Peppermint Hot Chocolate and discussing what activities they were hoping to enjoy over the holidays.

"On Boxing Day, we always go tobogganing on old Hobbs Hill just outside of town," Brendon told Matthew.

"Awesome!" Matthew answered.

"Well, don't be getting too excited, Matt—we won't be going. Grandma Tucker is coming on Boxing Day," Sarah informed him.

"But I don't want to just stay home—I want go and hang out with the guys," Matt argued.

"Well, that's not going to happen, and you know it," Sarah answered, raising her eyebrows.

"She's grumpy all the time and she smells like that stinky 'anti-stuff' spray I use when I sprain something."

Tessy and Marshall tried their best to hide a hearty chuckle.

"Well, dear, maybe your grandmother's grumpy because she is lonely; and, well, smelling like anti-inflammatory spray is almost a requirement when you get to our age or older."

"You don't smell like that. You always smell really good."

"Thank ye, dear, I'm glad to hear it. Maybe I can help with some of your grandmother's complaints while she's here. I'm actually looking forward to meeting her, as I've been invited over Boxing Day, too."

"Maybe Mom and Dad will let us go tobogganing for a bit while they are all visiting," Sarah offered Matthew.

"Hope so," Matthew scowled.

After everyone helped clean up and left to go get dressed for the party, Tessy ran upstairs to start getting ready as well. She had chosen a lovely, black velvet empire-cut jumper to go with a satin and lace white blouse. She laid them on the bed before entering her ensuite to run her bath. This was definitely an occasion that called for a soak in the big claw tub. She dribbled some of her favourite bath oil into the tub and had returned to her bedroom to disrobe when she noticed another sprig of holly on her pillow.

"Dermot, dear, what is it that you're trying to tell me? I can hear ye loud and strong but I just can't tell what it is you're trying to say. I guess you'll let me know when the time's right."

She picked up the holly and placed it in the vase on her nightstand with the other one, continued to undress, and went for her soak.

Tessy's doorbell chimed just as she was lighting the last of the candles in the dining room. She hurried to the foyer and opened the door to find Roger and Connie. "Merry Christmas!" chorused through the air as they all greeted each other.

"Come in, come in," Tessy motioned. "There's plenty of room in the cubby for your coats and boots. Can I help with anything?" Roger handed a bottle of wine to Tessy, and Connie was holding a beautifully wrapped box. "Now, you two, what have ye done, here?"

"We just brought the hostess a little something," Connie said as she gave her a hug.

"Well, ye know you're not to be doing that — it is my pleasure to have my wonderful friends and neighbours over for some holiday cheer."

"Oh, Tessy, everything looks absolutely gorgeous. Look at your tree!"

"Thank you, but I did have a little help from a couple of wee elves who stop by from time to time."

They had just entered the dining room to get some refreshments when the doorbell rang.

"Please help yourselves, and I'll be back in a jig."

Tessy reached the door to find that three other couples had arrived, and soon the house was full of happy guests, mingling and enjoying an evening of festive celebration. Danny and Betty Baker were the last to arrive as they made a grand entrance with their horses and sleigh ready to take the first bundled-up guests for a ride. This was always the biggest hit at Tessy's festive party.

As Tessy's Yuletide gathering was for the adult crowd only, Sarah and

Cherokee asked if they could take over the catering and kitchen duty. Tessy felt very confident that they would do a fine job and left them to it. They had arrived much earlier to prepare and set out the appetizers and to make sure they just kept coming.

The evening was full of laughter, food, fun, and festive songs. Guests would come and go for their enchanting sleigh ride over the lake and around town to see the lights. The evening proved to be crisp and calm with the sky so black and the moon and stars so bright one would almost suspect that it had been arranged from a higher source.

The last of the guests were leaving, and the girls had long since cleaned up and headed home by way of sleigh ride — an unexpected treat for sure! Tessy was wondering why Danny was still there, as she was pretty sure everyone had received their ride and she knew he had dropped Betty off at their house about an hour ago. Marshall snuggled up behind Tessy and gave her a hug. "Well, my lady, it is our turn to take a ride out into the moonlight."

"Oh, Marshall, I'm quite sure Danny is tired and would like to get the horses, as well as himself, off to bed."

Danny piped up, "Not at all, Tess. One more trip around town will be just fine, especially when you and Marshall are the passengers."

"Well, if you're sure. It would be a wonderful way to finish out the evening then, thank ye!"

Soon they were settled in the back of the sleigh nice and cozy under a plush quilt and gliding over the snow. They had been enjoying the ride in silence when Tessy said, "Look how the moonlight glistens over the snow like millions of tiny diamonds . . ."

"It's amazing that you would say that at this particular moment, my sweet lady."

"Why's that, my love?"

Marshall reached under the blanket and pulled out a small green velvet box. "Tessy McGuigan, you are the most beautiful, wonderful, magical woman I have ever met and I cannot imagine my life without you. Would you do me the honour of being my wife? I'd go down on one knee but I'm not quite sure how to do that in this sleigh right at the moment."

He opened the box, and there was a breathtakingly beautiful antique Celtic emerald and diamond ring.

Tessy was stunned. She could not believe what had just happened. A thousand thoughts were racing through her head. Yes, she knew she loved this man, without a doubt, but they had known each other only for five short months. He lived a province away. Was she being unfaithful to Dermot, her one true love until now. Then she smiled . . . Oh, Dermot . . . so this is what you've been so desperately trying to tell me with all your holly and tricks. Holly: a plant of protection, luck, for a man to increase his ability to attract a woman, and for Yule — your favourite time of the year. You sweet, wonderful spirit!

She looked up at Marshall. "YES! I don't know how this is all going to work out but I know that it is destined to be."

Marshall gathered her up in his arms and passionately kissed her again and again.

Danny was glad his horses knew the trail so well, as he was having a very hard time seeing through the tears in his eyes.

Yule Nog

1 1/2 cups (375 ml) cider (substitute rum or brandy if
    desired)
1/2 cup (125 ml) honey
2 Tbsp (30 ml) vanilla
8 cups (2 L) cream
2 tsp (10 ml) nutmeg
Cinnamon sticks

In a saucepan over medium heat, stir in the cider, honey, and vanilla
until honey is dissolved. Add cream and 1 tsp (5 ml) nutmeg and
whisk. Pour into pitcher, let cool, and refrigerate overnight. Serve
over ice with a sprinkle of nutmeg and a cinnamon stick.

27

"Attitute" and Patience

It was snowing quite heavily when Marshall arrived to pick up Tessy on Christmas Eve. The doorbell rang, and Tessy held up her hand to take one more affectionate look at her beautiful antique engagement ring. Was this really happening? Was she actually going to marry the amazing gentleman on the other side of that door? "Well, only if I open the door before the poor man freezes to death," she said out loud as she scurried to the foyer.

"Come in, come in. My, ye look like Jack Frost himself standing out there."

"Hello, my sweet bride-to-be," Marshall said as he took off his glove, picked up her hand, and brought it to his lips.

"Oh, you're cold!" Tessy replied as she vigorously rubbed his hand between hers.

"Now that I see you, not a bit!" Marshall smiled down at her and gave her a kiss. "I left the car running so it would be nice and warm for you. Are you about ready to go?"

"Aye, if ye could carry out this box of gifts, I'll get my coat on and bring the rest of the packages."

"Great. Oh, did you remember to bring the poems with you?" Marshall asked as he picked up the box.

"Aye, I popped them into one of these bags. It will sure be a relief to finally have this puzzle all figured out, ye rascal."

Marshall just chuckled as he closed the door behind him.

By the time they reached the Tuckers', it was snowing so hard the tire tracks were filling in as fast as they were made. Marshall pulled up to the door as close as he could to let Tessy out before parking the car. Tessy was greeted at the door as she came up the steps. The kids were hugging and fussing over her while trying to help her with all the packages.

"Kids, kids. Calm down. Give Tessy a chance to get in the door and catch her breath," Jim said, coming to her rescue. "Matt—here, take these parcels into the living room, please."

"Aye, thank ye, Jim. Merry Christmas to ye all. Marshall should be along with the rest in just a jig. My we're certainly getting our white Christmas, for sure."

Just as Marshall stomped in the door carrying a large box, Penny came around the corner. "Hello! Merry Christmas, Tessy," she said, giving Tessy a warm hug. "Come in, sit down and warm up . . . but first, may I have another look at that gorgeous ring?"

"Aye, I've had a hard time taking my eyes off it meself." Tessy glowed as she held out her left hand.

"Oh, Tessy, we couldn't be happier. I always knew my father had good taste and I'm not just talking about the diamond." Penny nudged Tessy while holding her hand.

"Thank ye, dear, and even if I talked to the good Lord himself I couldn't have wished for a more wonderful family to be joining. I am truly blessed."

"I'm just glad you said yes," Marshall piped. "For a minute there, I wasn't sure that would be your answer."

Everyone laughed as Jim handed them decorative cups of Olde English Wassail for the adults and hot cider for the kids.

"I would like to make a toast," Jim announced. "First, to Tessy, who has made a huge, positive impact on our family from our first day in Ladyslipper. It is a pleasure to — officially — now say you are truly family. And next, to Marshall and Tessy, may you spend many, many happy, prosperous years together and visit our home as often as possible. Cheers — or should I say *Slainte.*"

While the storm raged outside, everyone inside basked in the crackling fire before supper, playing games and enjoying their drinks, appetizers, and the company.

Penny had made what the kids call their favourite "Christmas Eve Casserole."

"Oh, Tessy, it's soooo delicious! You're going to just love it!" Emma grabbed Tessy's hand and started pulling her toward the dining room.

"I'm sure I will, sweetheart. It smells like a wee piece of heaven, it does."

After everyone was comfortably seated, Marshall looked around the table at his family; he reached for Tessy's hand and said, "I can't think of a better time to say a prayer of thanks for all the miracles who are sitting at this table." He continued on with a prayer of gratitude, squeezing Tessy's hand just a little firmer.

Well, little Emma was certainly right. The casserole *was* delicious, and Tessy raved, pleading for the recipe.

"Oh, thank you. It's really quite simple, actually," Penny offered, "but no problem — I can give you the recipe anytime."

"Can we go open presents now?" Emma begged.

"No, not yet, honey. We have to finish up here and then clean up the kitchen first."

"Aw, Mommy!" Emma pouted and crossed her arms.

"That's not attitude I'm seeing, is it?" Jim raised his eyebrows at his little daughter. "Because you know how Santa feels about attitude, right?"

"Oh, no, Daddy, I don't have 'attitute.' I promise, I don't."

"Good, I didn't think so. So maybe to keep you and your brother and sister busy, you can help clear some of these dishes and put them in the dishwasher."

"Yes, Daddy." Emma jumped down from her chair, picked up her plate, and immediately trotted off to the kitchen, with Matt and Sarah not far behind her.

"It's amazing how, from a month or so before Christmas, kids are just more than happy to co-operate and agree with just about anything you say," Jim laughed.

"Well, Jim, I think you and Penny have done a wonderful job raising my grandchildren. I think they are pretty amazing most of the time," Marshall pointed out.

"I guess we are extremely lucky they are good kids," Jim boasted.

"I should say. Fine wee darlings, every one," Tessy agreed. "And to think they'll be my grandchildren soon." Tessy suddenly stopped and stared at Marshall as tears welled up in her eyes. That fact had just truly dawned on her: She was to have grandchildren after all!

Marshall put his arm around Tessy and pulled her close. "And you'll be an amazing grandmother," he said as he kissed her forehead.

"Thank ye, love." Tessy smiled at him and dabbed her eyes with her napkin.

The kitchen was clean, and soon everyone was settled back in the living room with the children eagerly sitting on the floor in front of the Christmas tree.

"Now, just so Tessy knows the 'Christmas Eve Rules.' The children are allowed to open two gifts each tonight, then the rest, including the one from Santa—IF he comes—are opened in the morning," Jim said, looking pointedly at his youngest daughter.

"I know, Daddy," Emma softly agreed, nodding her head up and down and snuggling a little closer to her big sister. Sarah smiled and cuddled her.

"Excuse me, Jim. I have just one question then before we start but I'm not quite sure who to direct it to, you or Marshall. So does this mean I'll not be finding out about my riddles tonight?"

"Sorry, Tessy. It doesn't look promising for tonight," Marshall teased and gave Jim a wink.

"Well, I won't hold the children up any longer but I'll have a few choice words for you two when they're out of earshot, I will."

Marshall and Jim laughed heartily.

"You two behave yourselves. Leave Tessy alone and let the kids open their presents," Penny rebuked with a grin.

All three of the children decided they would like to open their gift from Tessy tonight. Little Emma opened hers first.

"Oh, Tessy! It's a magical crystal just like the one you have in your kitchen window. Will it make beautiful rainbows in my room like the ones at your house?"

"Yes, dear. We'll put it up in your room tomorrow and when the sun shines in you will have rainbows just like the ones at my house. There's also a book on faeries, a faery colouring book and some markers in the bottom of the box."

"Oh, Tessy! Thank you, thank you. I love you." Emma buried her head in Tessy's neck and hugged her tight.

"You're very welcome, sweetheart. I love you, too."

Matt was next. He took the box and gave it a shake.

"I wouldn't rattle it too hard, dear, although I did anticipate that you might so I wrapped it snug," Tessy laughed.

"Oh, sorry, Tessy," Matt flinched and then carefully set it down on his lap to open it. He took something out of the box and held it in his hand looking at it one way then the other. "What is it?"

"Dig a little deeper into the box and you should find an LCD magnifying glass that should help you out," Tessy instructed him.

He found it and held it close to solve the mystery. As he did, his eyes grew large. "Wow! Is this a real fossil?"

"Aye, it is, dear. It's called an ammonite."

"How old is it?"

"Oh, about 200 million years or more. It's from the Isle of Skye in Scotland around about the Jurassic Age. There's a wee pamphlet that comes with it in the box so you can read all about it, and you'll find a book on the Jurassic Age in there as well."

"Wow! This is so cool. Thanks, Tessy." Matt slowly exhaled as he dug back into the box to fish out the pamphlet.

Emma ran over to take a look. "That's a nice rock, Matt, but mine's more sparkly, and I bet yours doesn't make pretty rainbows," Emma gushed as she held up and gently swung her crystal for everyone to see.

Matt just rolled his eyes and shook his head.

"Okay, you two. That's enough," Penny intervened. "They are both wonderful, thoughtful gifts. Thank you so much, Tessy."

"I guess I'm next," Sarah said, rubbing her hands together. "I won't bother to shake mine," she said as she tossed a glance over to her brother.

"Very funny," Matt tossed back.

Sarah picked up the box discovering it was a bit heavier than she anticipated and balanced it on her lap. Inside she discovered two kits. One was full of crystals and gems, each in its own compartment, while the other kit was full of essential oils. "Oh, Tessy! This is wonderful! Thank you — but it is too much."

"Nonsense, dear. If you're embarking on your journey to alternative healing, you must start out with the proper tools. You'll find instruction books in there as well, with another one included on herbs. I'd be more than happy to give you and Cherokee a helping hand any way I can when you're ready to get started. Now, don't be going and calling Cherokee until after tomorrow, because I got her the exact same thing and I'm not sure when she'll be opening her gifts."

Sarah stood up, leaned over, and gave Tessy an affectionate hug. "Thank you! I can't wait to get started."

The children each opened one more gift then shortly thereafter disappeared into their bedrooms to get further acquainted with their new treasures, leaving the adults to some quiet time together.

"Have you two talked about any dates or anything yet?" Penny questioned.

"Heavens, no! I'm barely out of shock, dear," Tessy all but gasped.

Everyone laughed.

"Of course. It is early days, yet," Penny agreed.

"Well, it will never be too soon for me," Marshall piped.

"We'll get discussing it soon enough, my love," Tessy shook her head as she patted his hand. "However, there is something else I would like to talk to you about: these riddles you've been driving me crazy with for six weeks." She pulled out the tattered remains of the poems from a bag she had close by.

"Well, my dear, it seems that the children are the only ones allowed to open any gifts tonight and since there is one more gift to open in order for the poems to make any sense you'll have to wait until tomorrow. Sorry, I don't make the rules — right, Jim?"

"Don't get me in the middle of all this, you old fox," Jim laughed.

"Oh, I see where this is going, you two — one scoundrel hiding behind the other. Well, I think we'll be needing to discuss this a wee mite further."

"My, look at the time, my dear. The kids will have to be off to bed soon, and I still have to get you home, yet. I'll just go out and warm up the car," Marshall said, looking at his watch as he got up.

"I'll go with you and shovel the walk so you don't slip on the steps," Jim added as he, too, got up.

"Chickens, the two of ye!" Tessy called after them.

By the time the boys got back in the house, Tessy was at the door with her coat on saying her goodbyes to everyone.

"Well, we'll see ye bright and early tomorrow morning, then. You get some sleep, my wee ones, so Santa can sneak in and leave your presents under the tree. Night-night, my dears."

"But Sarah gets to stay up longer. How come Sarah gets to stay up and I have to go to bed? I want to stay up, too," Emma pouted as she crossed her arms.

"Again, that isn't attitude I am hearing from you, is it, little missy?" Jim shook his head at his daughter.

"No, Daddy. I don't have 'attitute.' Good night. I'm going to bed right now. Don't forget to tuck me in. 'Night, Tessy!" Emma yelled as she ran upstairs.

Marshall turned to Tessy. "Looks like Emma needs to work on her 'attitude' and you need to possibly work on your patience!" Then he ran out the door before she could whack him.

Christmas Breakfast-in-a-Pan

1 medium onion
1/2 cup (125 ml) finely chopped red pepper
1 cup (250 ml) fresh mushrooms, chopped
1 cup (250 ml) fresh spinach, chopped
1 large bag of frozen shredded hash browns (thawed enough to mix in)
1 16 oz. (455 g) container of cottage cheese
2 cups (500 ml) shredded cheddar cheese
2 cups (500 ml) cooked, cubed, ham or sausage
1 tsp (5 ml) thyme
1 tsp (5 ml) basil
12 eggs
1/2 cup (125 ml) milk

In a large bowl, combine everything except eggs and milk. Mix well and spread into a large sprayed or oiled casserole dish. Whisk eggs and milk and pour over mixture. Bake uncovered at 350°F (180°C) for approximately 1 hour. Serves 14.

28

All Things Revealed

Christmas morning was pristine. A Currier and Ives painting could not have done it any more justice. Everything was covered in a thick blanket of glistening diamonds, and the air was crisp and quiet . . . that is, until Tessy opened the door and the dogs tore out into the deep white ocean of snow. They bounced and frolicked, leaving clouds of fresh snow and tracks in their wake. Tessy stood at the door and couldn't help but laugh out loud. How did her life get to be so perfect? She knew Marshall would be there shortly to pick her up and she still needed to finish getting the Christmas Breakfast-in-a-Pan ready but she closed the door and first headed down the hall to the library.

"Merry Christmas, Dermot, my love," she said softly. "Well, ye did it. Ye made everyone's Christmas dreams come true, even for those of us who didn't really know what those dreams were and got in your way every step of the way. You are a true miracle worker, my dear, and I thank ye from the bottom of my heart. But what has happened doesn't mean I want ye to be going anywhere. I still need ye close by. I need your strength, your faith in me, and your love. Ye were and always will be my first love, and I won't be forgetting it. Well, I hope ye get to have Christmas where you are and they let ye have your wings, both on your back and your turkey. God bless ye, love." Just as she turned to walk out, she heard the tinkling of a Christmas bell. With that, she smiled, quietly closed the door, and scurried back to the kitchen to finish preparing her casserole.

Marshall and Tessy arrived at the Tuckers' and walked in to blissful chaos. The kids met them at the door jumping up and down and all talking at once. Apparently, Santa had arrived and, surprisingly, had brought them exactly what they wanted. So far, besides Santa's, only a few gifts had been opened, as they wanted to wait for Grandpa and Tessy before opening the rest.

The living room was filling up fast with wrappings, bags, and boxes of all colours and sizes as the children dug in with great gusto. Jim stopped playing honorary Santa long enough to get Marshall and Tessy a coffee with Irish cream, and they just sat back and enjoyed. The kids were getting close to the end when Jim announced it was time for the adults to open a few. He recruited Matt to help hand out the gifts while he rummaged under the tree looking for any strays left unopened after the children's frenzy. Matt was about to hand Tessy a small, flat box with her name on it when Marshall intercepted it. "If you don't mind, Matt, I'll take that one for now. Thank you."

Tessy glanced up from the parcel she was presently unwrapping and gave Marshall a puzzled look.

"Soon, my darling. Soon," Marshall smiled.

Lovely gifts of all shapes and sizes were exchanged and opened. Tessy received a beautiful cashmere wrap; a matching hat, scarf, and glove set; and from Marshall, a gorgeous set of emerald and diamond earrings to complement her engagement ring. Tessy brought special gifts for the Tuckers as well: An exquisite Irish bouclé cape for Penny, and a Celtic pocket watch for Jim, remarking that he would look quite distinguished wearing it. And for Marshall, a classic Donegal patchwork cap; a hand-carved Irish walking stick (what the Irish call a shillelagh), and a roll-collar fisherman knit cardigan.

Marshall roared with laughter when he opened his gifts. This puzzled Tessy, as she couldn't figure out why.

"Ye don't like the gifts, then, Marshall?" she questioned

"Like them? I love them! They are so perfect for what you are about to discover."

"Marshall Tayse. What on God's green earth are ye talking about?"

"Okay, I think it's time. Where are the poems I sent you?"

"I've them right here."

The whole family was intently listening while sitting on pins and needles.

"Good. Okay, let's start with the first one." He took the paper from Tessy and read aloud.

> In the six weeks to come you will find
> Little tokens to show you are on my mind.
> Each one has a purpose you'll see
> To bring you even closer to me.
> Now this fine horse is no grey mare
> For she belongs in a grand affair.

"Aye, and ye sent me a lovely china horse. So what does it mean?"

"Patience, my love. It will all make sense very soon. The next one reads,"

> Here's the next surprise it's number two
> a special little gift just for you.
> It will keep you guessing and amused
> with each one chase away your blues.
> As you can see it's a piggy bank at play
> So you can save for that rainy day.

"So, I did get that. I was to be saving some money but I still have no idea why."

"Next one, dear."

> This little gift may seem a little strange
> you might even think I may be deranged
> But don't give up and you will see
> these all connect as handy as can be
> This pack of gum don't use for glue
> just close your eyes and really chew.

Sarah remarked on this one. "Grandpa, seriously! A pack of chewing gum. Really?"

Everyone laughed.

"Okay, I admit it's a little 'out there' but it works. You'll see."

"Can't wait!" was her response.

"We're halfway there," and Marshall read out the remaining three riddles.

> We're into week four not long to go
> Though I do feel the time goes slow
> Looking forward to seeing you soon
> I see your face in every moon
> It's okay to take this mask and sleep
> For I will be there to share your dreams so deep.

> Not sure if you've guessed where this is going
> I want to keep it a surprise, it's not for showing
> Not long now and I'll be on my way
> Then in the snow we will frolic and play
> I hope the songs on this CD you'll like
> You can listen to them whether you rest or hike.

> One week from now I'll be in your arms
> Enjoying your laughter and all your charms
> This Christmas will be one of joy
> I will use every trick and every ploy
> To watch you pen in this journal your dreams,
> Your thoughts and all of your Irish schemes.

"There. Now, put them all together and what do you get?" Marshall seemed as pleased as punch with himself.

"Marshall, I've been going over and over them for six weeks. They don't make any more sense to me today than they did the day I received them."

"What do you guys think? Does it make sense to any of you?" Marshall questioned.

"Not a clue, Dad. So what does it mean?" Penny shook her head.

"Well, okay. Tessy, dear, it's time for you to unwrap your last Christmas present. Here." He handed Tessy the little flat box about the size a pair of leather gloves would fit nicely in.

Everyone held their breath in anticipation as Tessy opened it. Inside was a leaflet. She pulled it out of the box and unfolded it. Was this really what she thought it was? Was she seeing clearly?

"We can't wait any longer, Tessy. What is it?" Penny cried.

"Two tickets to Ireland in June!" she whispered as she stared up at Marshall.

"YES!" Marshall all but yelped as he picked her up and swung her around. "And June for a very good reason, my love. Now do the riddles make sense?"

"No, well, at least not all of them."

"Okay. Look further into the brochure. What do you see?"

"Oh, my stars! There's two tickets to the Irish Derby in June, as well. Oh, Marshall!"

"Yes. Exactly . . . so . . . Okay. Let's go over them one more time — Poem 1 . . . Irish Derby . . . hence the horse; Poem 2 . . . piggy bank . . . no-brainer; Poem 3 . . . Sarah, I'll explain this one for you. When you take off and land in an airplane your ears always pop, right? So you have a pack of chewing gum with you because when you chew gum, they don't pop. Poem 4 . . . mask . . . well, since it's such a long flight over there, it's always easier to take a nap with an eye mask. Poem 5 . . . CD . . . again, on a long flight, sometimes it's nice to just sit back and listen to your own music. And that CD holds some pretty special memories along with it." He picked up Tessy's hand and gave it a kiss. "Last, but not least, Poem 6 . . . the journal . . . I am going to enjoy watching my bride write in it every night while we're over in Ireland, and many, many more nights after."

"Wow, Grandpa. That is ingenious! Good job!" Sarah said in awe.

"Well, maybe not ingenious; clever, perhaps," Marshall boasted, pushing out his chest.

Everyone laughed.

Tessy took Marshall's face in her hands and beamed up at him. "Aye, clever and crafty as a fox, but thoughtful — and more wonderful than all the stars in the heavens." She pulled his face to hers and planted a solid kiss on his lips.

Jim said, "Well, well . . . congratulations, you two. I know you will have a wonderful time. Now that the mystery is finally over, how about we hit the kitchen for some of Tessy's Christmas Breakfast-in-a-Pan? I'm starving!"

As everyone headed out to the kitchen, Marshall and Tessy remained alone in the living room for a few minutes.

"Marshall, I can't thank you enough for all my wonderful gifts. A trip to Ireland, how did ye know I was so homesick and needed to step back to my homeland? And to be taking you with me. I have so much to show you and all the folks ye have to meet. Ye might be thinking twice about going once you figure out what that's going to entail."

"Oh, I think I will chance it as long as you are by my side, my lovely lady of Ladyslipper."

"Are you two lovebirds coming? It's going fast," Jim called around the corner.

Later that evening, after a very full Christmas day, Marshall drove Tessy home and helped her into the house with her parcels.

"Would ye care to come in for a nightcap, love?" asked Tessy.

"Well, I would love to come in for a while but after that huge turkey supper, I'm not sure I could put one more thing in my mouth," Marshall answered, holding his stomach.

"Well, then, how about a nice cup of tea to help calm your grumbling tummy?"

"That sounds wonderful."

"Good. Then if ye could go in to the living room, plug in the Christmas lights, and light some of the candles, I'll go off to the kitchen and fetch some tea."

"You got it. Shall I put your opened gifts under the tree?" Marshall asked as he walked through to the living room.

"Aye, thank ye," Tessy called from down the hall.

Tessy returned to the living room to find a romantic warm glow about the room. She set the tray down in front of Marshall, who was comfortably settled on the couch. Tessy snuggled in close beside him, poured them each a fragrant, steaming cup, and they sat in silence for a moment enjoying the solitude after the day's blissful mayhem.

"Mmmm, this is heavenly, and so are you," Marshall said as he nestled into her neck. They kissed and cuddled for a bit; then Marshall pulled slightly away so he could see Tessy's eyes.

"You know, if it weren't for the children, I wouldn't be leaving tonight," he said with a cocky smirk and a mischievous twinkle in his eye. The answer he received was one he was not expecting.

"Aye, and if it weren't for the children, I wouldn't want ye to be leaving tonight," she smiled; then continued, "but . . . Winnipeg is just a wink away." Then she winked at Marshall and gave him an impish grin.

"Ohhh, you are a very wise woman." Marshall nestled back into her neck then whispered into her ear. "Soooo . . . when am I booking your flight?"

Tessy just laughed.

After Marshall finally did leave, Tessy returned to the living room to reflect and quietly enjoy the ambience. She retrieved the tickets to Ireland, sat staring at them and softly stroking them. Ireland, her beloved homeland . . . and she was going there in just a few short months with the most wonderful man. She thought back to what had taken place over the past six months. How her life had completely changed in what seemed the wink of an eye. Gratitude filled her heart. She held up her left hand and admired the precious gems that danced in the candlelight. She gave thanks to the Divine for her past, the present, and the future that she now knew was destined to be. She realized she truly had become so much more than a wise woman. She spotted a fresh sprig of holly on the coffee table and she began to laugh out loud. "God love ye, Dermot McGuigan." Then she got up, blew out all the candles, and headed upstairs to dream of love, lore, and leprechauns.

Acknowledgements

First, a huge thank you to Tim Gordon and his amazing crew at General Store Publishing House for giving me this wonderful opportunity and for pairing me up with editor "extraordinaire" Jane Karchmar. Jane, your talent, patience, and kindness were above and beyond and is so appreciated. You are incredible!

Thank you to my parents, Bob and Helen Gugin, for raising such a loving, supportive family. Can't wait to see you on the other side! Thanks with love to my son, Robin, for the Irish tidbits and your constant, enthusiastic encouragement. Love and thank you to our daughter, Sabrina; sons, Darren, Chris, and Robin; and daughters-in-law Holly and Jo-anne, and our nine beautiful grandchildren: Without you, life would have no meaning. To my daughter-in-law, Holly, for your support, hours of reading, and delightful comments! Thanks to my brother, Craig, for the directions, and his wife, Karen, for the wonderful recipe suggestions; to my brother Jim, for lovingly watching over us from above and to my sister-in-law Kathy for keeping his memory alive; to my brother-in-law, Bill, for helping me with my never-ending financial questions and woes; to sister-in-law Shar for just being you and telling me you wouldn't read my book until all the recipes were done!

My thanks to Monica, for accompanying me on my journey to the mystical realms of beyond and for the hours of proofreading; to my dear friend Nancy for your love and never-ending support; to my "bestest" friend, Darlene, for your honesty and opinions — we might not always see eye-to-eye on some beliefs, but isn't it nice that judgment is never held and love is always present?

Abrah, thank you for opening my life into the world of herbs and oils and giving me the confidence to use these treasures from Mother Earth with love, respect, and gratitude. Dale, thank you for showing me how to pet a bee . . . rest in peace, my friend.

Last, but certainly not least, a huge thank you to my Grade 12 English teachers, Judy (Richardson) Wesley and Jean Tully, for not giving up on me nor letting me give up on myself. You told me if I would just put some effort into it, I could do it — as long as I had a dictionary close by . . . who'd-a-thunk!

About the Author

Elaine Gugin Maddex is a wife, mother, grandmother, and first-time author. She was born and raised in the small town of Minnedosa, Manitoba, where as a small child she daily followed her grandmother about, "helping" tend her massive gardens. Elaine is a kitchen herbalist and enjoys spending a great deal of time in her herb and perennial gardens. She is presently working on her next book and is looking forward to sharing it with you soon. Elaine lives on an acreage in Alberta with her husband, two dogs, two cats, and a wide array of wild birds and local critters.

TO ORDER MORE COPIES:

email the author at guginmaddex@gmail.com
or contact Red Tuque Books Inc. at www.redtuquebooks.ca